- HERGÉ -
★

THE ADVENTURES OF TINTIN

CIGARS OF
THE PHARAOH

L B

Little, Brown and Company
New York   Boston

Original Album: *Cigars of the Pharaoh*
Renewed Art Copyright © 1946, 1974 by Casterman, Belgium
Text Copyright © 1959 by Egmont UK Limited

Additional Material
Art Copyright © Hergé/Moulinsart 2011
Text Copyright © Moulinsart 2011

www.casterman.com
www.tintin.com

Little, Brown and Company
Hachette Book Group
237 Park Avenue, New York, NY 10017
Visit our website at www.lb-kids.com

The publisher is not responsible for websites (or their content) that are not owned by the publisher.

First Edition: July 2011

The characters and events portrayed in this book are fictitious. Any similarity to real persons,
living or dead, is coincidental and not intended by the author.

ISBN: 978-0-316-13388-3
2011921034
SC
Printed in China

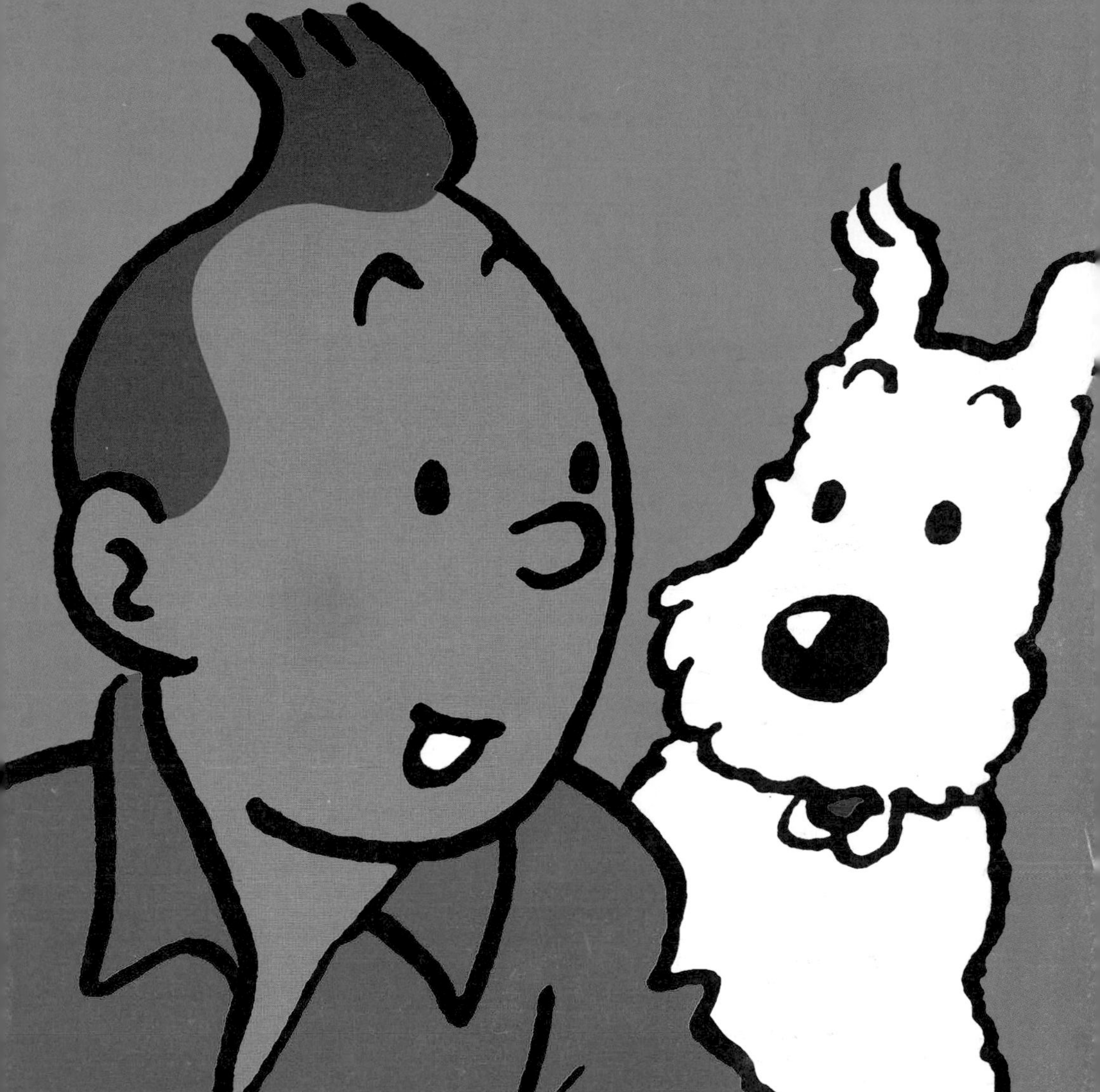

Tintin and Snowy

Brave reporter Tintin and his trusty hound Snowy love traveling around the world on exciting adventures.

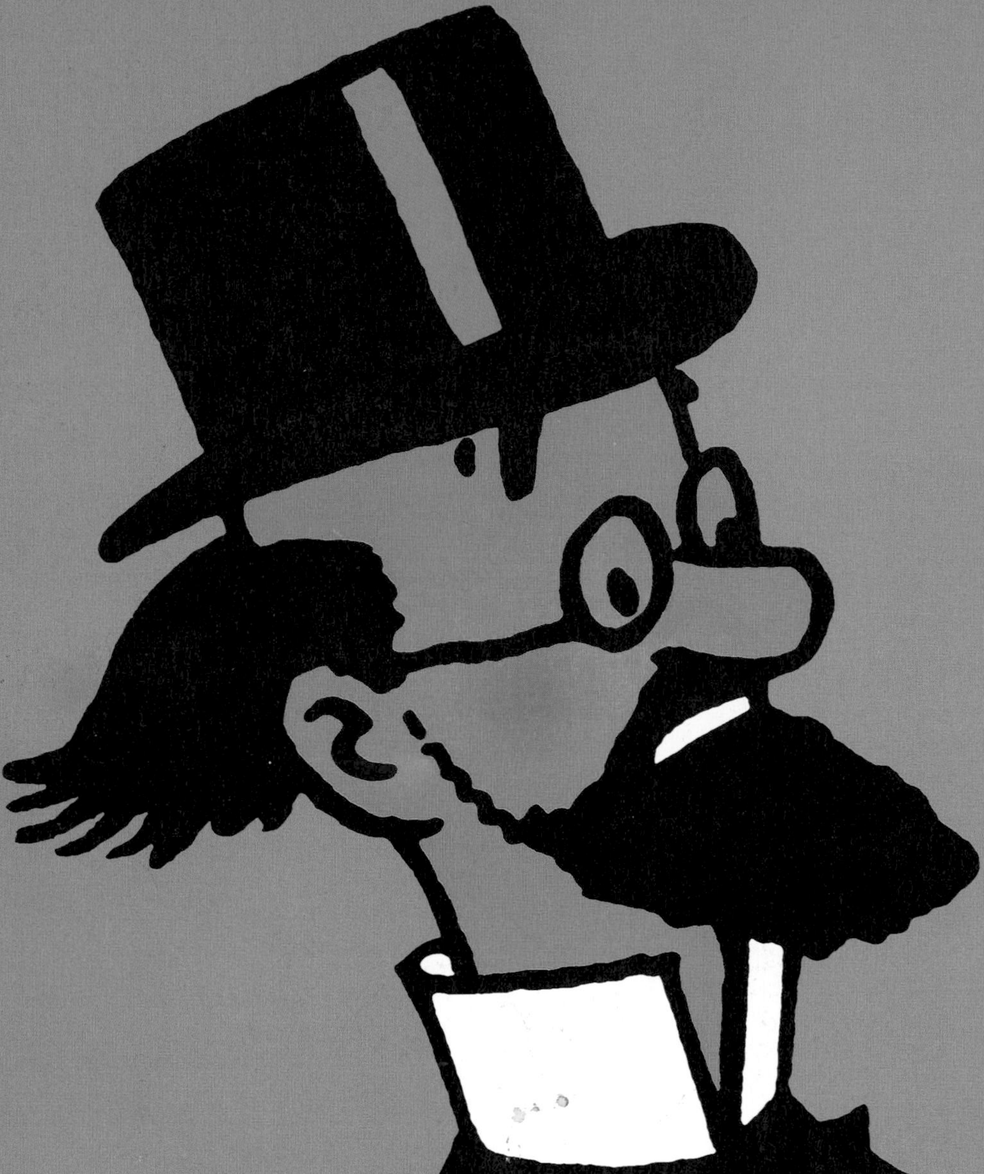

Sophocles Sarcophagus

Doctor Sarcophagus only has one thing on his mind throughout this adventure: Ancient Egyptian pharaohs!

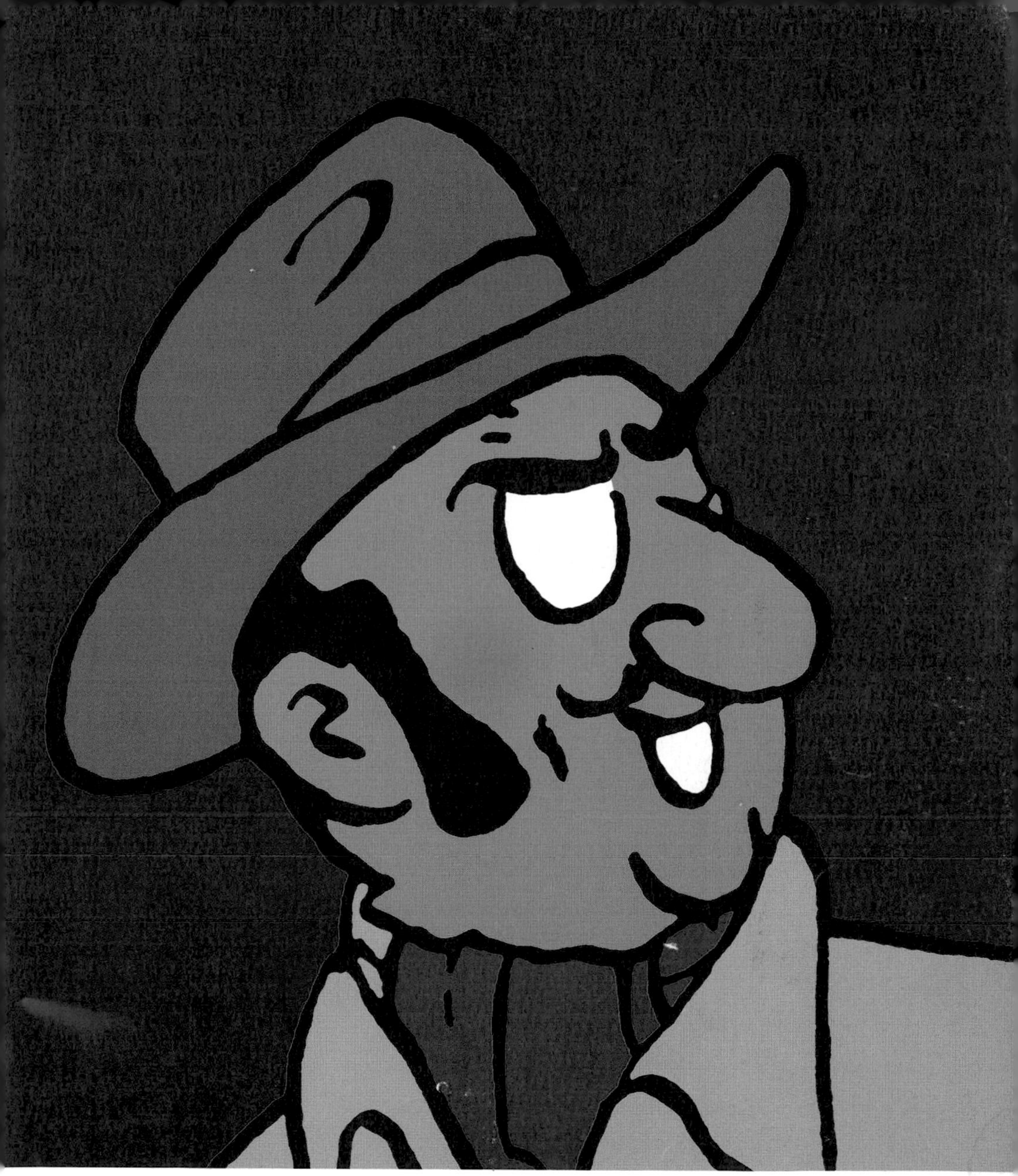

Rastapopoulos

Tintin's first meeting with the "King of Cosmos Pictures" doesn't go well.
Later on Rastapopoulos seems friendly enough,
but remains a man of mystery.

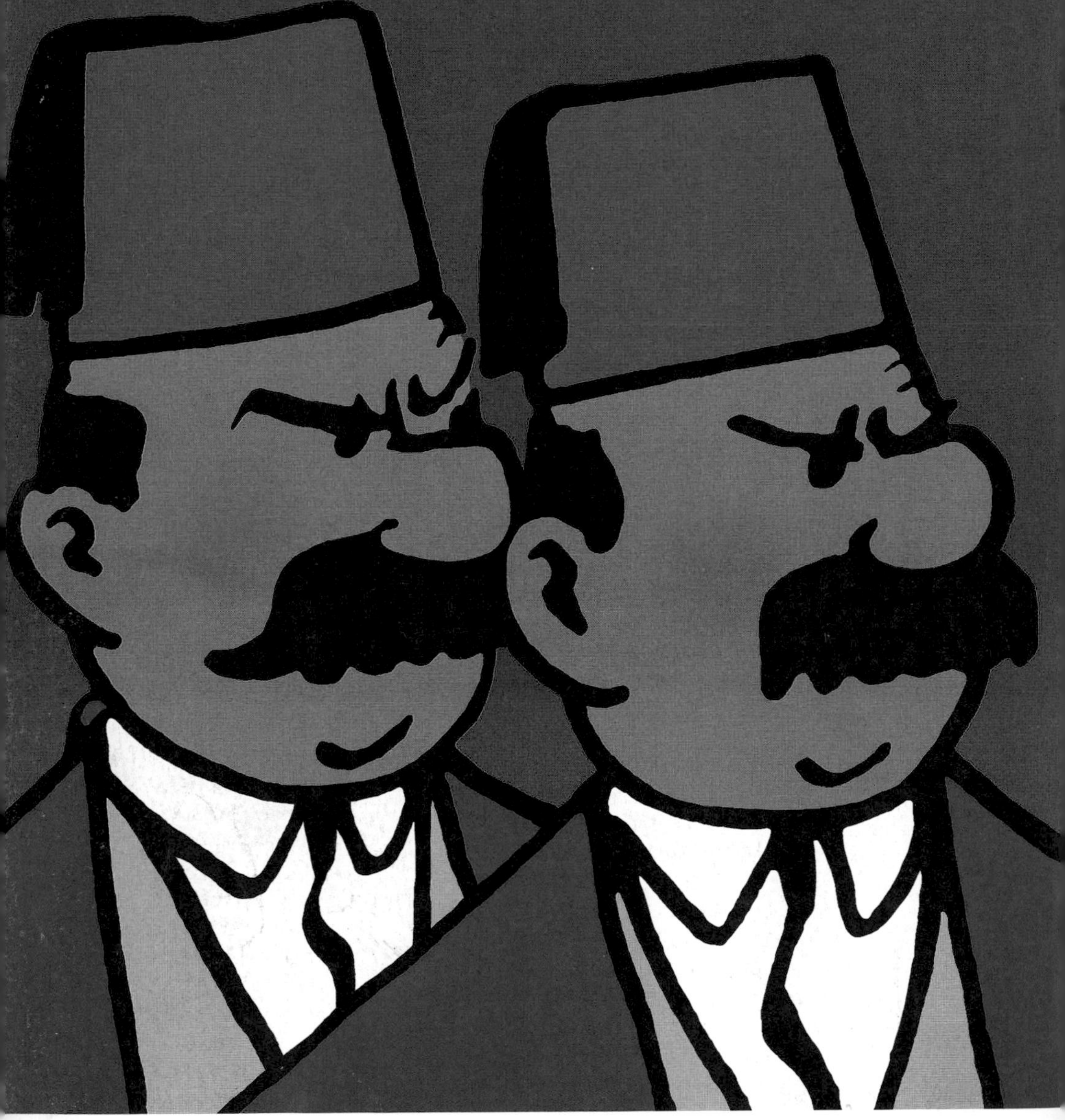

Thomson and Thompson

The world's silliest police detectives make their first appearance in this Tintin story. Right from the start, their investigations are in a hopeless muddle!

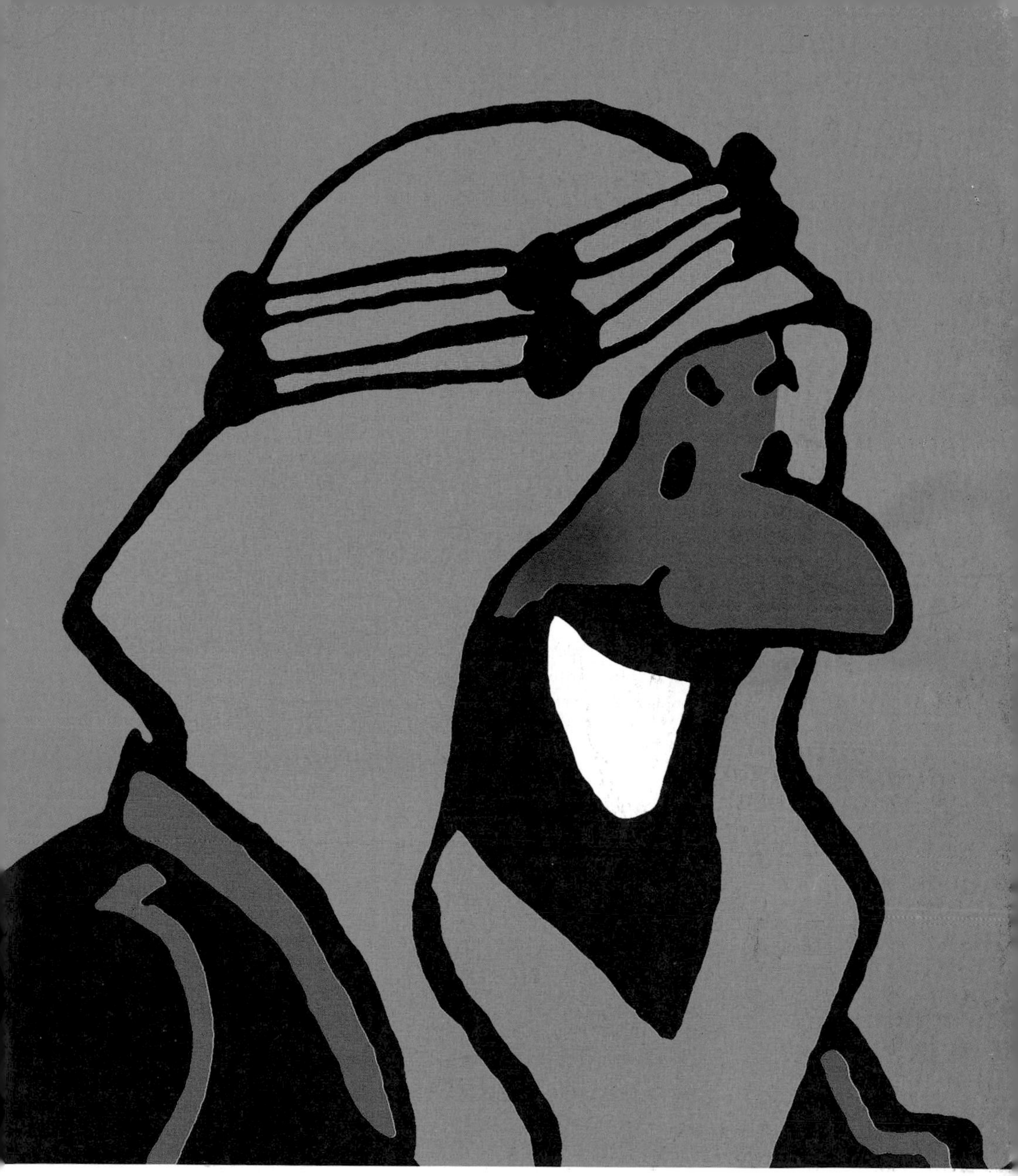

Sheik Patrash Pasha

The tribal sheik seems threatening at first, but his anger turns to joy when he realizes who his attendants have captured!

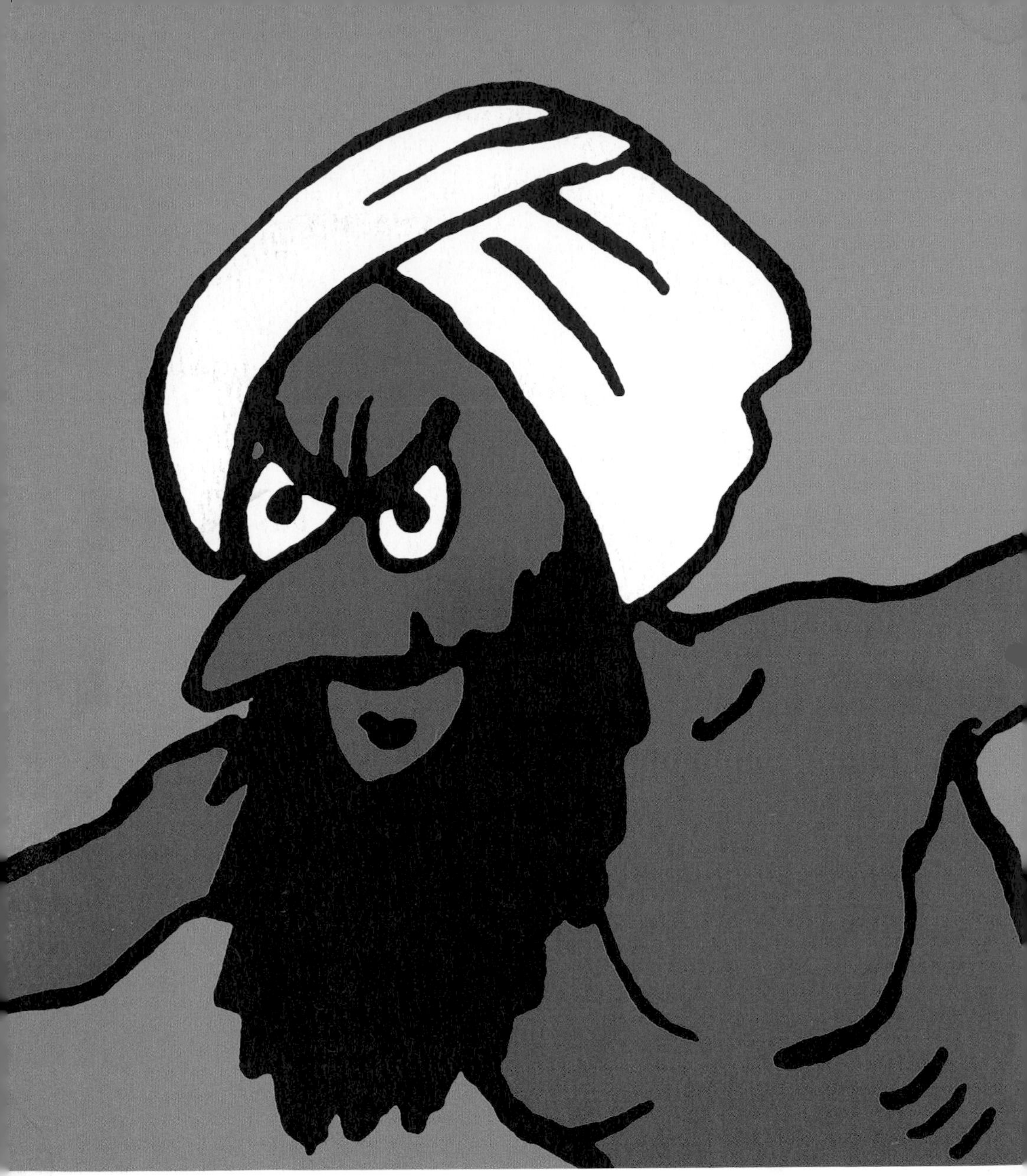

The fakir

Weapons are no match for the malevolent fakir:
one look into his eyes and you are under his hypnotic power!

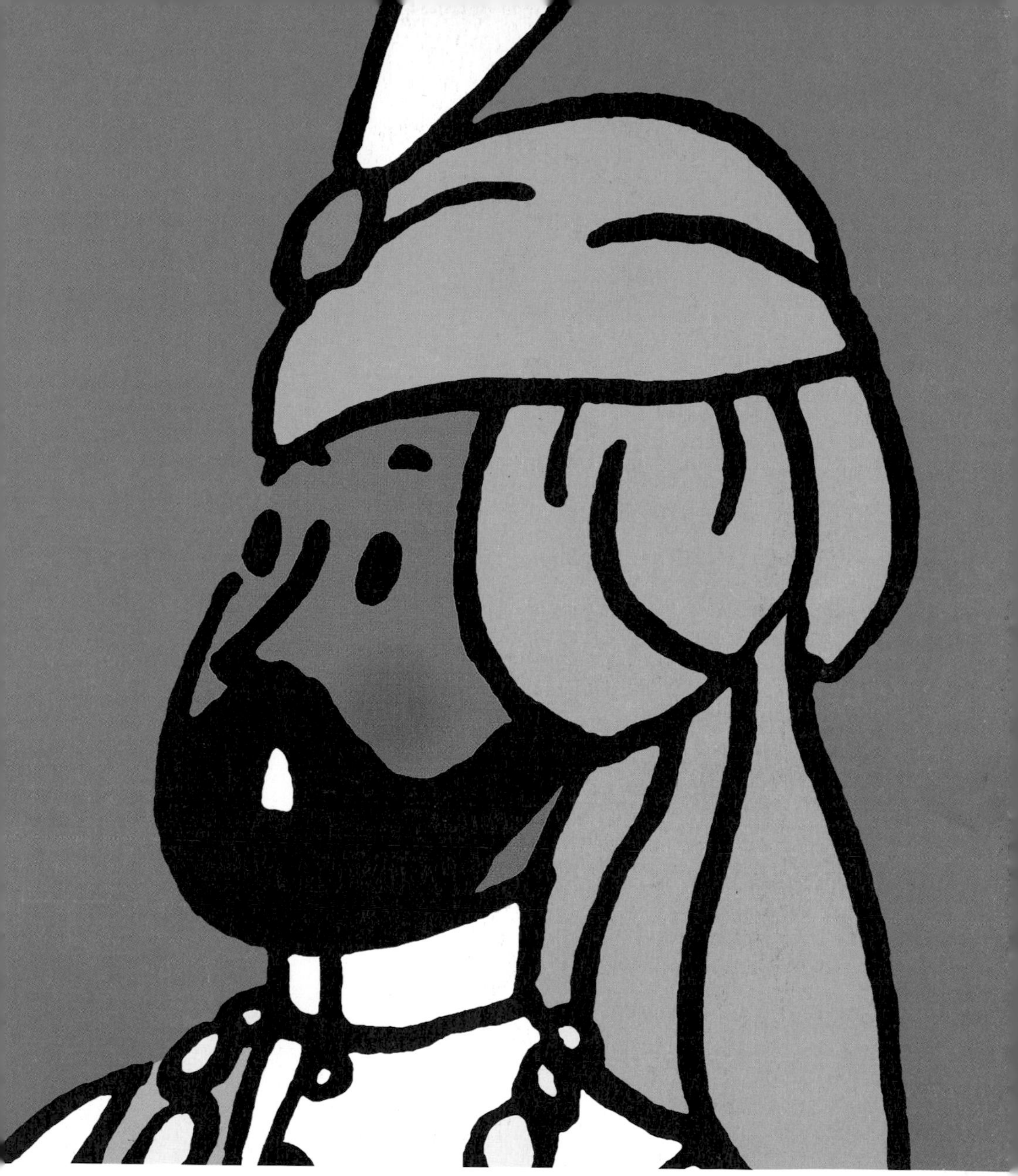

The Maharaja of Gaipajama

The dignified Maharaja of Gaipajama welcomes Tintin into his palace, and the heroic reporter returns his kindness.

CIGARS OF THE PHARAOH

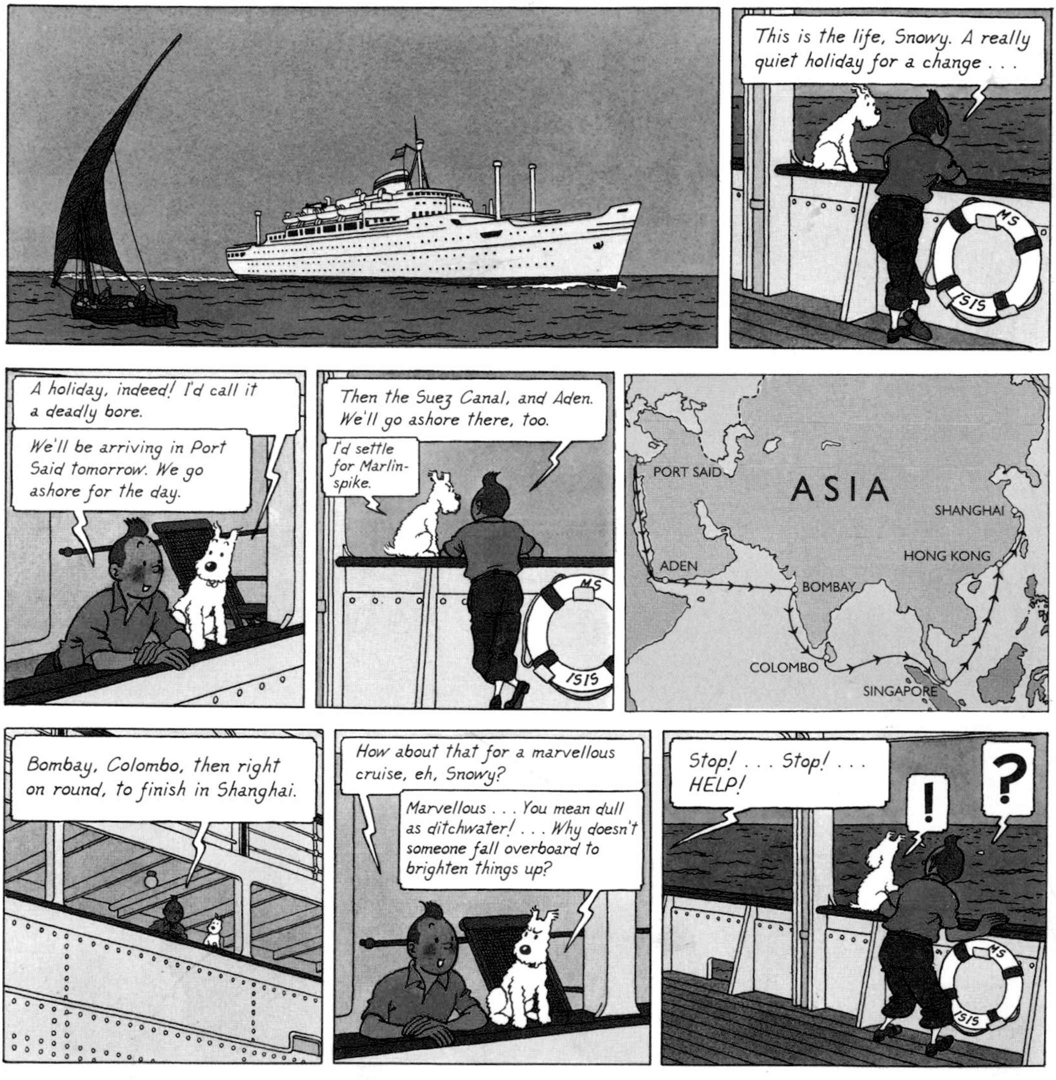
This is the life, Snowy. A really quiet holiday for a change . . .
A holiday, indeed! I'd call it a deadly bore.
We'll be arriving in Port Said tomorrow. We go ashore for the day.
Then the Suez Canal, and Aden. We'll go ashore there, too.
I'd settle for Marlinspike.
PORT SAID
ASIA
SHANGHAI
HONG KONG
ADEN
BOMBAY
COLOMBO
SINGAPORE
Bombay, Colombo, then right on round, to finish in Shanghai.
How about that for a marvellous cruise, eh, Snowy?
Marvellous . . . You mean dull as ditchwater! . . . Why doesn't someone fall overboard to brighten things up?
Stop! . . . Stop! . . . HELP!
!
?

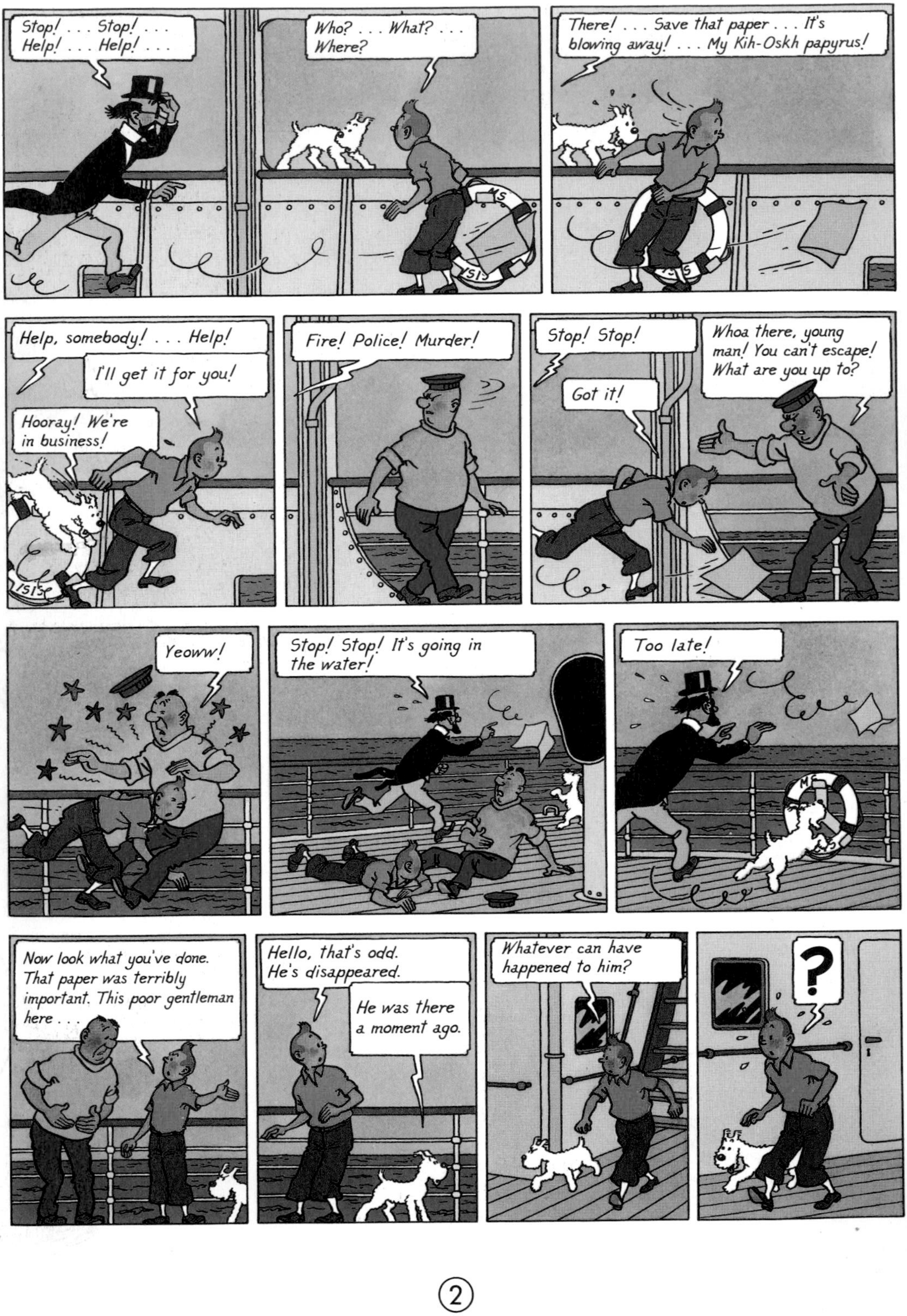
Stop! . . . Stop! . . . Help! . . . Help! . . .
Who? . . . What? . . . Where?
There! . . . Save that paper . . . It's blowing away! . . . My Kih-Oskh papyrus!
MS
ISIS
Help, somebody! . . . Help!
I'll get it for you!
Hooray! We're in business!
ISIS
Fire! Police! Murder!
Stop! Stop!
Got it!
Whoa there, young man! You can't escape! What are you up to?
Yeoww!
Stop! Stop! It's going in the water!
Too late!
Now look what you've done. That paper was terribly important. This poor gentleman here . . .
Hello, that's odd. He's disappeared.
He was there a moment ago.
Whatever can have happened to him?
?

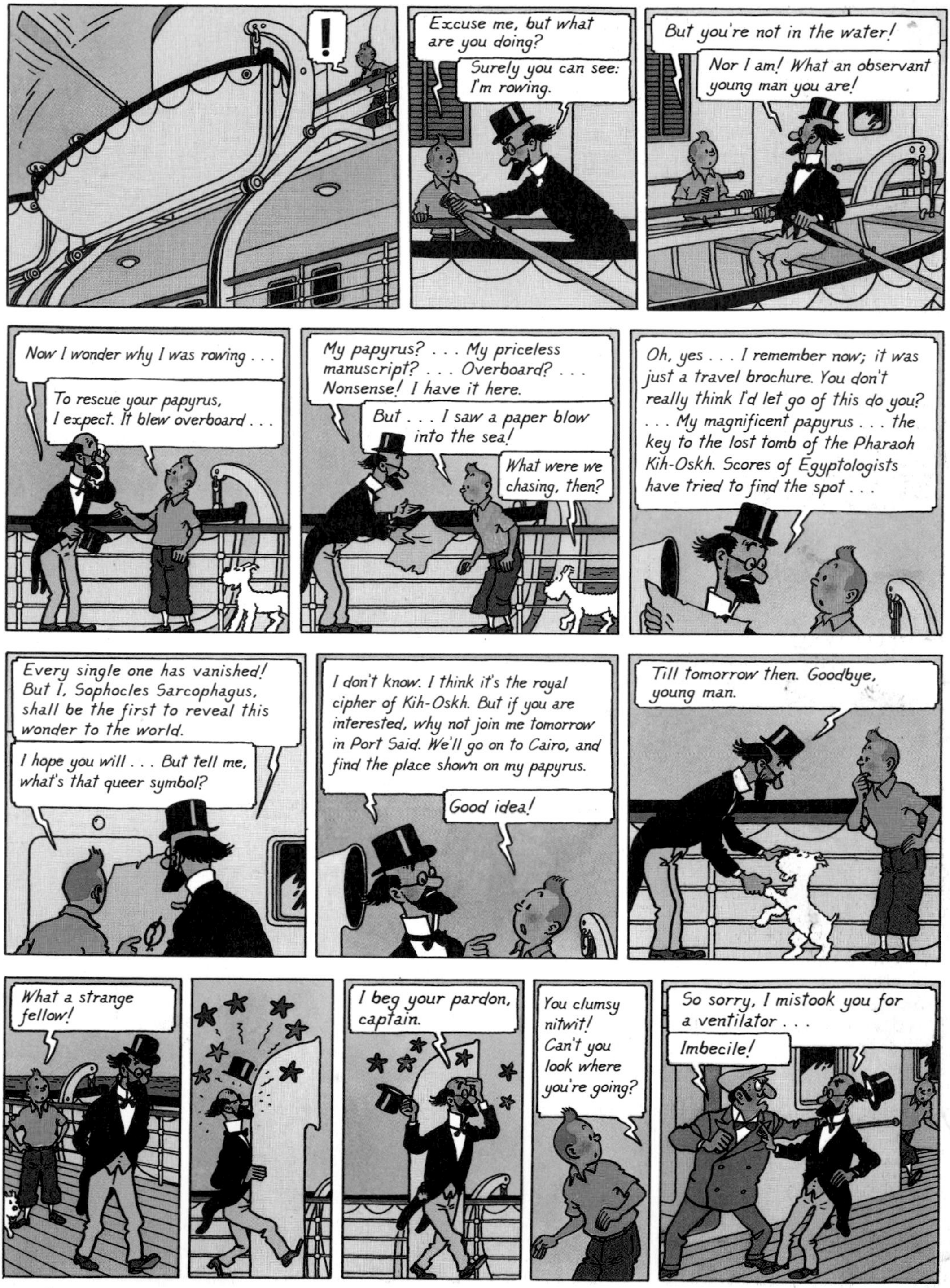
!
Excuse me, but what are you doing?
Surely you can see: I'm rowing.
But you're not in the water!
Nor I am! What an observant young man you are!
Now I wonder why I was rowing . . .
To rescue your papyrus, I expect. It blew overboard . . .
My papyrus? . . . My priceless manuscript? . . . Overboard? . . . Nonsense! I have it here.
But . . . I saw a paper blow into the sea!
What were we chasing, then?
Oh, yes . . . I remember now; it was just a travel brochure. You don't really think I'd let go of this do you? . . . My magnificent papyrus . . . the key to the lost tomb of the Pharaoh Kih-Oskh. Scores of Egyptologists have tried to find the spot . . .
Every single one has vanished! But I, Sophocles Sarcophagus, shall be the first to reveal this wonder to the world.
I hope you will . . . But tell me, what's that queer symbol?
I don't know. I think it's the royal cipher of Kih-Oskh. But if you are interested, why not join me tomorrow in Port Said. We'll go on to Cairo, and find the place shown on my papyrus.
Good idea!
Till tomorrow then. Goodbye, young man.
What a strange fellow!
I beg your pardon, captain.
You clumsy nitwit! Can't you look where you're going?
So sorry, I mistook you for a ventilator . . .
Imbecile!

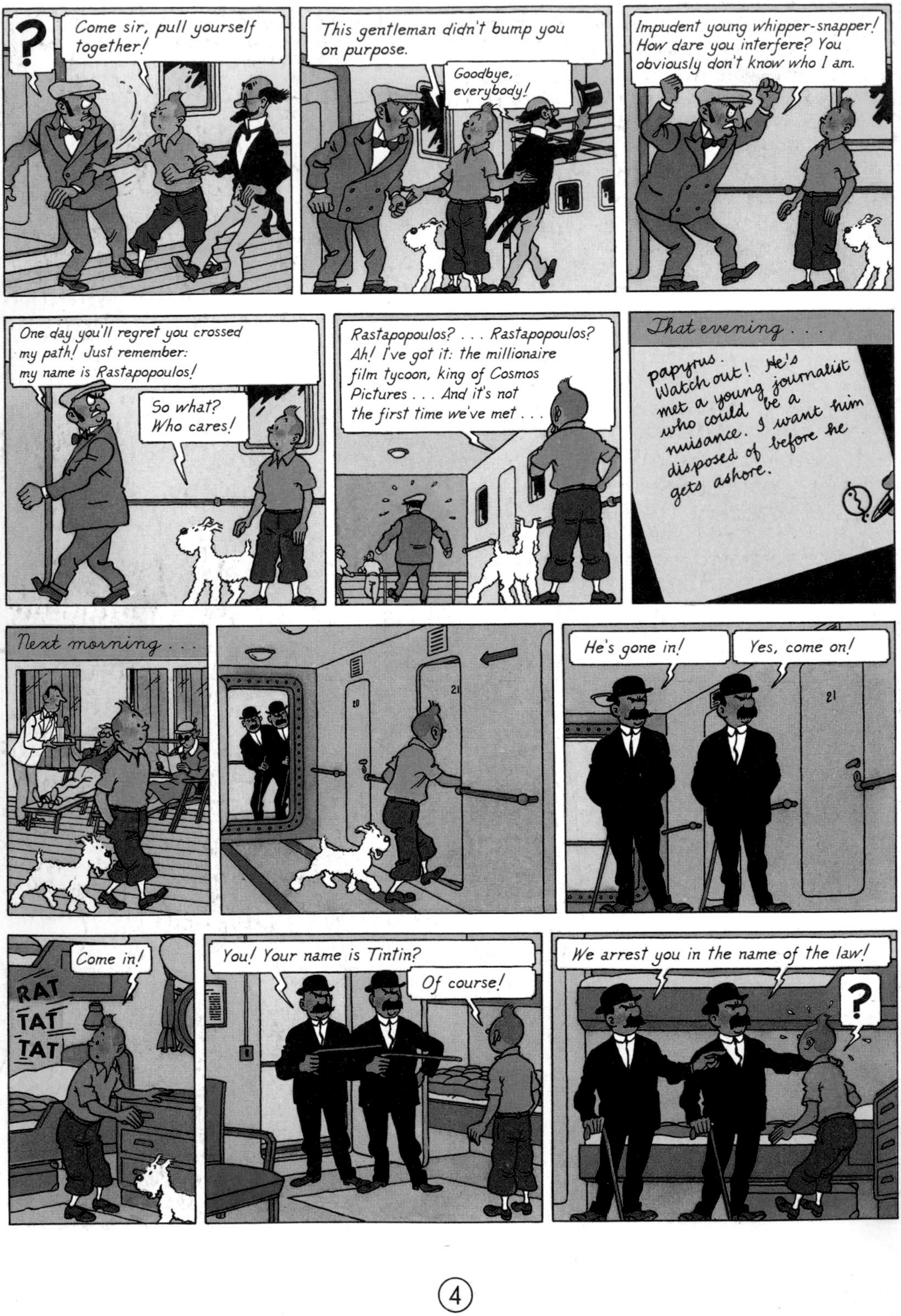
?
Come sir, pull yourself together!
This gentleman didn't bump you on purpose.
Goodbye, everybody!
Impudent young whipper-snapper! How dare you interfere? You obviously don't know who I am.
One day you'll regret you crossed my path! Just remember: my name is Rastapopoulos!
So what? Who cares!
Rastapopoulos? . . . Rastapopoulos? Ah! I've got it: the millionaire film tycoon, king of Cosmos Pictures . . . And it's not the first time we've met . . .
That evening . . .
papyrus. Watch out! He's met a young journalist who could be a nuisance. I want him disposed of before he gets ashore.
Next morning . . .
20
21
He's gone in!
Yes, come on!
21
Come in!
RAT TAT TAT
You! Your name is Tintin?
Of course!
We arrest you in the name of the law!
?

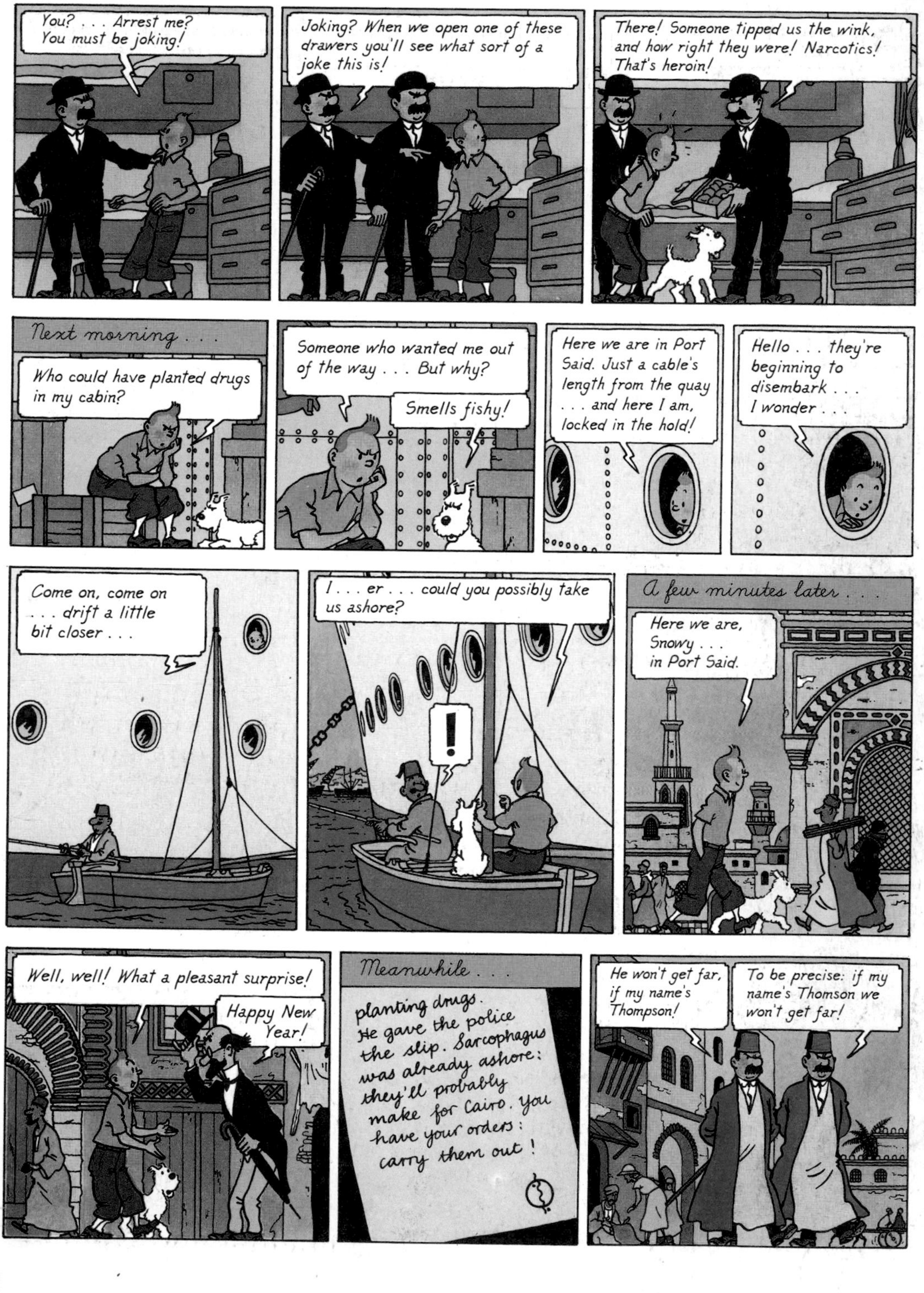
You? . . . Arrest me? You must be joking!
Joking? When we open one of these drawers you'll see what sort of a joke this is!
There! Someone tipped us the wink, and how right they were! Narcotics! That's heroin!
Next morning . . .
Who could have planted drugs in my cabin?
Someone who wanted me out of the way . . . But why?
Smells fishy!
Here we are in Port Said. Just a cable's length from the quay . . . and here I am, locked in the hold!
Hello . . . they're beginning to disembark . . . I wonder . . .
Come on, come on . . . drift a little bit closer . . .
I . . . er . . . could you possibly take us ashore?
!
A few minutes later . . .
Here we are, Snowy . . . in Port Said.
Well, well! What a pleasant surprise!
Happy New Year!
Meanwhile . . .
planting drugs. He gave the police the slip. Sarcophagus was already ashore: they'll probably make for Cairo. You have your orders: carry them out!
He won't get far, if my name's Thompson!
To be precise: if my name's Thomson we won't get far!

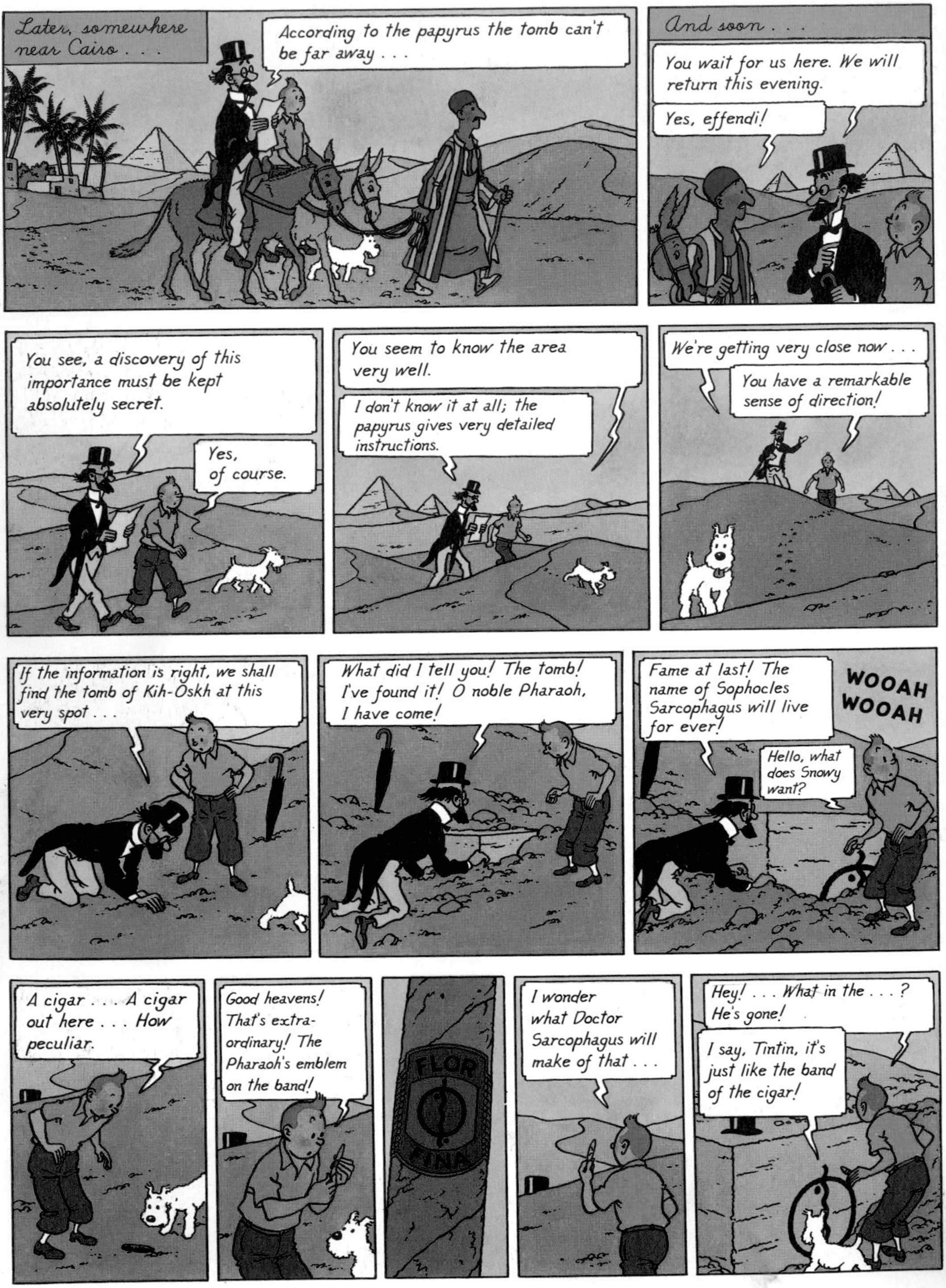
Later, somewhere near Cairo . . .
According to the papyrus the tomb can't be far away . . .
And soon . . .
You wait for us here. We will return this evening.
Yes, effendi!
You see, a discovery of this importance must be kept absolutely secret.
Yes, of course.
You seem to know the area very well.
I don't know it at all; the papyrus gives very detailed instructions.
We're getting very close now . . .
You have a remarkable sense of direction!
If the information is right, we shall find the tomb of Kih-Oskh at this very spot . . .
What did I tell you! The tomb! I've found it! O noble Pharaoh, I have come!
Fame at last! The name of Sophocles Sarcophagus will live for ever!
WOOAH WOOAH
Hello, what does Snowy want?
A cigar . . . A cigar out here . . . How peculiar.
Good heavens! That's extra-ordinary! The Pharaoh's emblem on the band!
FLOR FINA
I wonder what Doctor Sarcophagus will make of that . . .
Hey! . . . What in the . . . ? He's gone!
I say, Tintin, it's just like the band of the cigar!

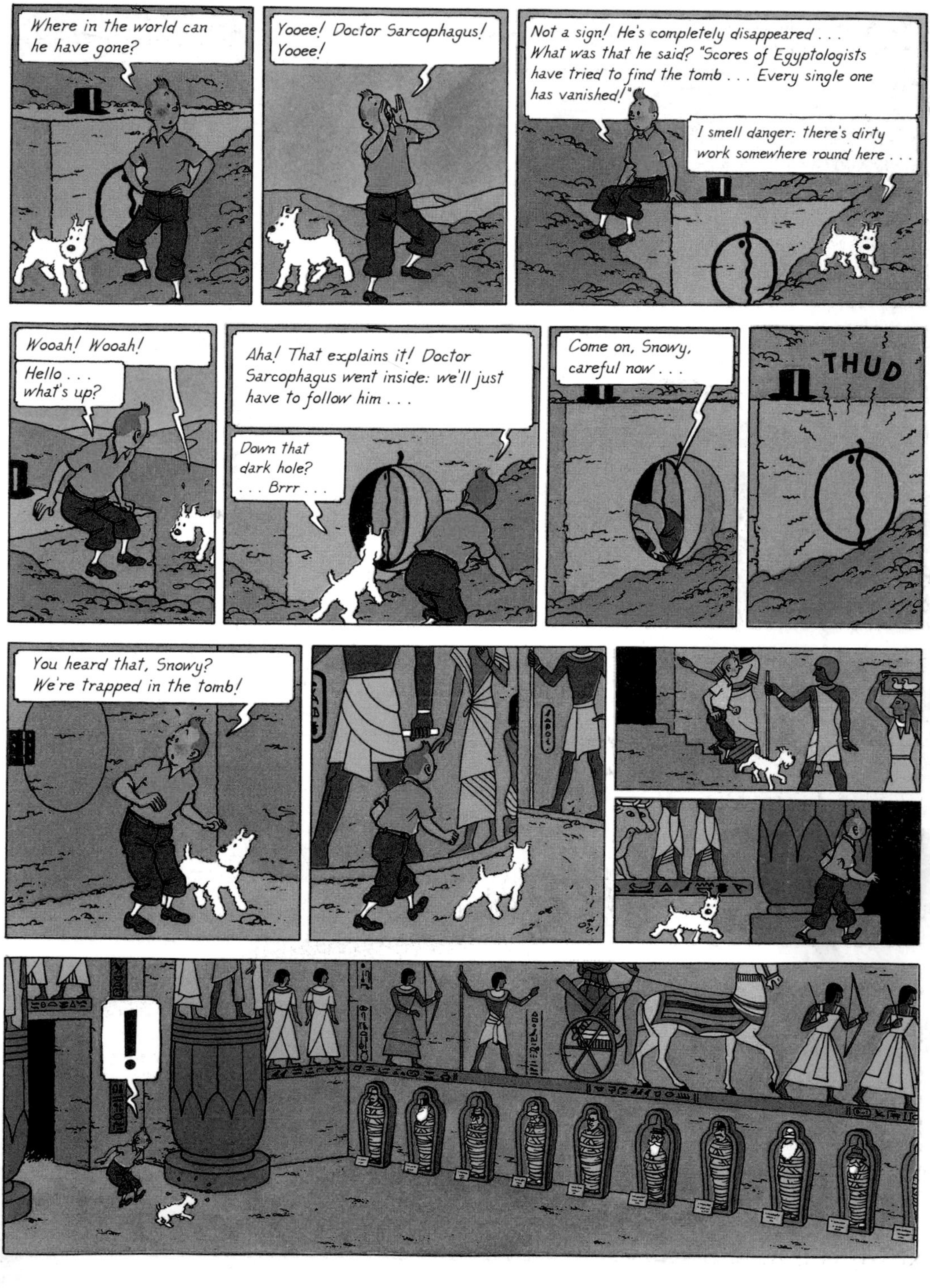
Where in the world can he have gone?
Yooee! Doctor Sarcophagus! Yooee!
Not a sign! He's completely disappeared . . . What was that he said? "Scores of Egyptologists have tried to find the tomb . . . Every single one has vanished!"
I smell danger: there's dirty work somewhere round here . . .
Wooah! Wooah!
Hello . . . what's up?
Aha! That explains it! Doctor Sarcophagus went inside: we'll just have to follow him . . .
Down that dark hole? . . . Brrr . . .
Come on, Snowy, careful now . . .
THUD
You heard that, Snowy? We're trapped in the tomb!
!

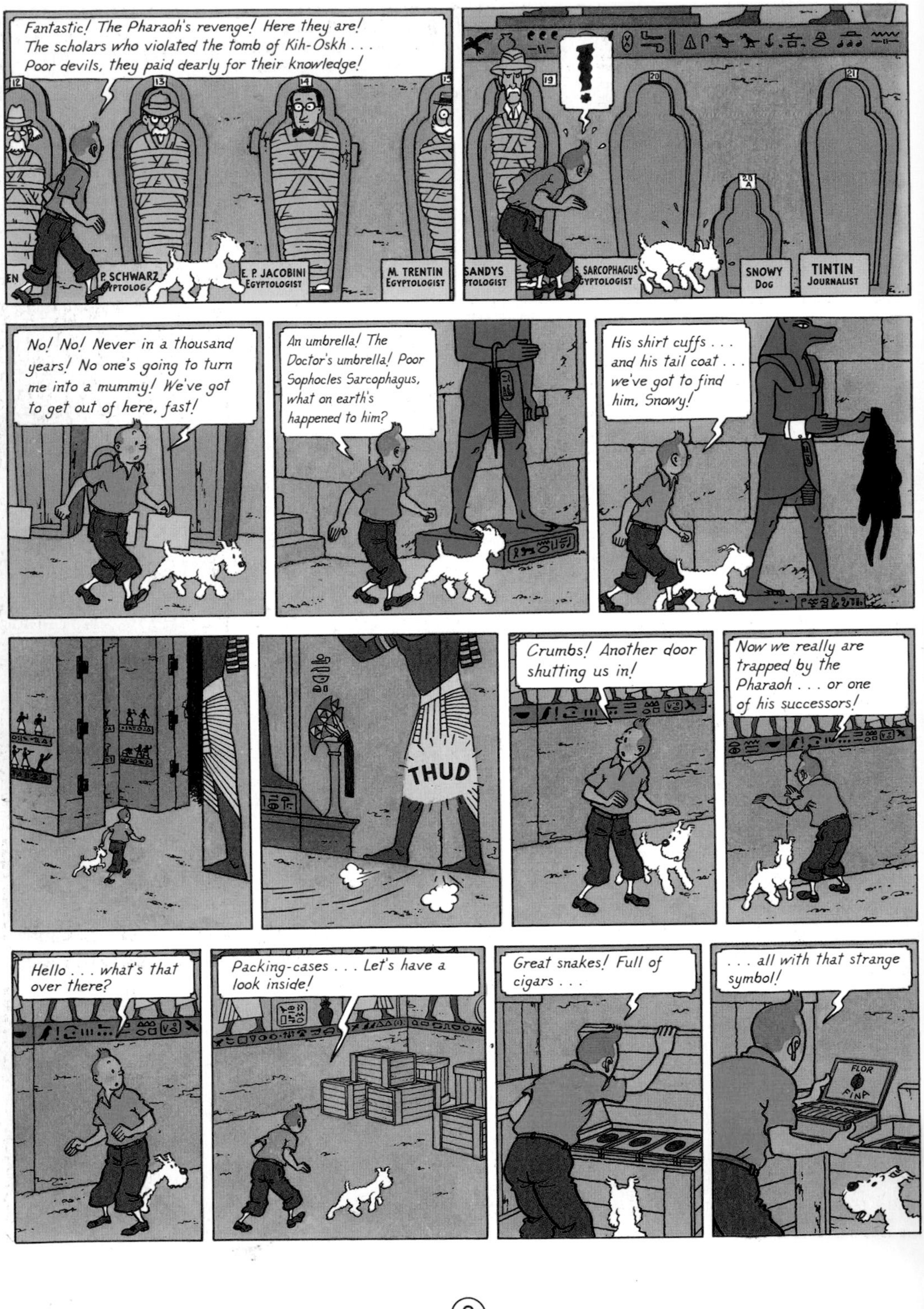

Fantastic! The Pharaoh's revenge! Here they are! The scholars who violated the tomb of Kih-Oskh . . . Poor devils, they paid dearly for their knowledge!
P. SCHWARZ
E. P. JACOBINI
EGYPTOLOGIST
M. TRENTIN
EGYPTOLOGIST
S. SARCOPHAGUS
SNOWY
DOG
TINTIN
JOURNALIST
No! No! Never in a thousand years! No one's going to turn me into a mummy! We've got to get out of here, fast!
An umbrella! The Doctor's umbrella! Poor Sophocles Sarcophagus, what on earth's happened to him?
His shirt cuffs . . . and his tail coat . . . we've got to find him, Snowy!
THUD
Crumbs! Another door shutting us in!
Now we really are trapped by the Pharaoh . . . or one of his successors!
Hello . . . what's that over there?
Packing-cases . . . Let's have a look inside!
Great snakes! Full of cigars . . .
. . . all with that strange symbol!
FLOR FINA

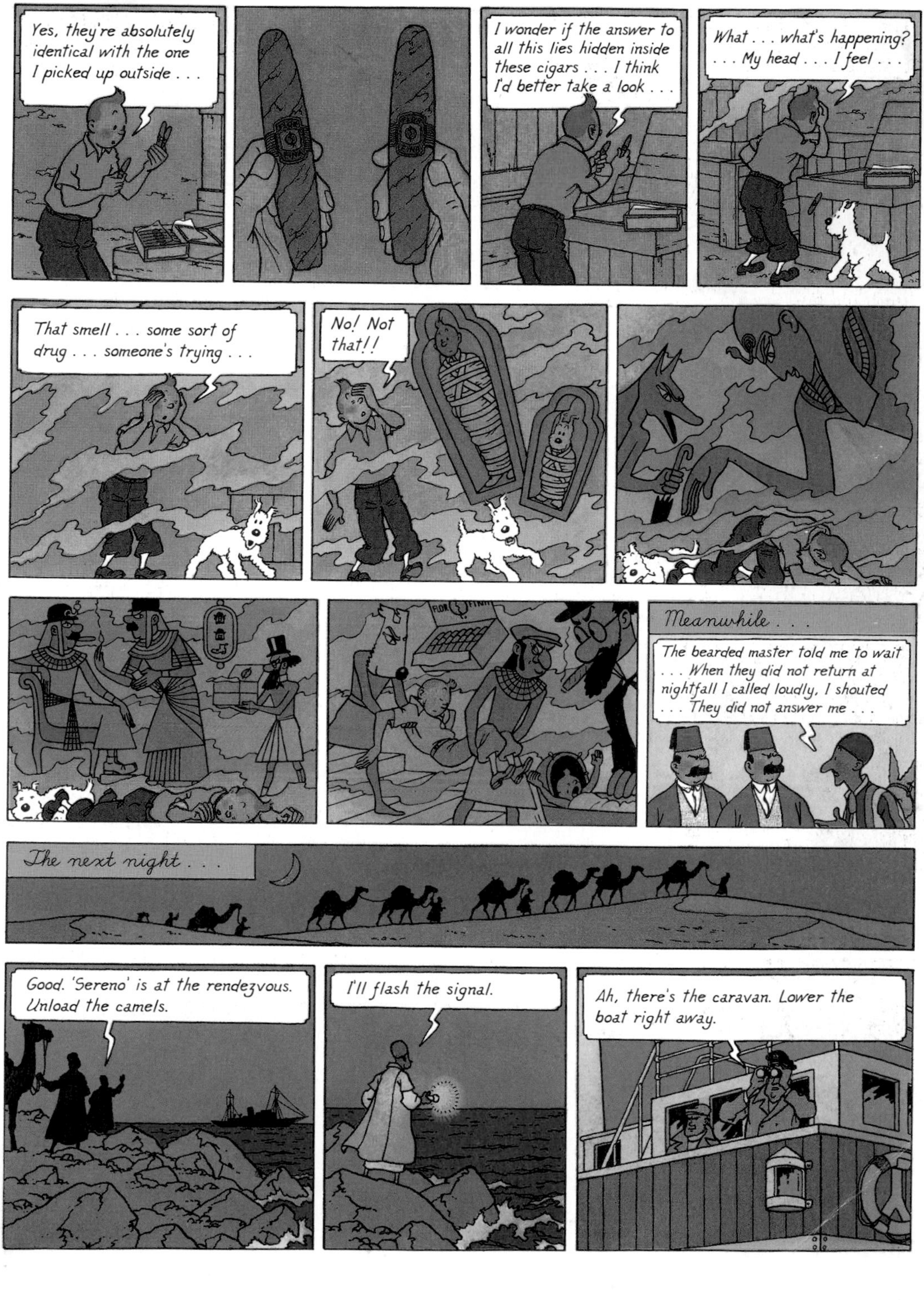
Yes, they're absolutely identical with the one I picked up outside . . .
I wonder if the answer to all this lies hidden inside these cigars . . . I think I'd better take a look . . .
What . . . what's happening? . . . My head . . . I feel . . .
That smell . . . some sort of drug . . . someone's trying . . .
No! Not that!!
Meanwhile . . .
The bearded master told me to wait . . . When they did not return at nightfall I called loudly, I shouted . . . They did not answer me . . .
The next night . . .
Good. 'Sereno' is at the rendezvous. Unload the camels.
I'll flash the signal.
Ah, there's the caravan. Lower the boat right away.

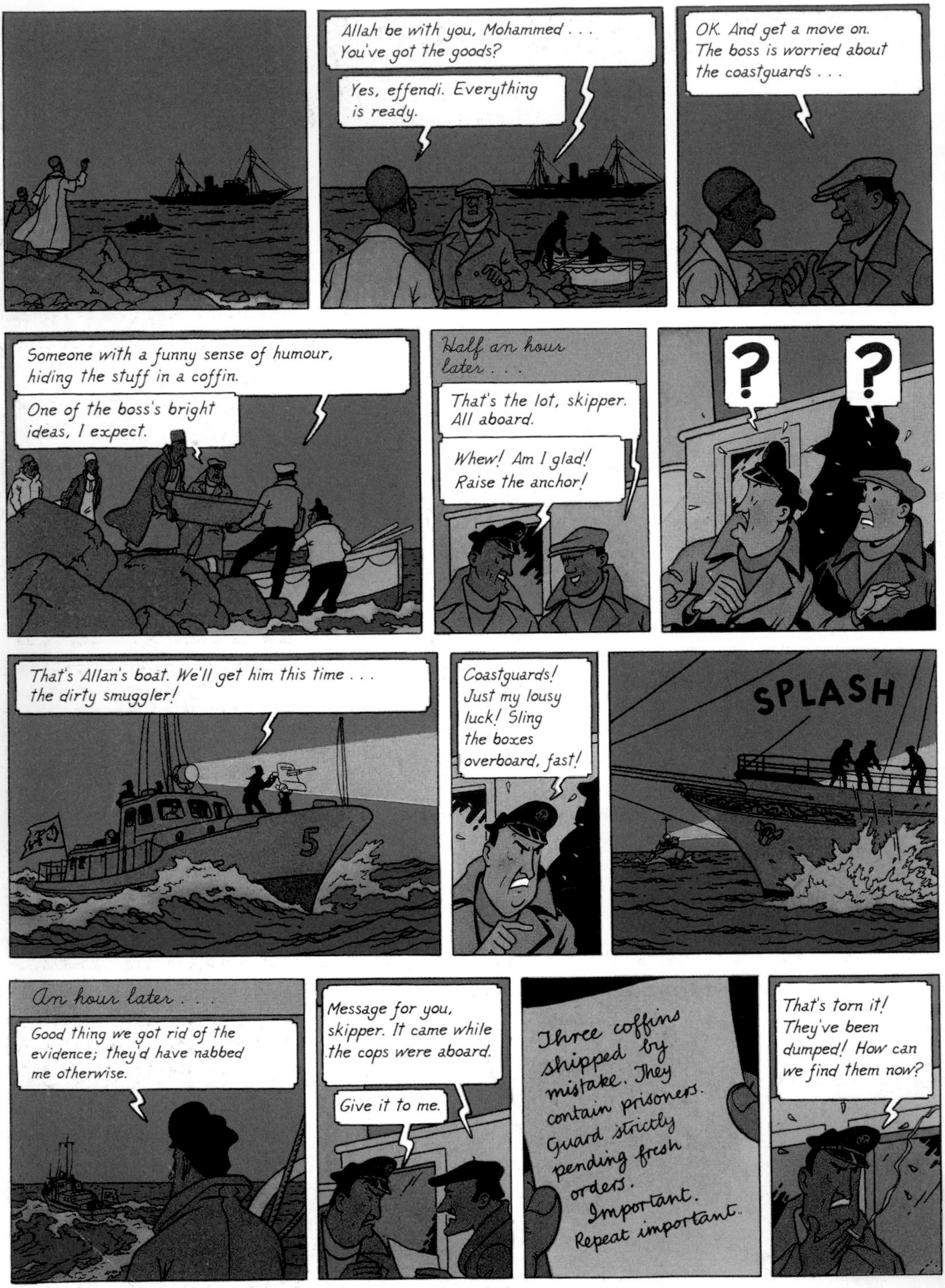

Allah be with you, Mohammed . . . You've got the goods?
Yes, effendi. Everything is ready.
OK. And get a move on. The boss is worried about the coastguards . . .
Someone with a funny sense of humour, hiding the stuff in a coffin.
One of the boss's bright ideas, I expect.
Half an hour later . . .
That's the lot, skipper. All aboard.
Whew! Am I glad! Raise the anchor!
?
?
That's Allan's boat. We'll get him this time . . . the dirty smuggler!
5
Coastguards! Just my lousy luck! Sling the boxes overboard, fast!
SPLASH
An hour later . . .
Good thing we got rid of the evidence; they'd have nabbed me otherwise.
Message for you, skipper. It came while the cops were aboard.
Give it to me.
Three coffins shipped by mistake. They contain prisoners. Guard strictly pending fresh orders. Important. Repeat important.
That's torn it! They've been dumped! How can we find them now?

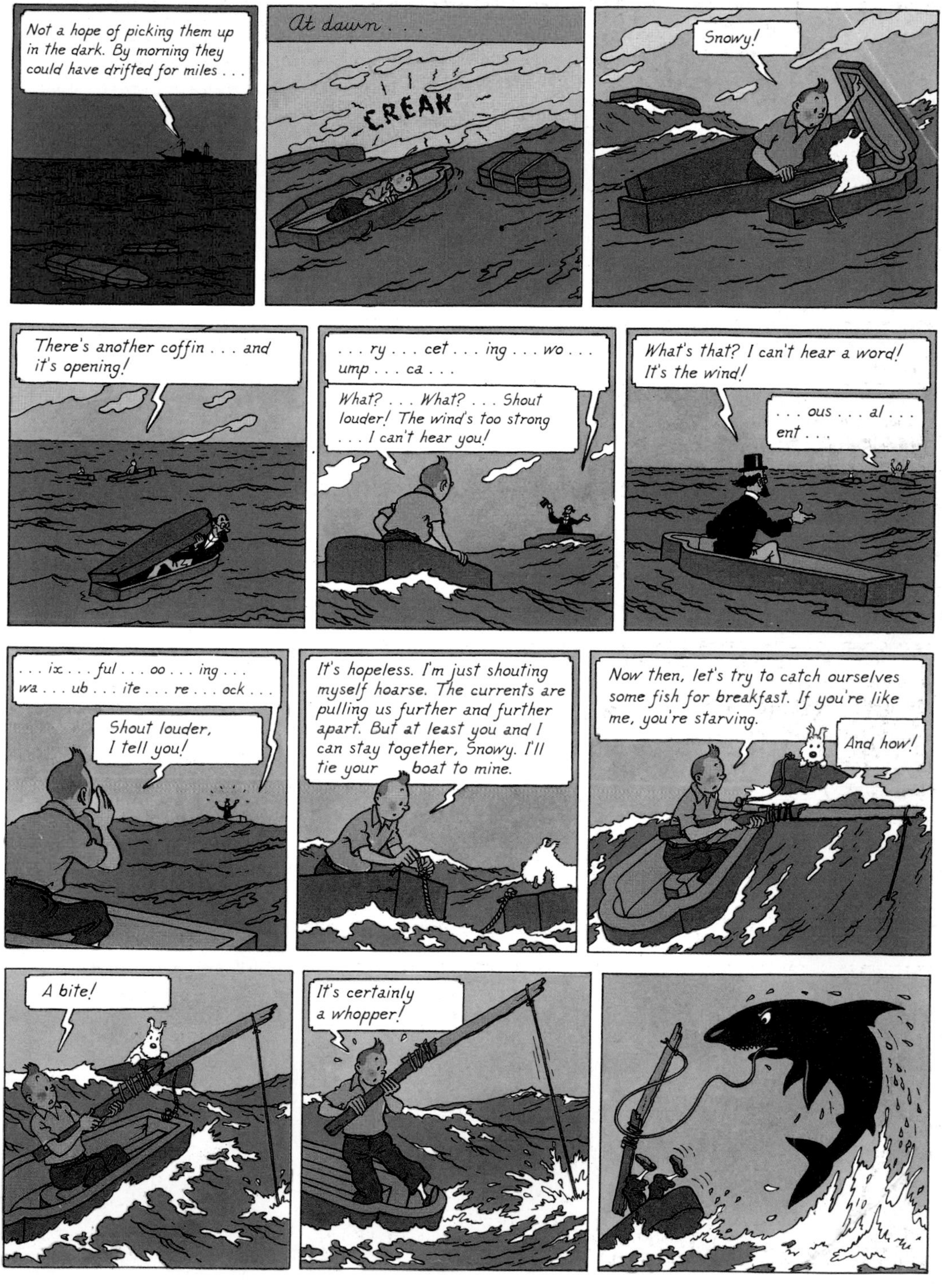
Not a hope of picking them up in the dark. By morning they could have drifted for miles . . .
At dawn . . .
CREAK
Snowy!
There's another coffin . . . and it's opening!
. . . ry . . . cet . . . ing . . . wo . . . ump . . . ca . . .
What? . . . What? . . . Shout louder! The wind's too strong . . . I can't hear you!
What's that? I can't hear a word! It's the wind!
. . . ous . . . al . . . ent . . .
. . . ix . . . ful . . . oo . . . ing . . . wa . . . ub . . . ite . . . re . . . ock . . .
Shout louder, I tell you!
It's hopeless. I'm just shouting myself hoarse. The currents are pulling us further and further apart. But at least you and I can stay together, Snowy. I'll tie your boat to mine.
Now then, let's try to catch ourselves some fish for breakfast. If you're like me, you're starving.
And how!
A bite!
It's certainly a whopper!

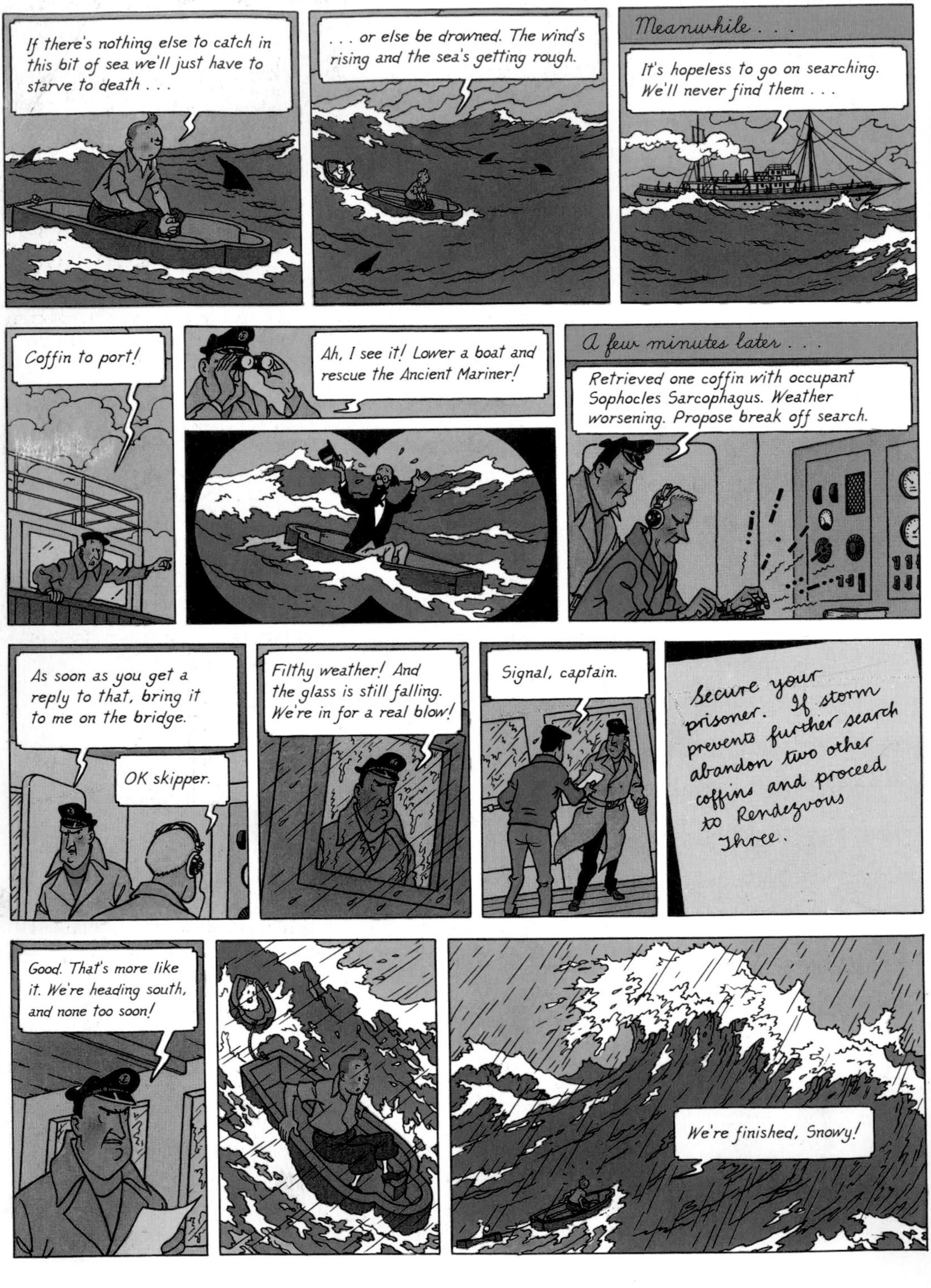
If there's nothing else to catch in this bit of sea we'll just have to starve to death . . .
. . . or else be drowned. The wind's rising and the sea's getting rough.
Meanwhile . . .
It's hopeless to go on searching. We'll never find them . . .
Coffin to port!
Ah, I see it! Lower a boat and rescue the Ancient Mariner!
A few minutes later . . .
Retrieved one coffin with occupant Sophocles Sarcophagus. Weather worsening. Propose break off search.
As soon as you get a reply to that, bring it to me on the bridge.
OK skipper.
Filthy weather! And the glass is still falling. We're in for a real blow!
Signal, captain.
Secure your prisoner. If storm prevents further search abandon two other coffins and proceed to Rendezvous Three.
Good. That's more like it. We're heading south, and none too soon!
We're finished, Snowy!

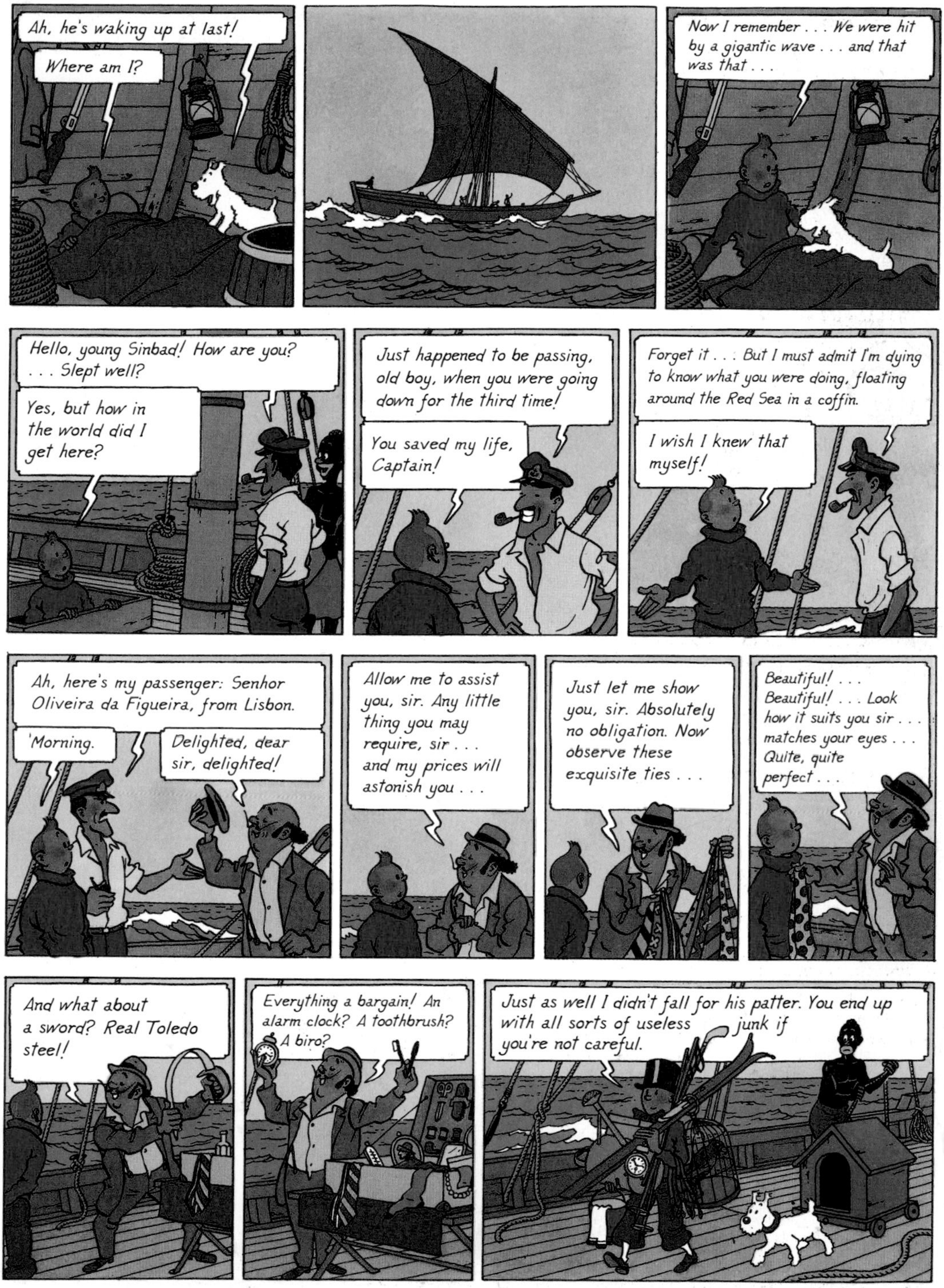

Ah, he's waking up at last!
Where am I?
Now I remember . . . We were hit by a gigantic wave . . . and that was that . . .
Hello, young Sinbad! How are you? . . . Slept well?
Yes, but how in the world did I get here?
Just happened to be passing, old boy, when you were going down for the third time!
You saved my life, Captain!
Forget it . . . But I must admit I'm dying to know what you were doing, floating around the Red Sea in a coffin.
I wish I knew that myself!
Ah, here's my passenger: Senhor Oliveira da Figueira, from Lisbon.
'Morning.
Delighted, dear sir, delighted!
Allow me to assist you, sir. Any little thing you may require, sir . . . and my prices will astonish you . . .
Just let me show you, sir. Absolutely no obligation. Now observe these exquisite ties . . .
Beautiful! . . . Beautiful! . . . Look how it suits you sir . . . matches your eyes . . . Quite, quite perfect . . .
And what about a sword? Real Toledo steel!
Everything a bargain! An alarm clock? A toothbrush? A biro?
Just as well I didn't fall for his patter. You end up with all sorts of useless junk if you're not careful.

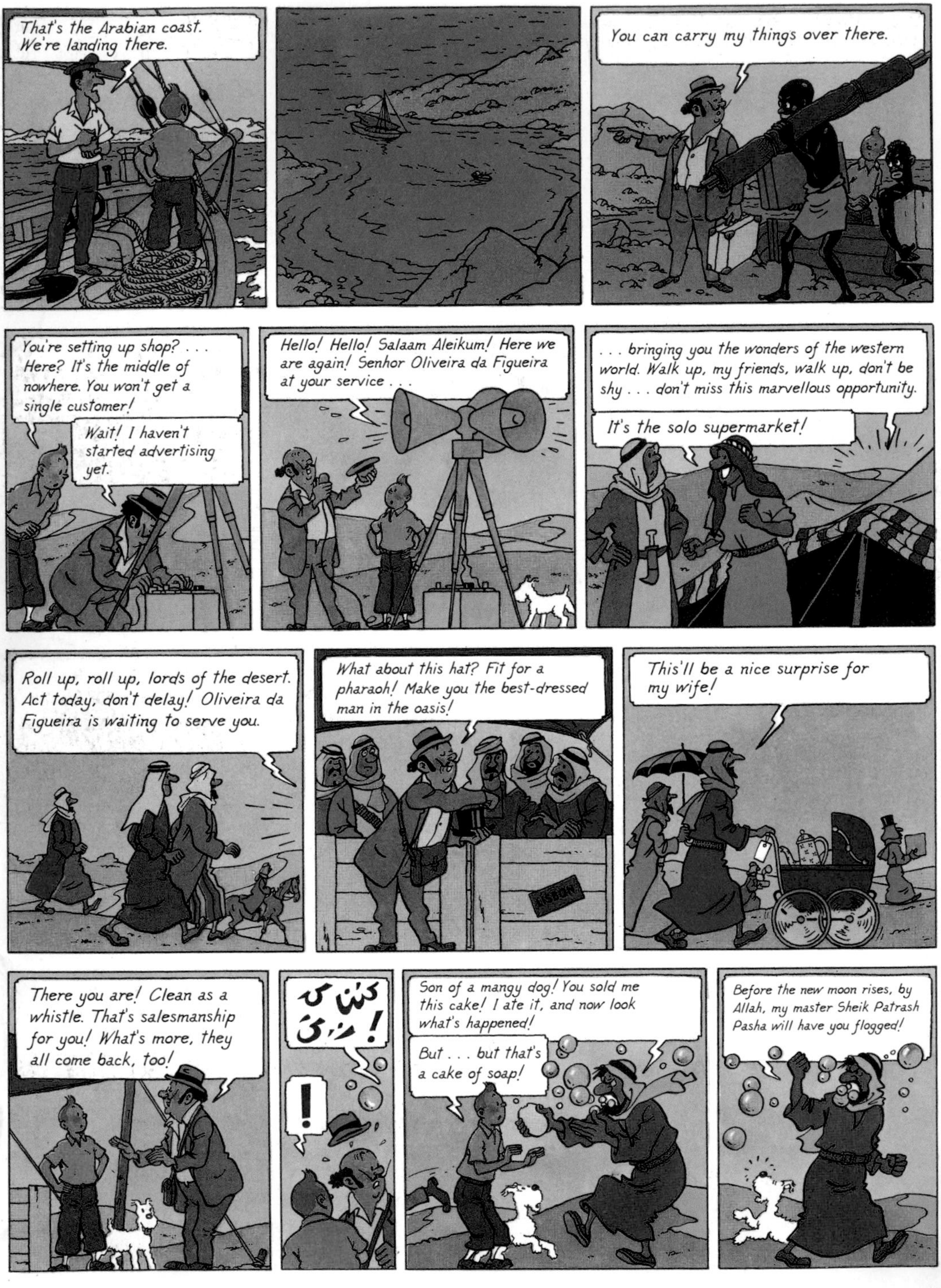
That's the Arabian coast. We're landing there.
You can carry my things over there.
You're setting up shop? . . . Here? It's the middle of nowhere. You won't get a single customer!
Wait! I haven't started advertising yet.
Hello! Hello! Salaam Aleikum! Here we are again! Senhor Oliveira da Figueira at your service . . .
. . . bringing you the wonders of the western world. Walk up, my friends, walk up, don't be shy . . . don't miss this marvellous opportunity.
It's the solo supermarket!
Roll up, roll up, lords of the desert. Act today, don't delay! Oliveira da Figueira is waiting to serve you.
What about this hat? Fit for a pharaoh! Make you the best-dressed man in the oasis!
LISBOA
This'll be a nice surprise for my wife!
There you are! Clean as a whistle. That's salesmanship for you! What's more, they all come back, too!
!
Son of a mangy dog! You sold me this cake! I ate it, and now look what's happened!
But . . . but that's a cake of soap!
Before the new moon rises, by Allah, my master Sheik Patrash Pasha will have you flogged!

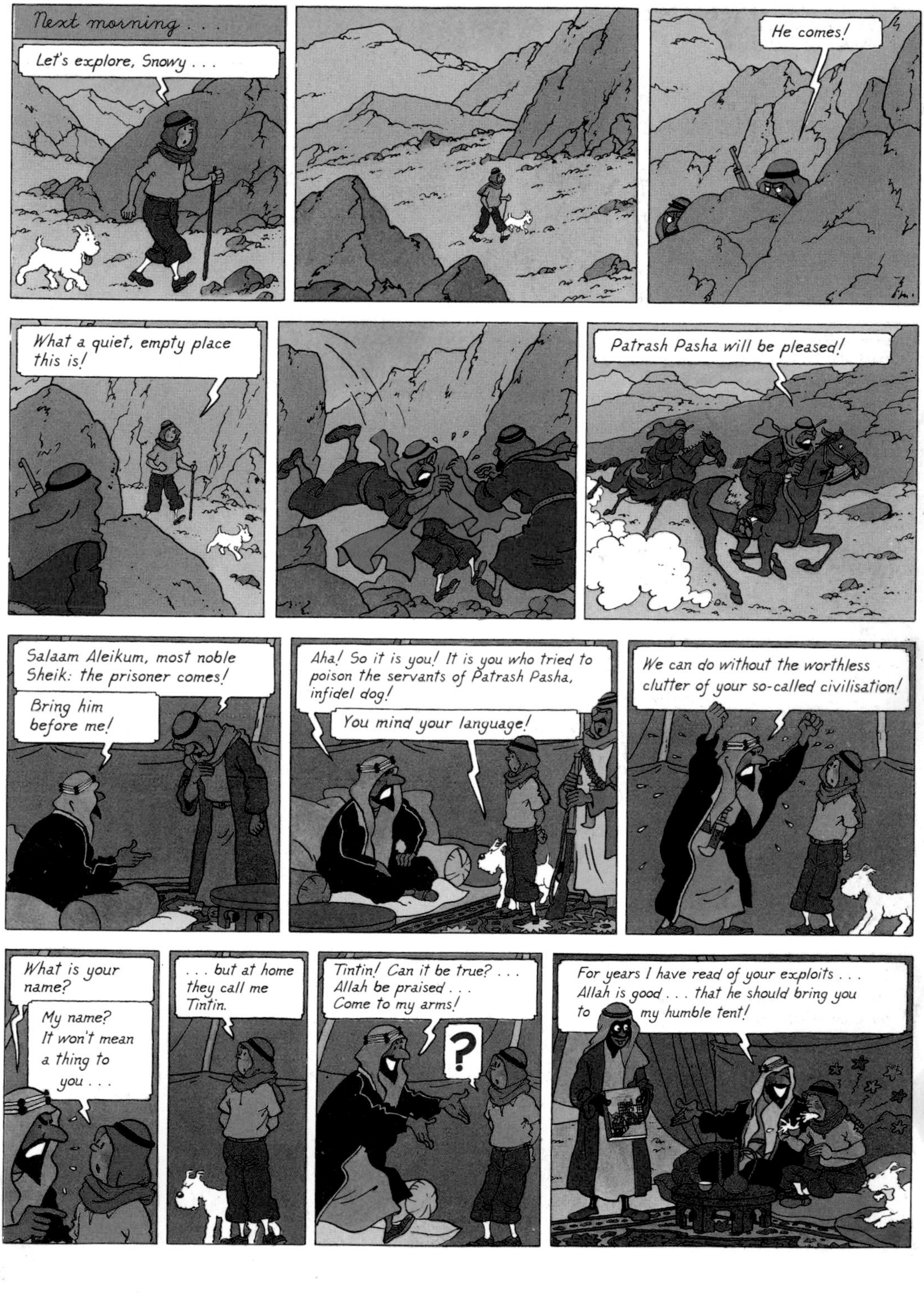

Next morning . . .
Let's explore, Snowy . . .
He comes!
What a quiet, empty place this is!
Patrash Pasha will be pleased!
Salaam Aleikum, most noble Sheik: the prisoner comes!
Bring him before me!
Aha! So it is you! It is you who tried to poison the servants of Patrash Pasha, infidel dog!
You mind your language!
We can do without the worthless clutter of your so-called civilisation!
What is your name?
My name? It won't mean a thing to you . . .
. . . but at home they call me Tintin.
Tintin! Can it be true? . . . Allah be praised . . . Come to my arms!
?
For years I have read of your exploits . . . Allah is good . . . that he should bring you to my humble tent!

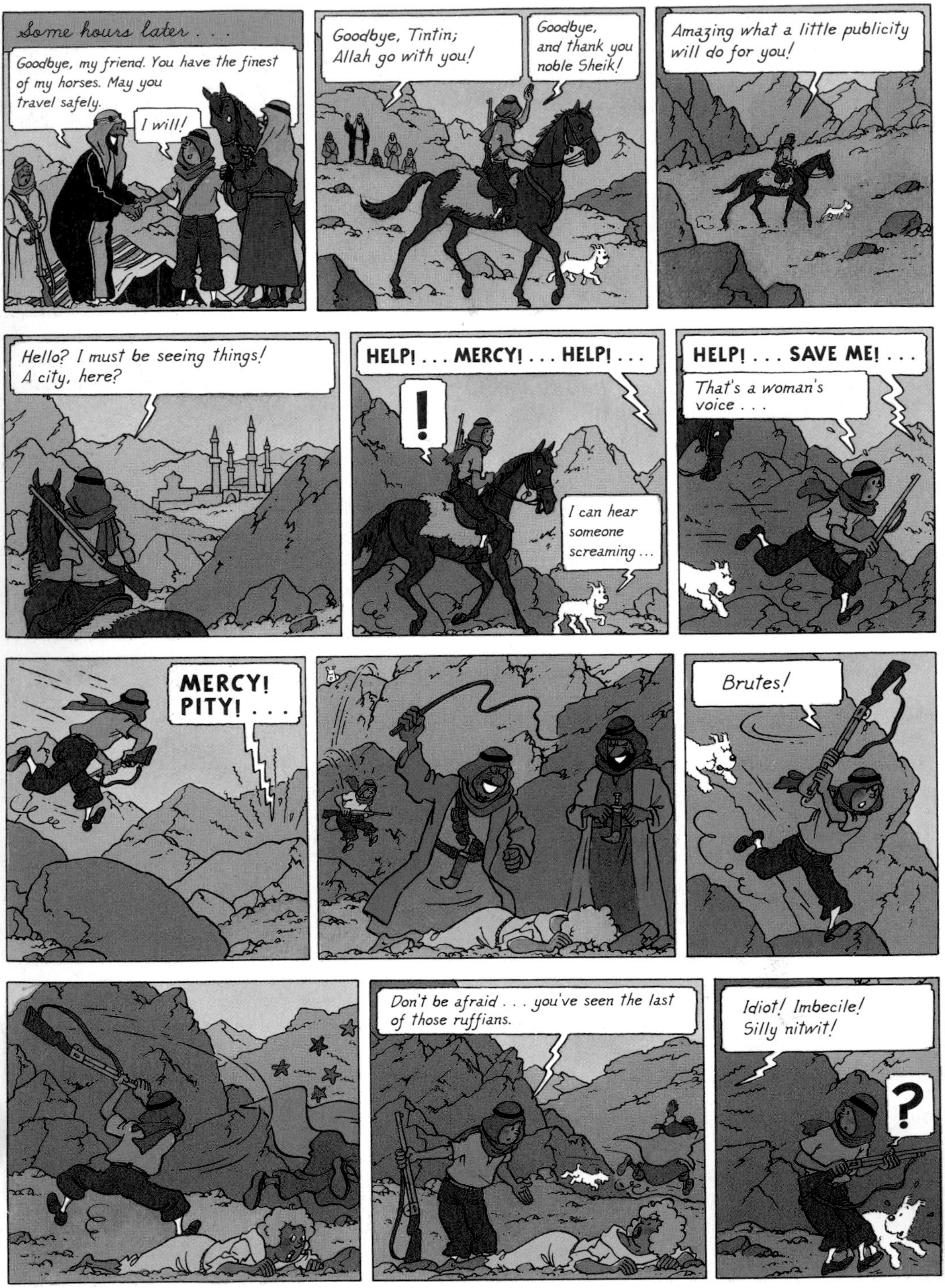
Some hours later . . .
Goodbye, my friend. You have the finest of my horses. May you travel safely.
I will!
Goodbye, Tintin; Allah go with you!
Goodbye, and thank you noble Sheik!
Amazing what a little publicity will do for you!
Hello? I must be seeing things! A city, here?
HELP! . . . MERCY! . . . HELP! . . .
!
I can hear someone screaming . . .
HELP! . . . SAVE ME! . . .
That's a woman's voice . . .
MERCY! PITY! . . .
Brutes!
Don't be afraid . . . you've seen the last of those ruffians.
Idiot! Imbecile! Silly nitwit!
?

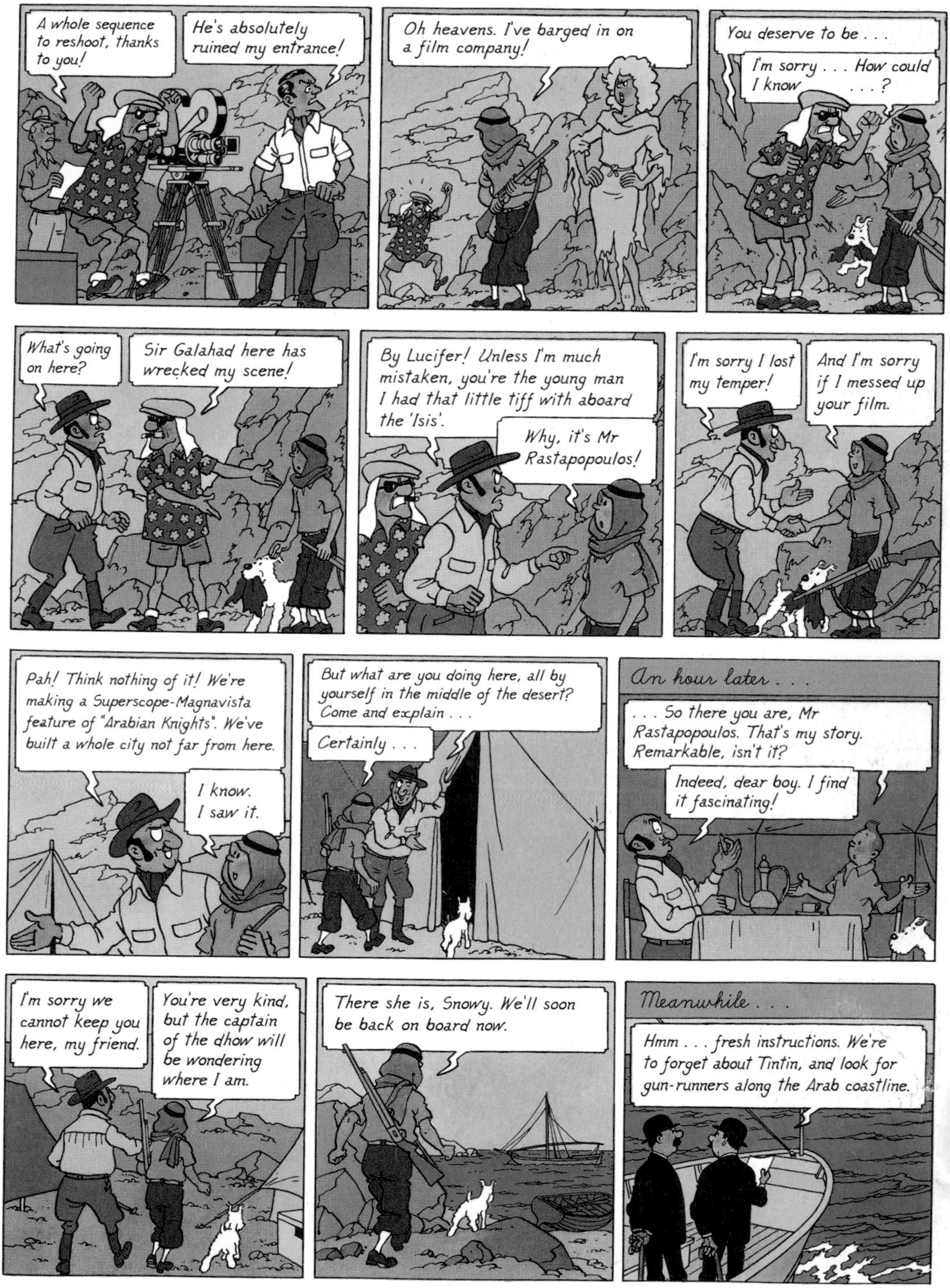
A whole sequence to reshoot, thanks to you!
He's absolutely ruined my entrance!
Oh heavens. I've barged in on a film company!
You deserve to be . . .
I'm sorry . . . How could I know . . . ?
What's going on here?
Sir Galahad here has wrecked my scene!
By Lucifer! Unless I'm much mistaken, you're the young man I had that little tiff with aboard the 'Isis'.
Why, it's Mr Rastapopoulos!
I'm sorry I lost my temper!
And I'm sorry if I messed up your film.
Pah! Think nothing of it! We're making a Superscope-Magnavista feature of "Arabian Knights". We've built a whole city not far from here.
I know. I saw it.
But what are you doing here, all by yourself in the middle of the desert? Come and explain . . .
Certainly . . .
An hour later . . .
. . . So there you are, Mr Rastapopoulos. That's my story. Remarkable, isn't it?
Indeed, dear boy. I find it fascinating!
I'm sorry we cannot keep you here, my friend.
You're very kind, but the captain of the dhow will be wondering where I am.
There she is, Snowy. We'll soon be back on board now.
Meanwhile . . .
Hmm . . . fresh instructions. We're to forget about Tintin, and look for gun-runners along the Arab coastline.

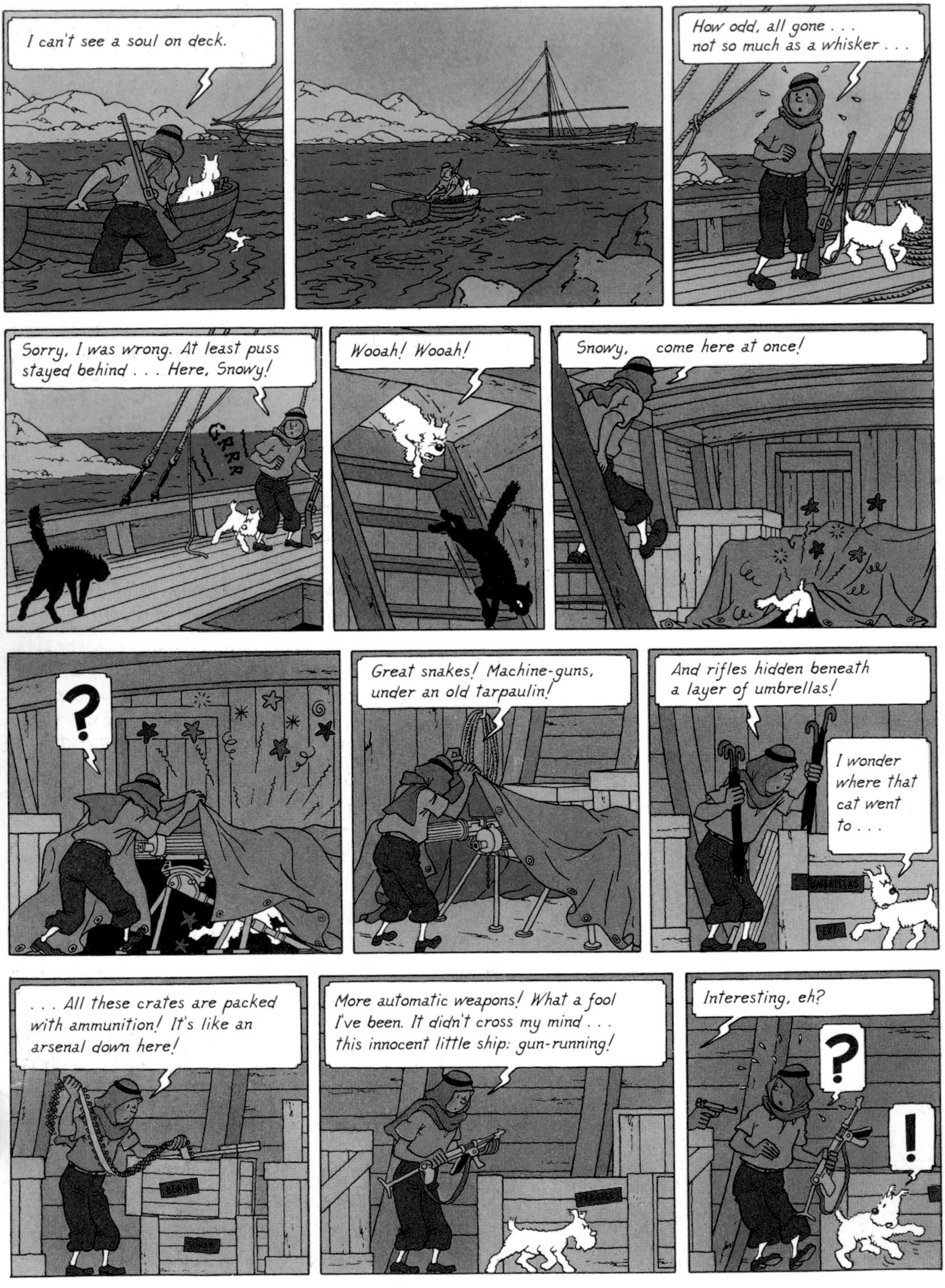

I can't see a soul on deck.
How odd, all gone . . . not so much as a whisker . . .
Sorry, I was wrong. At least puss stayed behind . . . Here, Snowy!
GRRR
Wooah! Wooah!
Snowy, come here at once!
?
Great snakes! Machine-guns, under an old tarpaulin!
And rifles hidden beneath a layer of umbrellas!
I wonder where that cat went to . . .
. . . All these crates are packed with ammunition! It's like an arsenal down here!
More automatic weapons! What a fool I've been. It didn't cross my mind . . . this innocent little ship: gun-running!
Interesting, eh?
?
!

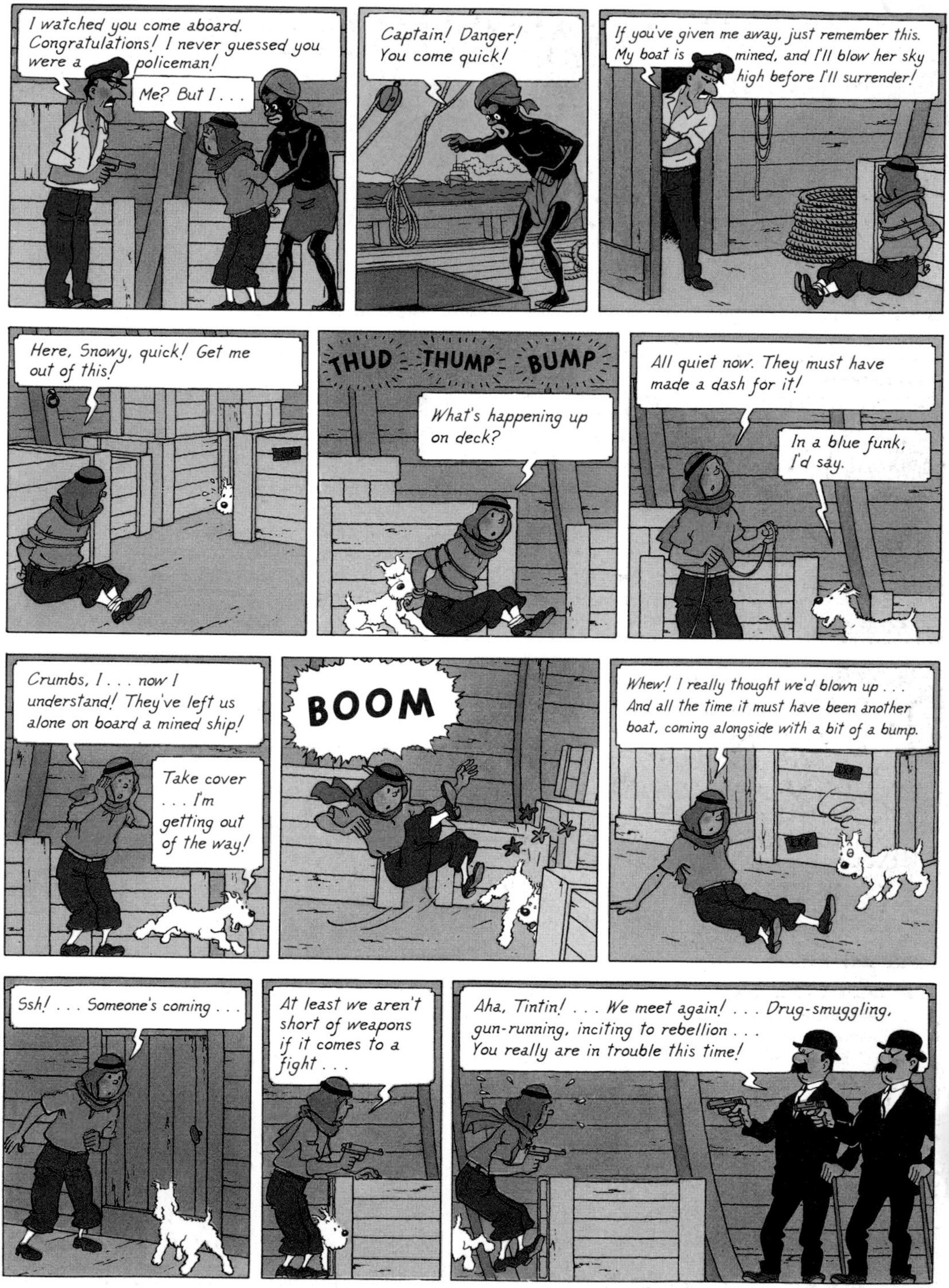
I watched you come aboard. Congratulations! I never guessed you were a policeman!
Me? But I . . .
Captain! Danger! You come quick!
If you've given me away, just remember this. My boat is mined, and I'll blow her sky high before I'll surrender!
Here, Snowy, quick! Get me out of this!
THUD THUMP BUMP
What's happening up on deck?
All quiet now. They must have made a dash for it!
In a blue funk, I'd say.
Crumbs, I . . . now I understand! They've left us alone on board a mined ship!
Take cover . . . I'm getting out of the way!
BOOM
Whew! I really thought we'd blown up . . . And all the time it must have been another boat, coming alongside with a bit of a bump.
Ssh! . . . Someone's coming . . .
At least we aren't short of weapons if it comes to a fight . . .
Aha, Tintin! . . . We meet again! . . . Drug-smuggling, gun-running, inciting to rebellion . . . You really are in trouble this time!

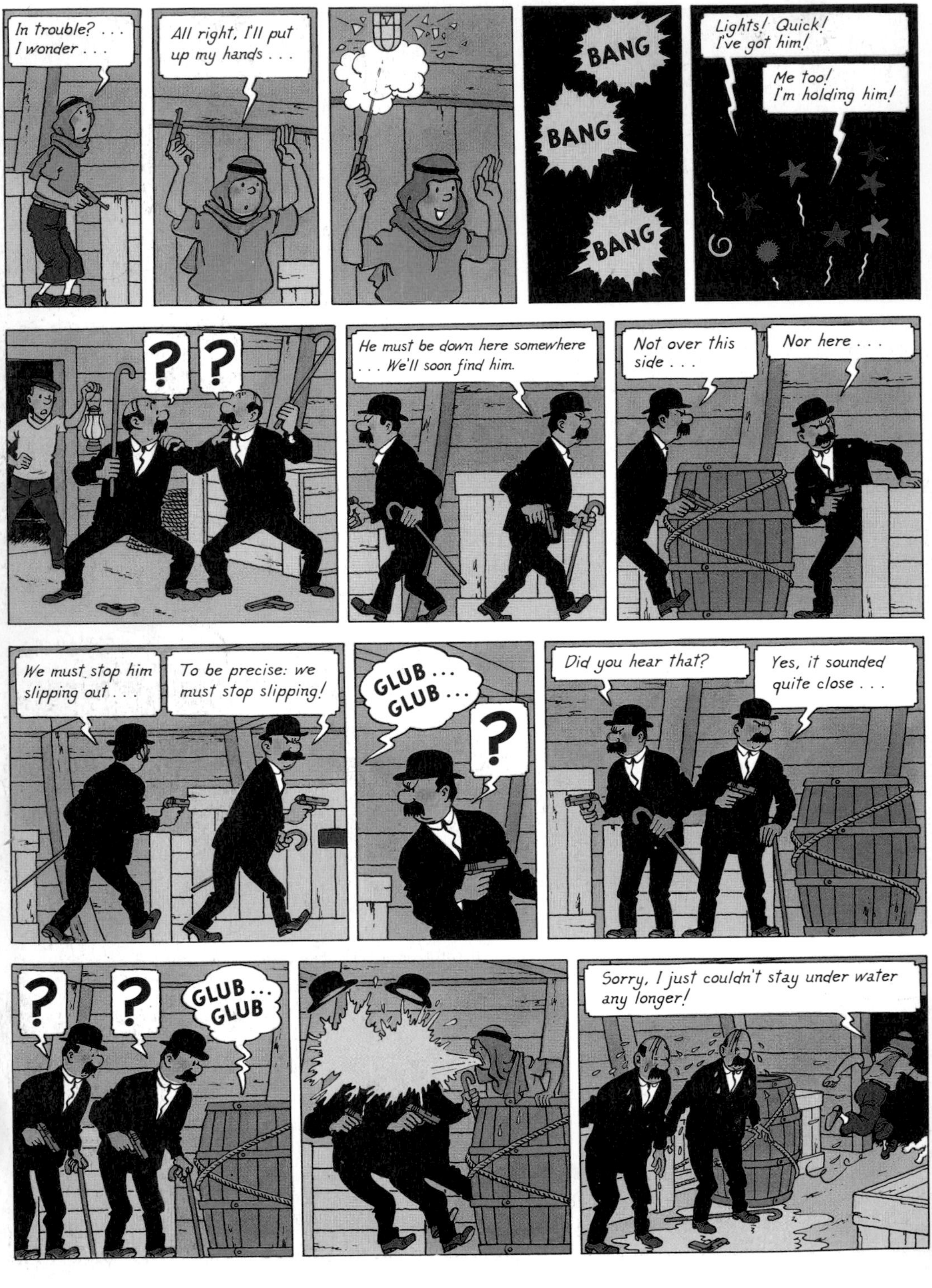
In trouble? . . .
I wonder . . .
All right, I'll put up my hands . . .
BANG
BANG
BANG
Lights! Quick! I've got him!
Me too! I'm holding him!
?
?
He must be down here somewhere . . . We'll soon find him.
Not over this side . . .
Nor here . . .
We must stop him slipping out . . .
To be precise: we must stop slipping!
GLUB . . . GLUB . . .
?
Did you hear that?
Yes, it sounded quite close . . .
?
?
GLUB . . . GLUB
Sorry, I just couldn't stay under water any longer!

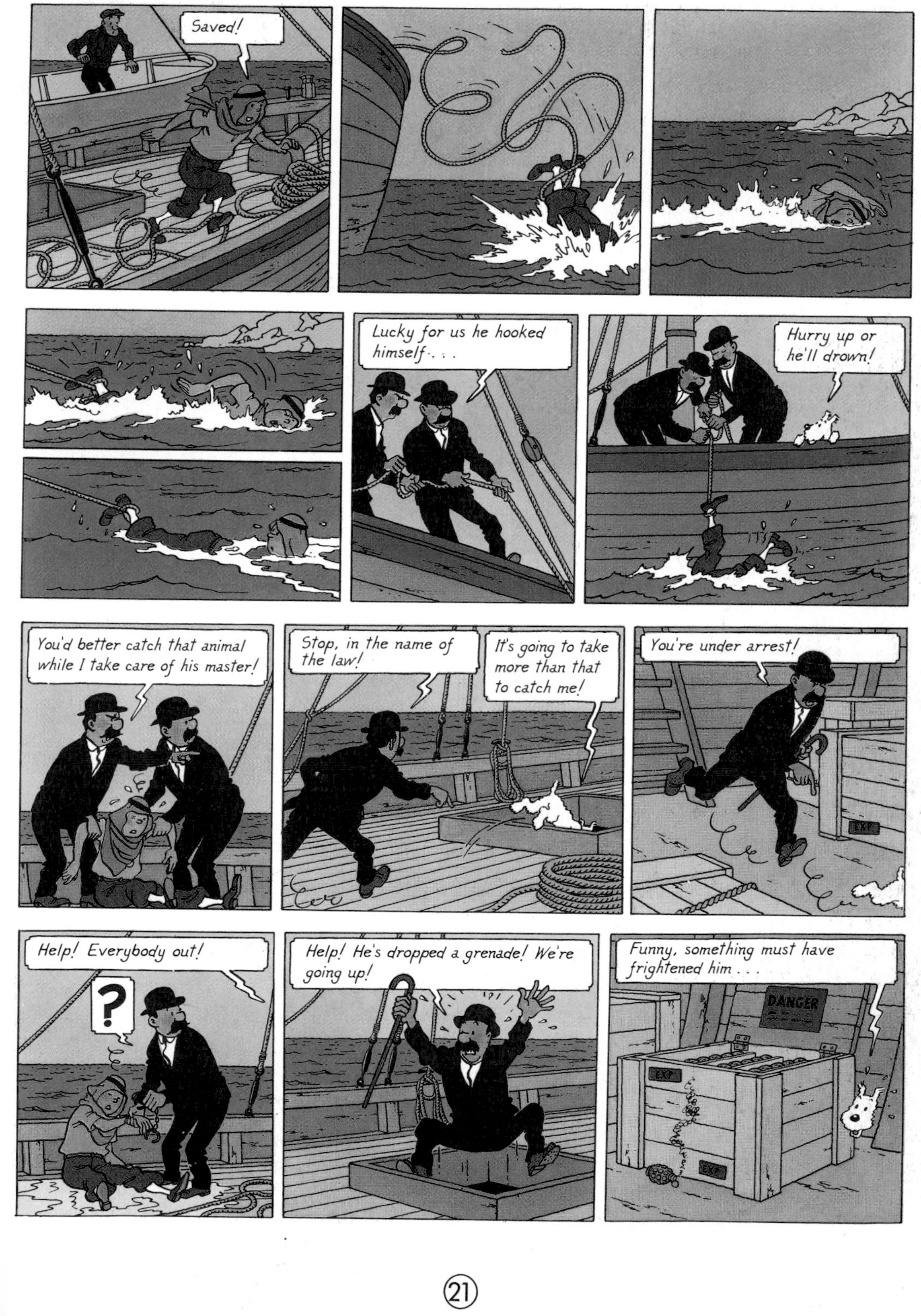

Saved!
Lucky for us he hooked himself . . .
Hurry up or he'll drown!
You'd better catch that animal while I take care of his master!
Stop, in the name of the law!
It's going to take more than that to catch me!
You're under arrest!
Help! Everybody out!
?
Help! He's dropped a grenade! We're going up!
Funny, something must have frightened him . . .
DANGER
EXP

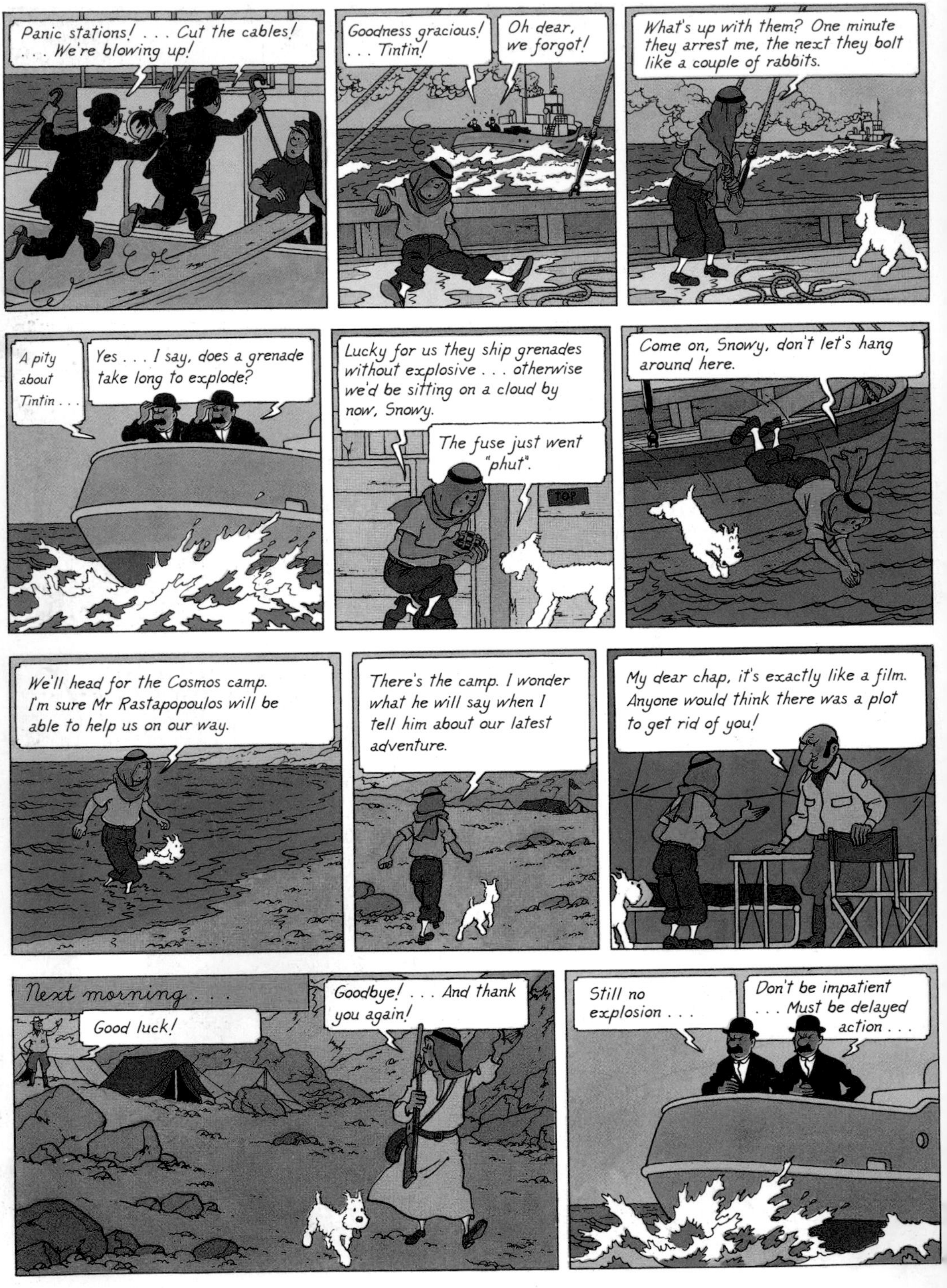
Panic stations! . . . Cut the cables! . . . We're blowing up!
Goodness gracious! . . . Tintin!
Oh dear, we forgot!
What's up with them? One minute they arrest me, the next they bolt like a couple of rabbits.
A pity about Tintin . . .
Yes . . . I say, does a grenade take long to explode?
Lucky for us they ship grenades without explosive . . . otherwise we'd be sitting on a cloud by now, Snowy.
The fuse just went "phut".
TOP
Come on, Snowy, don't let's hang around here.
We'll head for the Cosmos camp. I'm sure Mr Rastapopoulos will be able to help us on our way.
There's the camp. I wonder what he will say when I tell him about our latest adventure.
My dear chap, it's exactly like a film. Anyone would think there was a plot to get rid of you!
Next morning . . .
Good luck!
Goodbye! . . . And thank you again!
Still no explosion . . .
Don't be impatient . . . Must be delayed action . . .

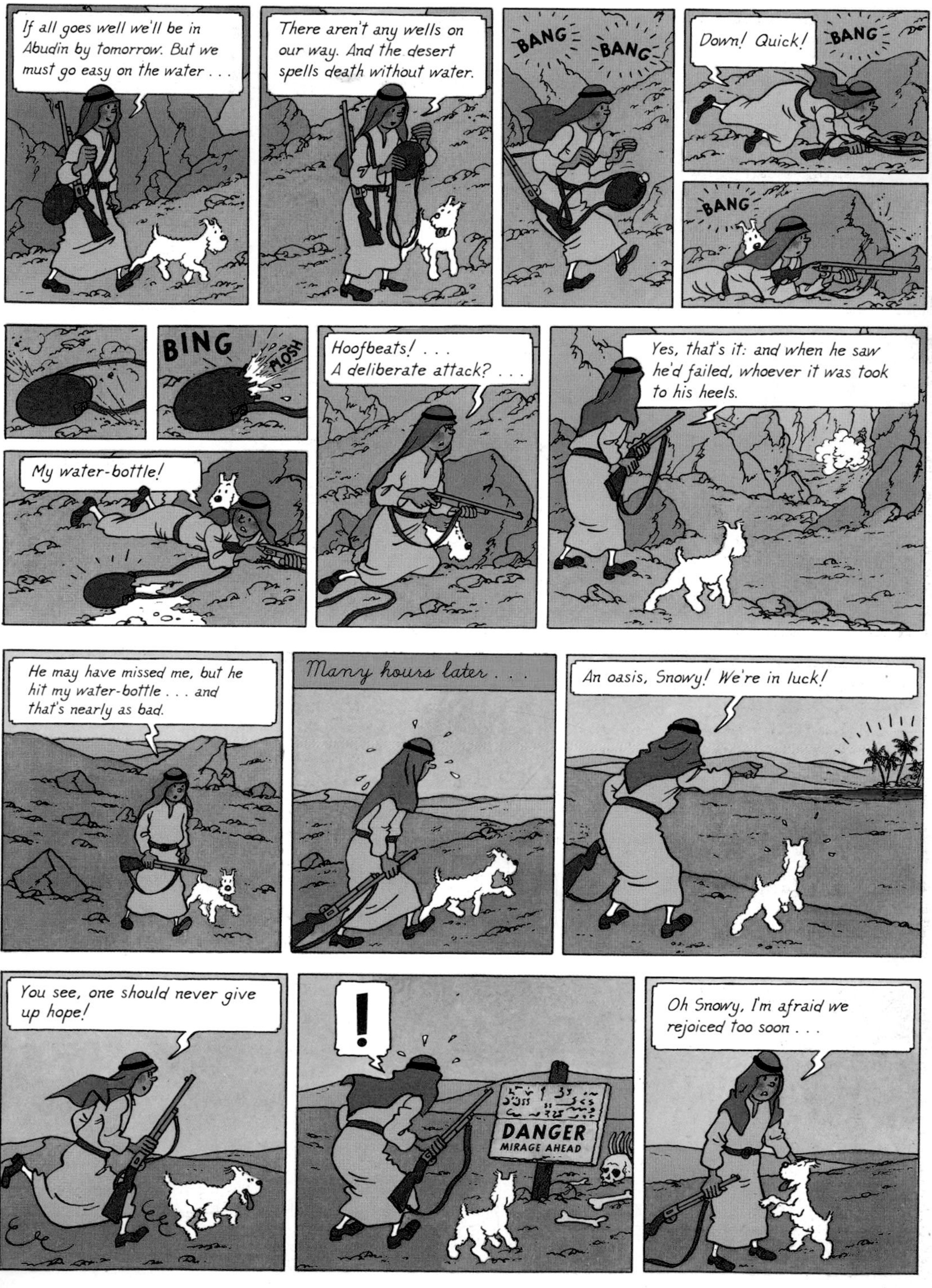
If all goes well we'll be in Abudin by tomorrow. But we must go easy on the water . . .
There aren't any wells on our way. And the desert spells death without water.
BANG
BANG
Down! Quick!
BANG
BANG
BING
PLOSH
My water-bottle!
Hoofbeats! . . . A deliberate attack? . . .
Yes, that's it: and when he saw he'd failed, whoever it was took to his heels.
He may have missed me, but he hit my water-bottle . . . and that's nearly as bad.
Many hours later . . .
An oasis, Snowy! We're in luck!
You see, one should never give up hope!
!
DANGER
MIRAGE AHEAD
Oh Snowy, I'm afraid we rejoiced too soon . . .

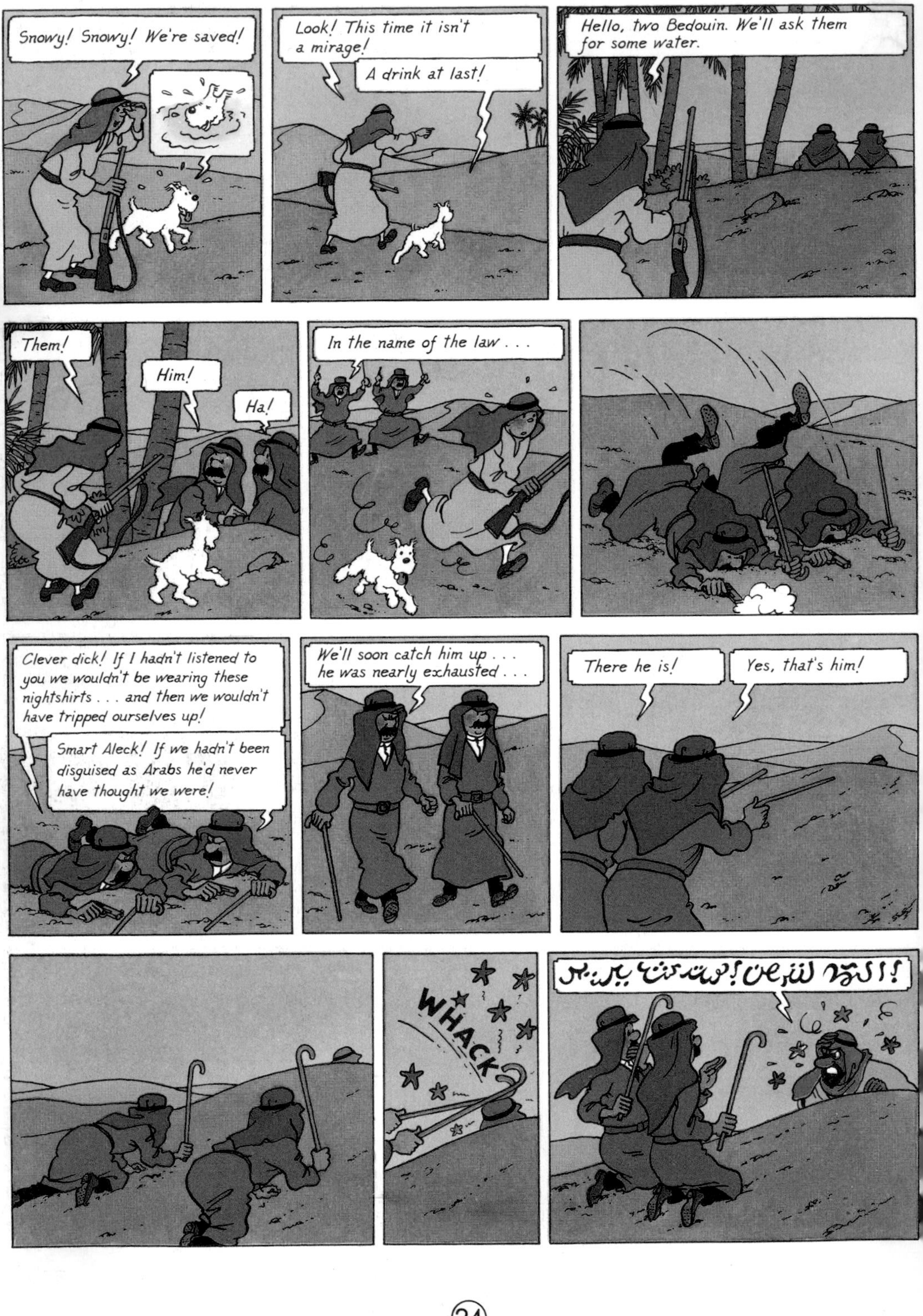
Snowy! Snowy! We're saved!
Look! This time it isn't a mirage!
A drink at last!
Hello, two Bedouin. We'll ask them for some water.
Them!
Him!
Ha!
In the name of the law . . .
Clever dick! If I hadn't listened to you we wouldn't be wearing these nightshirts . . . and then we wouldn't have tripped ourselves up!
Smart Aleck! If we hadn't been disguised as Arabs he'd never have thought we were!
We'll soon catch him up . . . he was nearly exhausted . . .
There he is!
Yes, that's him!
WHACK

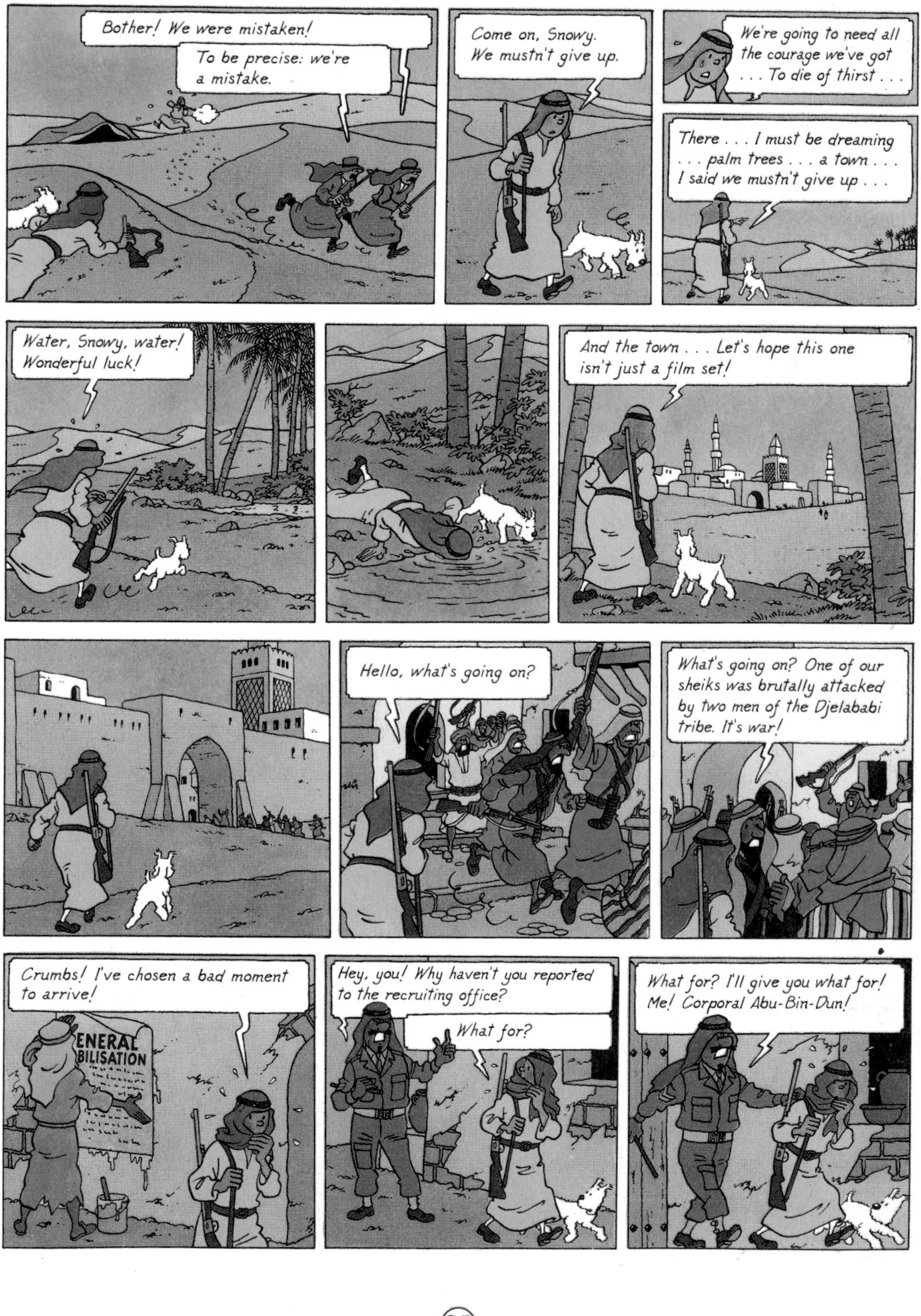

Bother! We were mistaken!
To be precise: we're a mistake.
Come on, Snowy. We mustn't give up.
We're going to need all the courage we've got . . . To die of thirst . . .
There . . . I must be dreaming . . . palm trees . . . a town . . . I said we mustn't give up . . .
Water, Snowy, water! Wonderful luck!
And the town . . . Let's hope this one isn't just a film set!
Hello, what's going on?
What's going on? One of our sheiks was brutally attacked by two men of the Djelababi tribe. It's war!
Crumbs! I've chosen a bad moment to arrive!
ENERAL
BILISATION
Hey, you! Why haven't you reported to the recruiting office?
What for?
What for? I'll give you what for! Me! Corporal Abu-Bin-Dun!

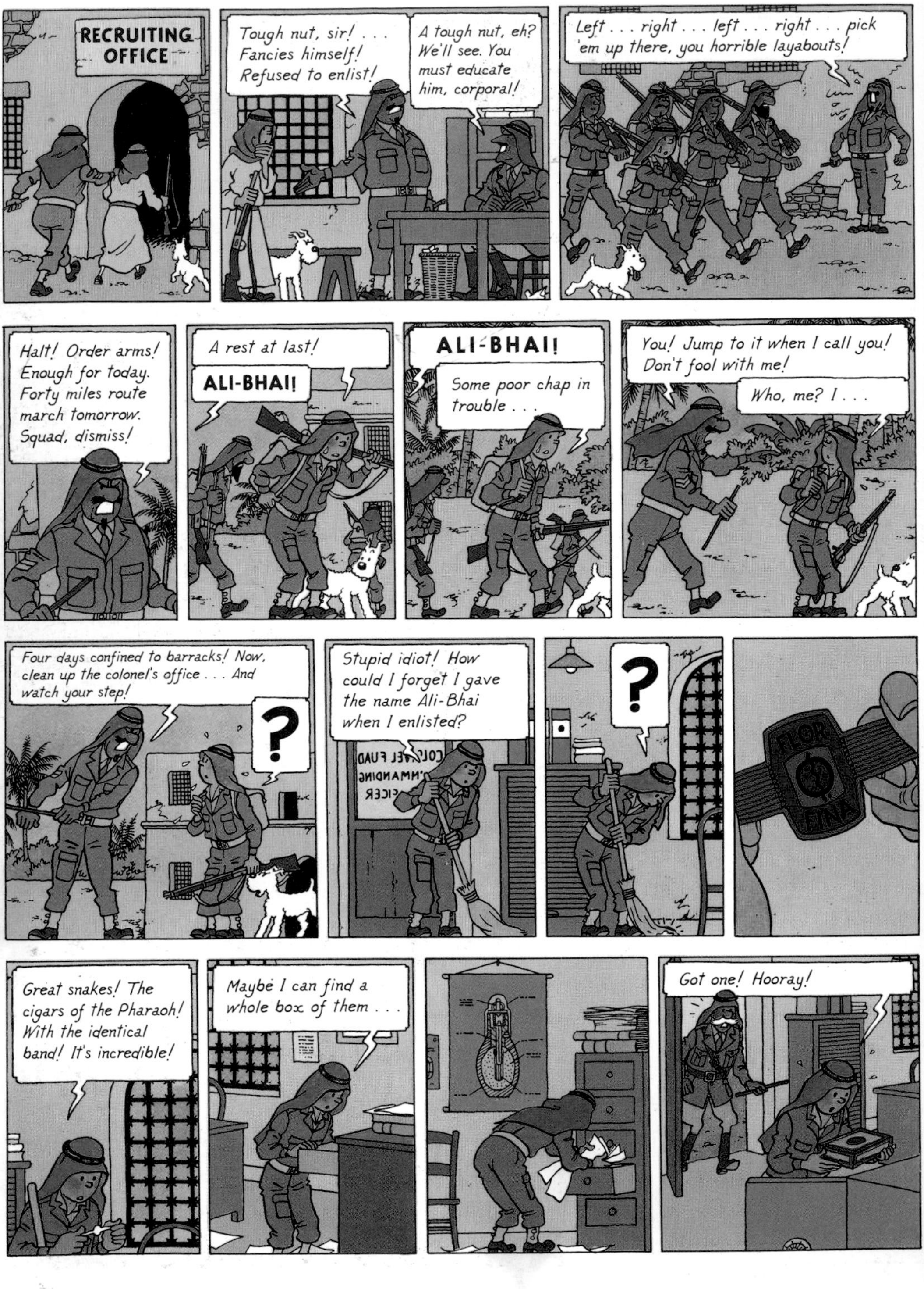

RECRUITING OFFICE
Tough nut, sir! . . . Fancies himself! Refused to enlist!
A tough nut, eh? We'll see. You must educate him, corporal!
Left . . . right . . . left . . . right . . . pick 'em up there, you horrible layabouts!
Halt! Order arms! Enough for today. Forty miles route march tomorrow. Squad, dismiss!
A rest at last!
ALI-BHAI!
ALI-BHAI!
Some poor chap in trouble . . .
You! Jump to it when I call you! Don't fool with me!
Who, me? I . . .
Four days confined to barracks! Now, clean up the colonel's office . . . And watch your step!
?
Stupid idiot! How could I forget I gave the name Ali-Bhai when I enlisted?
?
Great snakes! The cigars of the Pharaoh! With the identical band! It's incredible!
Maybe I can find a whole box of them . . .
Got one! Hooray!

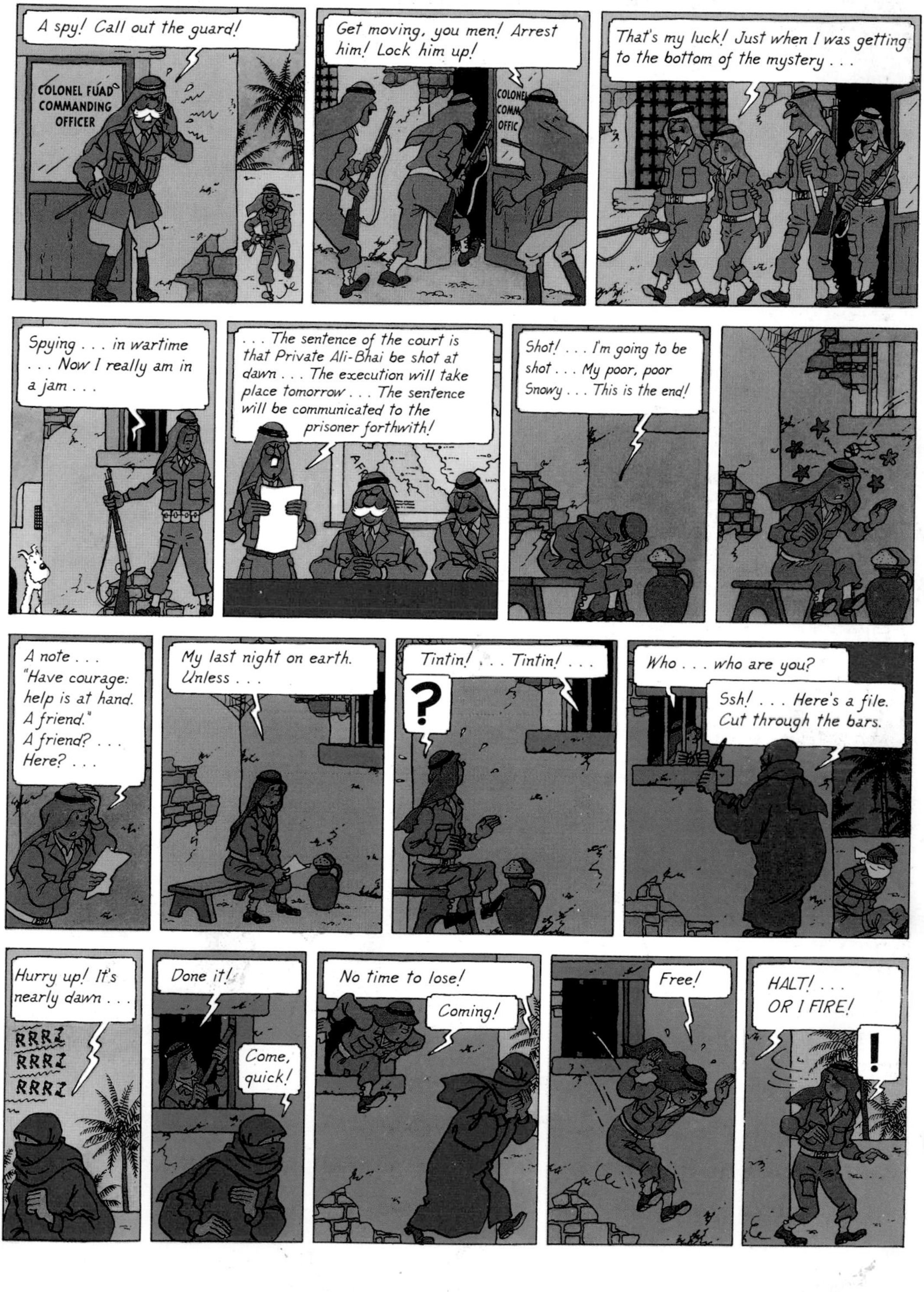
A spy! Call out the guard!
COLONEL FUAD COMMANDING OFFICER
Get moving, you men! Arrest him! Lock him up!
That's my luck! Just when I was getting to the bottom of the mystery . . .
Spying . . . in wartime . . . Now I really am in a jam . . .
. . . The sentence of the court is that Private Ali-Bhai be shot at dawn . . . The execution will take place tomorrow . . . The sentence will be communicated to the prisoner forthwith!
Shot! . . . I'm going to be shot . . . My poor, poor Snowy . . . This is the end!
A note . . . "Have courage: help is at hand. A friend." A friend? . . . Here? . . .
My last night on earth. Unless . . .
Tintin! . . . Tintin! . . .
?
Who . . . who are you?
Ssh! . . . Here's a file. Cut through the bars.
Hurry up! It's nearly dawn . . .
RRRZ RRRZ RRRZ
Done it!
Come, quick!
No time to lose!
Coming!
Free!
HALT! . . . OR I FIRE!
!

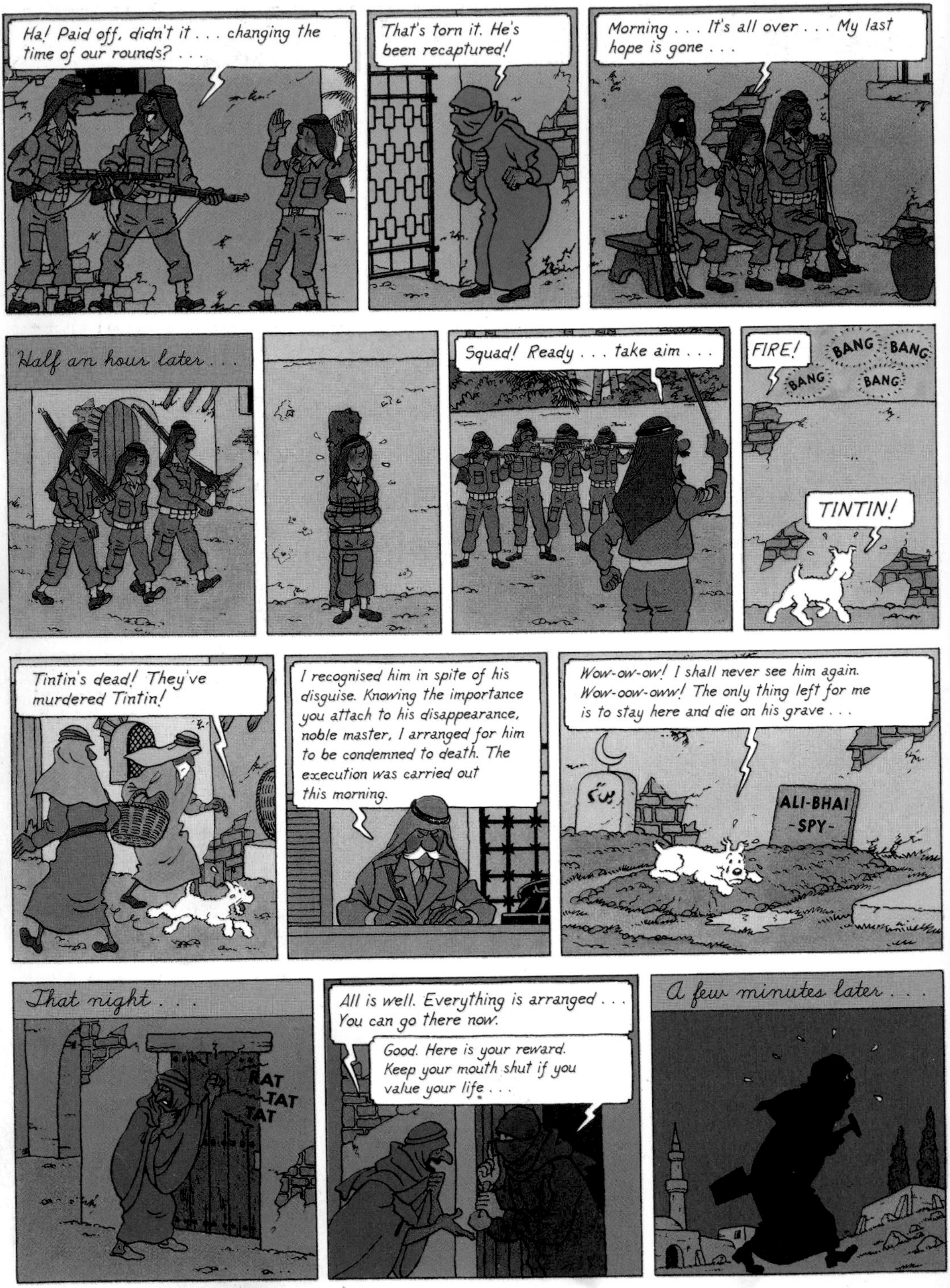
Ha! Paid off, didn't it . . . changing the time of our rounds? . . .
That's torn it. He's been recaptured!
Morning . . . It's all over . . . My last hope is gone . . .
Half an hour later . . .
Squad! Ready . . . take aim . . .
FIRE!
BANG
BANG
BANG
BANG
TINTIN!
Tintin's dead! They've murdered Tintin!
I recognised him in spite of his disguise. Knowing the importance you attach to his disappearance, noble master, I arranged for him to be condemned to death. The execution was carried out this morning.
Wow-ow-ow! I shall never see him again. Wow-oow-oww! The only thing left for me is to stay here and die on his grave . . .
ALI-BHAI -SPY-
That night . . .
RAT TAT TAT
All is well. Everything is arranged . . . You can go there now.
Good. Here is your reward. Keep your mouth shut if you value your life . . .
A few minutes later . . .

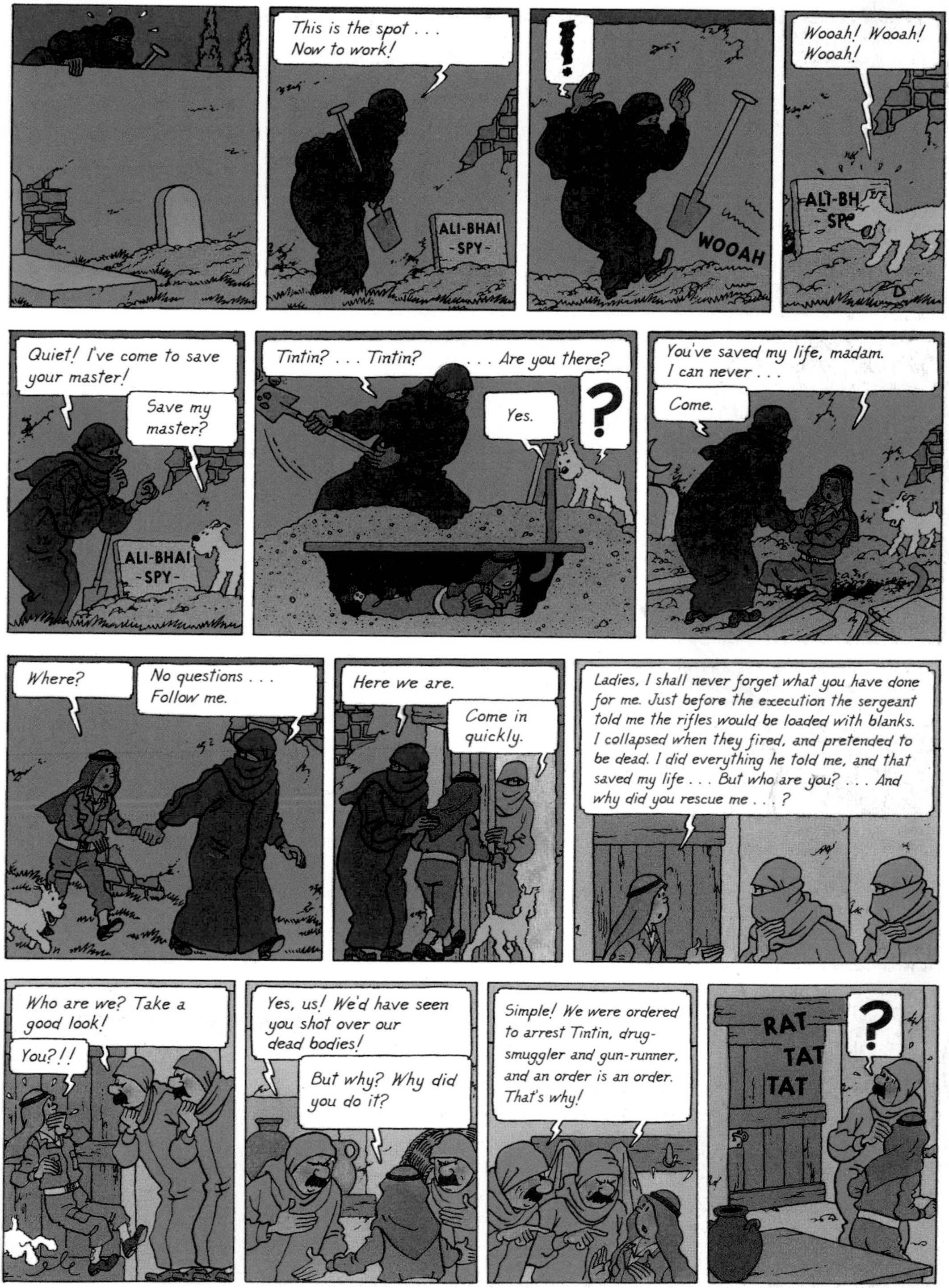
This is the spot . . . Now to work!
!!!
Wooah! Wooah! Wooah!
WOOAH
ALI-BHAI -SPY-
Quiet! I've come to save your master!
Save my master?
Tintin? . . . Tintin? . . . Are you there?
Yes.
?
You've saved my life, madam. I can never . . .
Come.
Where?
No questions . . . Follow me.
Here we are.
Come in quickly.
Ladies, I shall never forget what you have done for me. Just before the execution the sergeant told me the rifles would be loaded with blanks. I collapsed when they fired, and pretended to be dead. I did everything he told me, and that saved my life . . . But who are you? . . . And why did you rescue me . . . ?
Who are we? Take a good look!
You?!!
Yes, us! We'd have seen you shot over our dead bodies!
But why? Why did you do it?
Simple! We were ordered to arrest Tintin, drug-smuggler and gun-runner, and an order is an order. That's why!
RAT TAT TAT
?

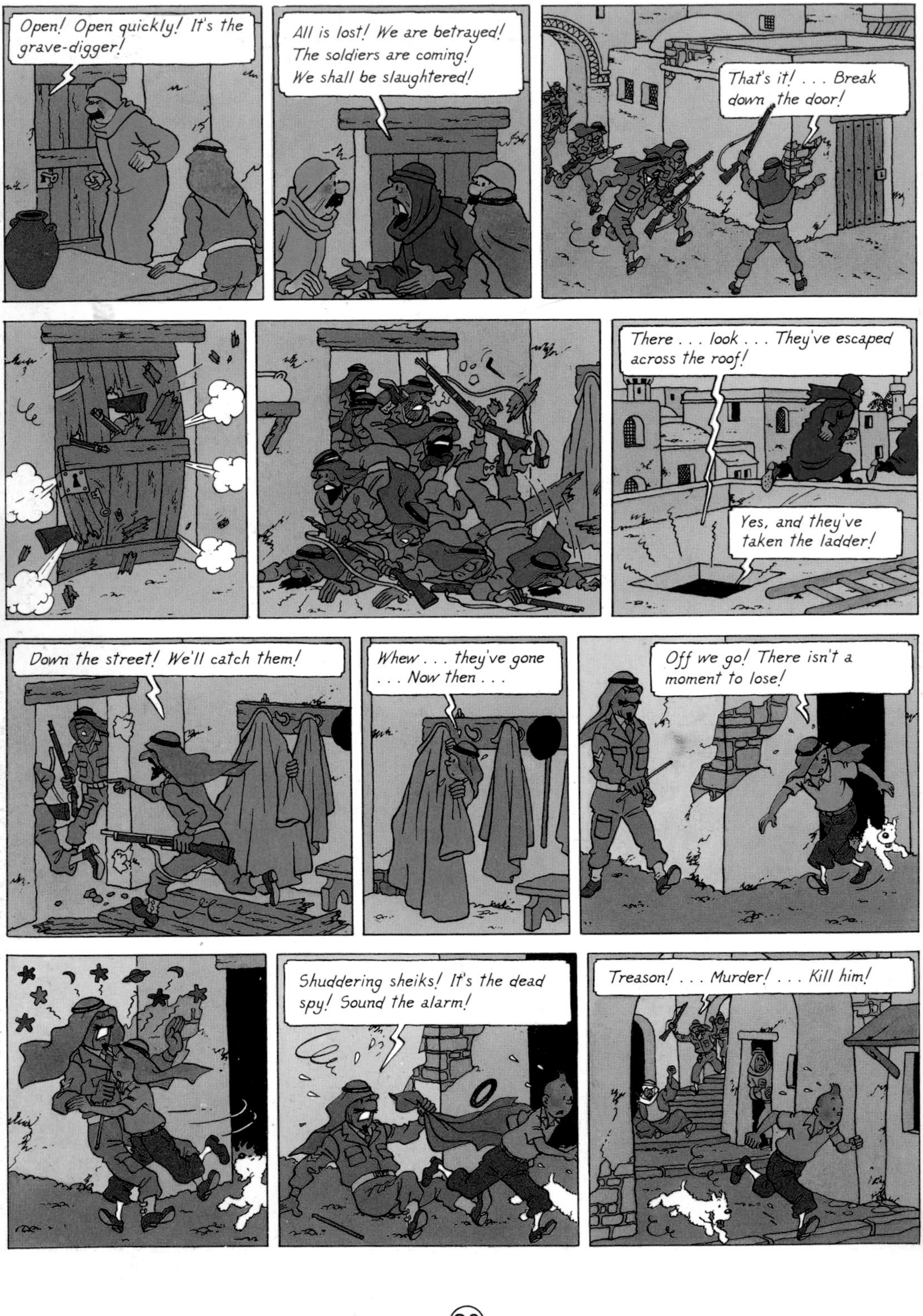
Open! Open quickly! It's the grave-digger!
All is lost! We are betrayed! The soldiers are coming! We shall be slaughtered!
That's it! . . . Break down the door!
There . . . look . . . They've escaped across the roof!
Yes, and they've taken the ladder!
Down the street! We'll catch them!
Whew . . . they've gone . . . Now then . . .
Off we go! There isn't a moment to lose!
Shuddering sheiks! It's the dead spy! Sound the alarm!
Treason! . . . Murder! . . . Kill him!

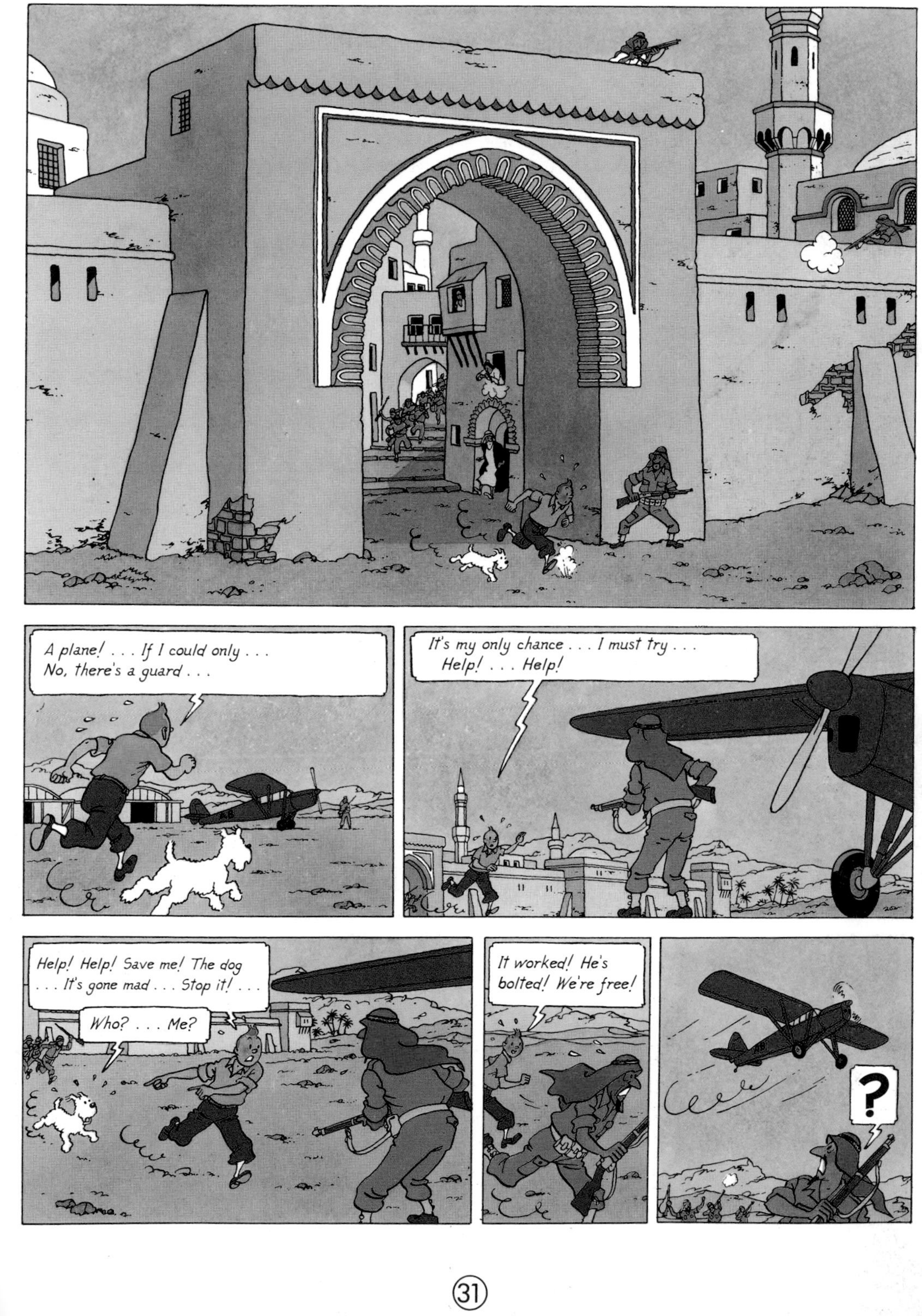
A plane! . . . If I could only . . .
No, there's a guard . . .
It's my only chance . . . I must try . . .
Help! . . . Help!
Help! Help! Save me! The dog . . . It's gone mad . . . Stop it! . . .
Who? . . . Me?
It worked! He's bolted! We're free!
?

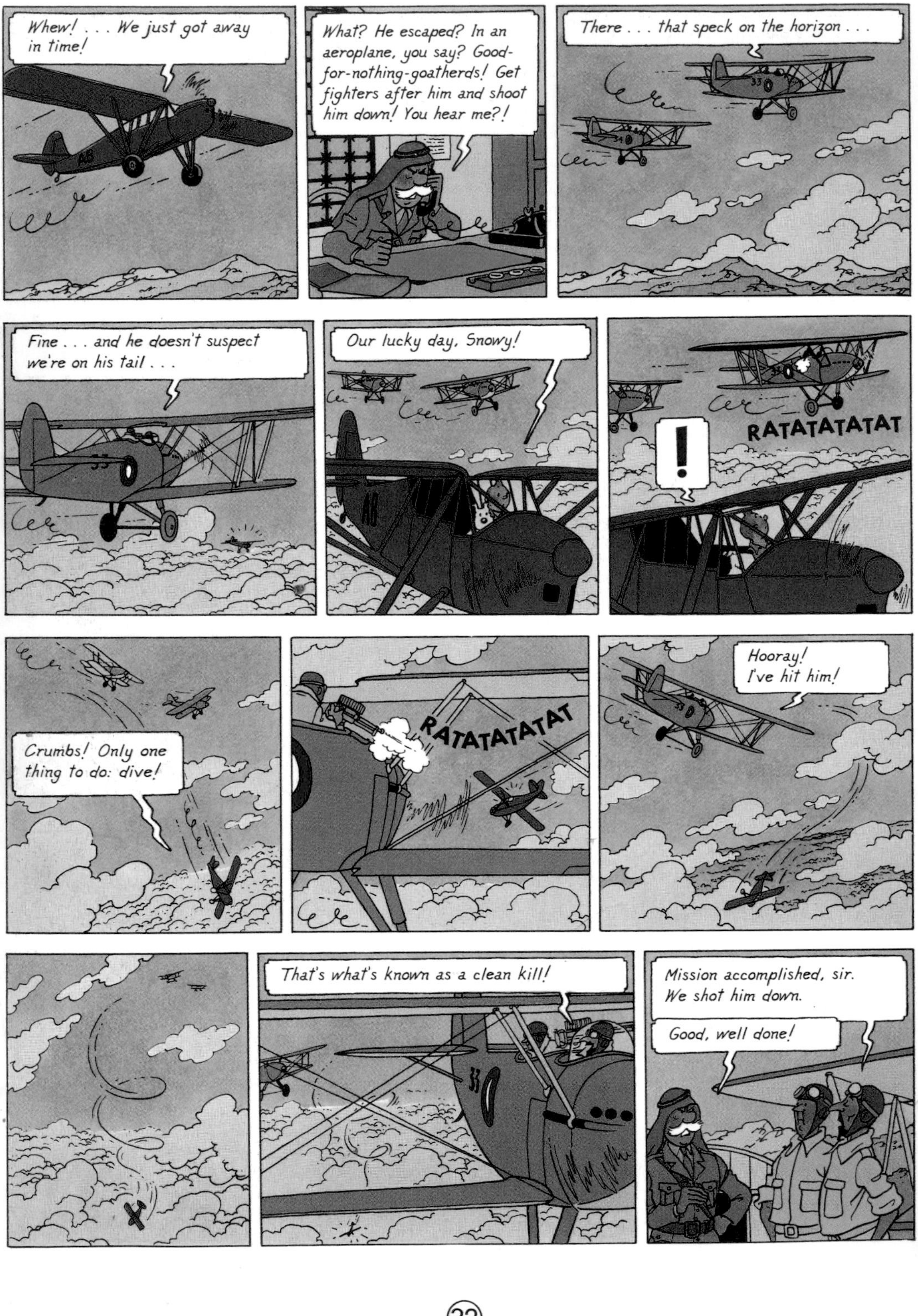

Whew! . . . We just got away in time!
What? He escaped? In an aeroplane, you say? Good-for-nothing-goatherds! Get fighters after him and shoot him down! You hear me?!
There . . . that speck on the horizon . . .
Fine . . . and he doesn't suspect we're on his tail . . .
Our lucky day, Snowy!
RATATATATAT
!
Crumbs! Only one thing to do: dive!
RATATATATAT
Hooray! I've hit him!
That's what's known as a clean kill!
Mission accomplished, sir. We shot him down.
Good, well done!

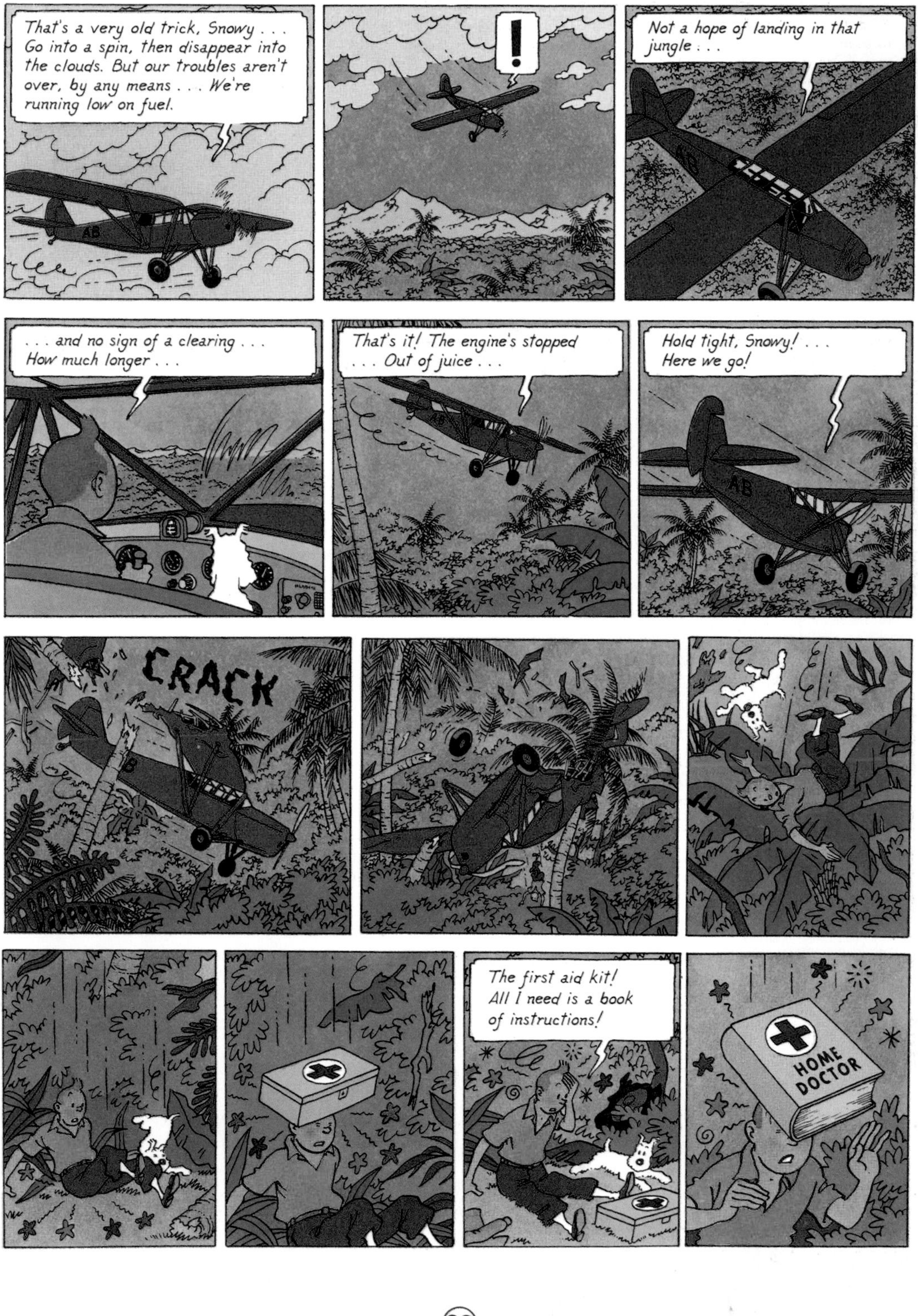
That's a very old trick, Snowy . . . Go into a spin, then disappear into the clouds. But our troubles aren't over, by any means . . . We're running low on fuel.
!
Not a hope of landing in that jungle . . .
. . . and no sign of a clearing . . . How much longer . . .
That's it! The engine's stopped . . . Out of juice . . .
Hold tight, Snowy! . . . Here we go!
CRACK
The first aid kit! All I need is a book of instructions!
HOME DOCTOR

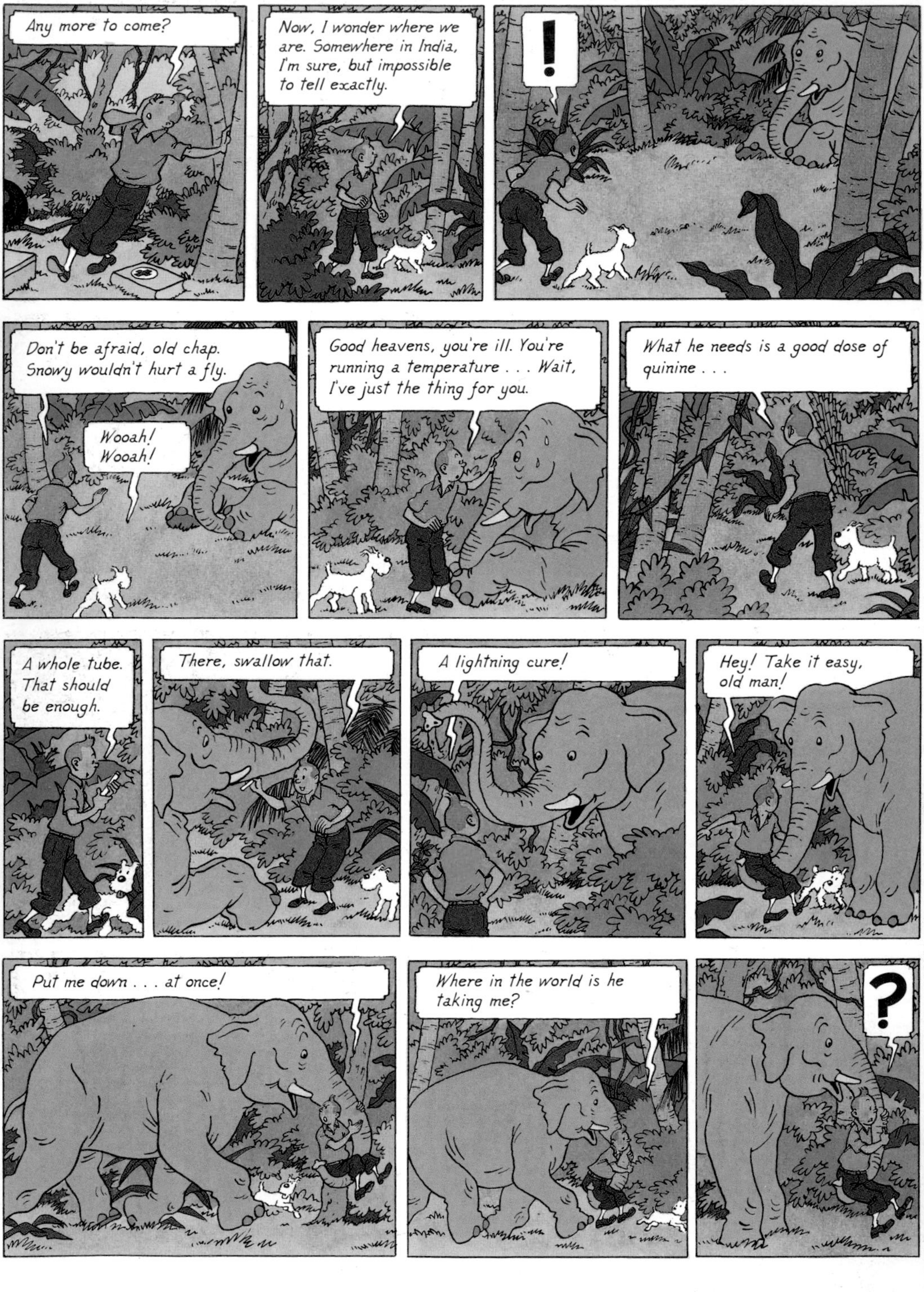
Any more to come?
Now, I wonder where we are. Somewhere in India, I'm sure, but impossible to tell exactly.
!
Don't be afraid, old chap. Snowy wouldn't hurt a fly.
Wooah! Wooah!
Good heavens, you're ill. You're running a temperature . . . Wait, I've just the thing for you.
What he needs is a good dose of quinine . . .
A whole tube. That should be enough.
There, swallow that.
A lightning cure!
Hey! Take it easy, old man!
Put me down . . . at once!
Where in the world is he taking me?
?

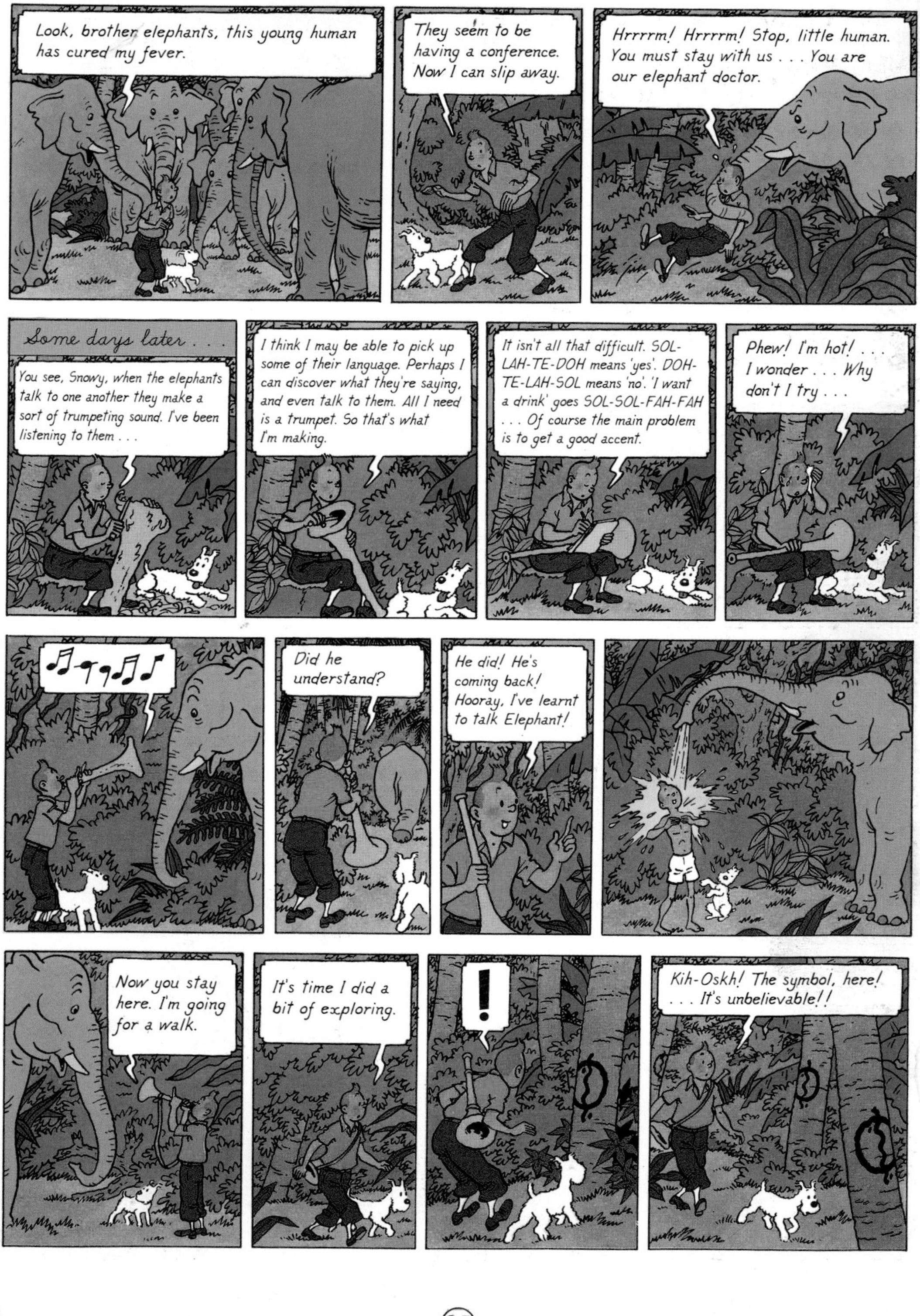
Look, brother elephants, this young human has cured my fever.
They seem to be having a conference. Now I can slip away.
Hrrrrm! Hrrrrm! Stop, little human. You must stay with us . . . You are our elephant doctor.
Some days later . . .
You see, Snowy, when the elephants talk to one another they make a sort of trumpeting sound. I've been listening to them . . .
I think I may be able to pick up some of their language. Perhaps I can discover what they're saying, and even talk to them. All I need is a trumpet. So that's what I'm making.
It isn't all that difficult. SOL-LAH-TE-DOH means 'yes'. DOH-TE-LAH-SOL means 'no'. 'I want a drink' goes SOL-SOL-FAH-FAH . . . Of course the main problem is to get a good accent.
Phew! I'm hot! . . . I wonder . . . Why don't I try . . .
Did he understand?
He did! He's coming back! Hooray, I've learnt to talk Elephant!
Now you stay here. I'm going for a walk.
It's time I did a bit of exploring.
!
Kih-Oskh! The symbol, here! . . . It's unbelievable!!

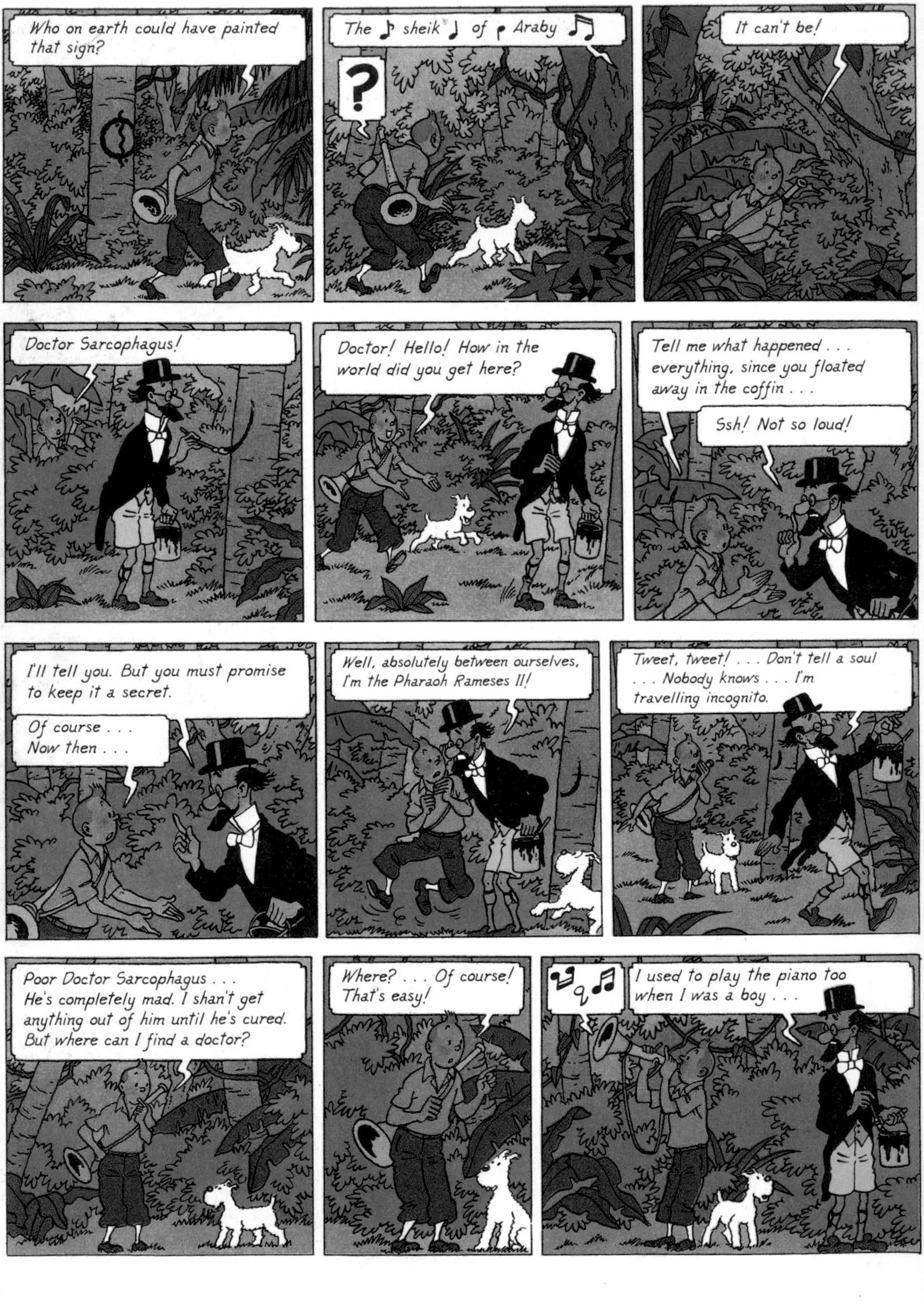
Who on earth could have painted that sign?
The ♪ sheik ♩ of Araby ♫
?
It can't be!
Doctor Sarcophagus!
Doctor! Hello! How in the world did you get here?
Tell me what happened . . . everything, since you floated away in the coffin . . .
Ssh! Not so loud!
I'll tell you. But you must promise to keep it a secret.
Of course . . . Now then . . .
Well, absolutely between ourselves, I'm the Pharaoh Rameses II!
Tweet, tweet! . . . Don't tell a soul . . . Nobody knows . . . I'm travelling incognito.
Poor Doctor Sarcophagus . . . He's completely mad. I shan't get anything out of him until he's cured. But where can I find a doctor?
Where? . . . Of course! That's easy!
I used to play the piano too when I was a boy . . .

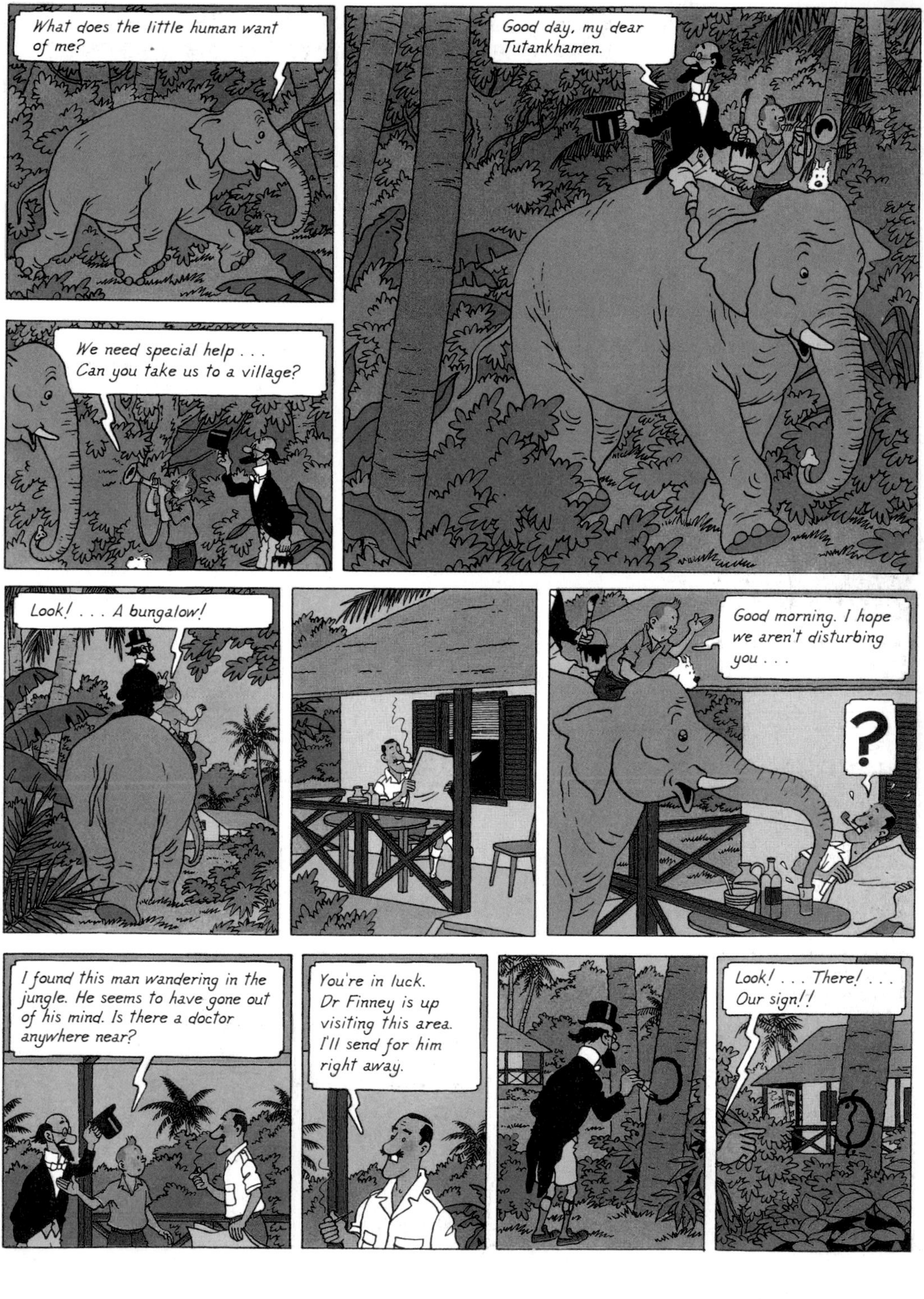
What does the little human want of me?
Good day, my dear Tutankhamen.
We need special help . . . Can you take us to a village?
Look! . . . A bungalow!
Good morning. I hope we aren't disturbing you . . .
?
I found this man wandering in the jungle. He seems to have gone out of his mind. Is there a doctor anywhere near?
You're in luck. Dr Finney is up visiting this area. I'll send for him right away.
Look! . . . There! . . . Our sign!!

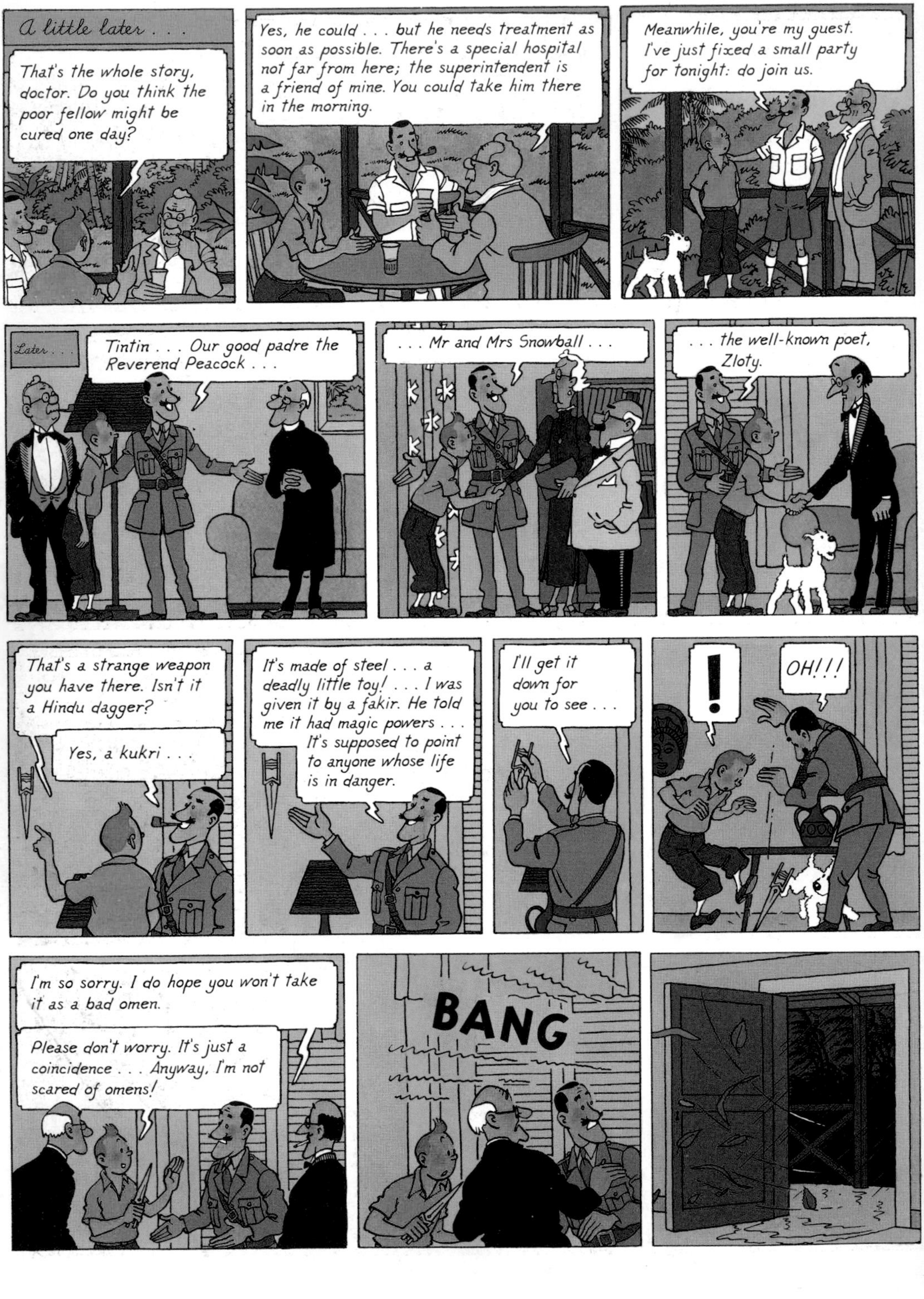
A little later . . .
That's the whole story, doctor. Do you think the poor fellow might be cured one day?
Yes, he could . . . but he needs treatment as soon as possible. There's a special hospital not far from here; the superintendent is a friend of mine. You could take him there in the morning.
Meanwhile, you're my guest. I've just fixed a small party for tonight: do join us.
Later . . .
Tintin . . . Our good padre the Reverend Peacock . . .
. . . Mr and Mrs Snowball . . .
. . . the well-known poet, Zloty.
That's a strange weapon you have there. Isn't it a Hindu dagger?
Yes, a kukri . . .
It's made of steel . . . a deadly little toy! . . . I was given it by a fakir. He told me it had magic powers . . . It's supposed to point to anyone whose life is in danger.
I'll get it down for you to see . . .
!
OH!!!
I'm so sorry. I do hope you won't take it as a bad omen.
Please don't worry. It's just a coincidence . . . Anyway, I'm not scared of omens!
BANG

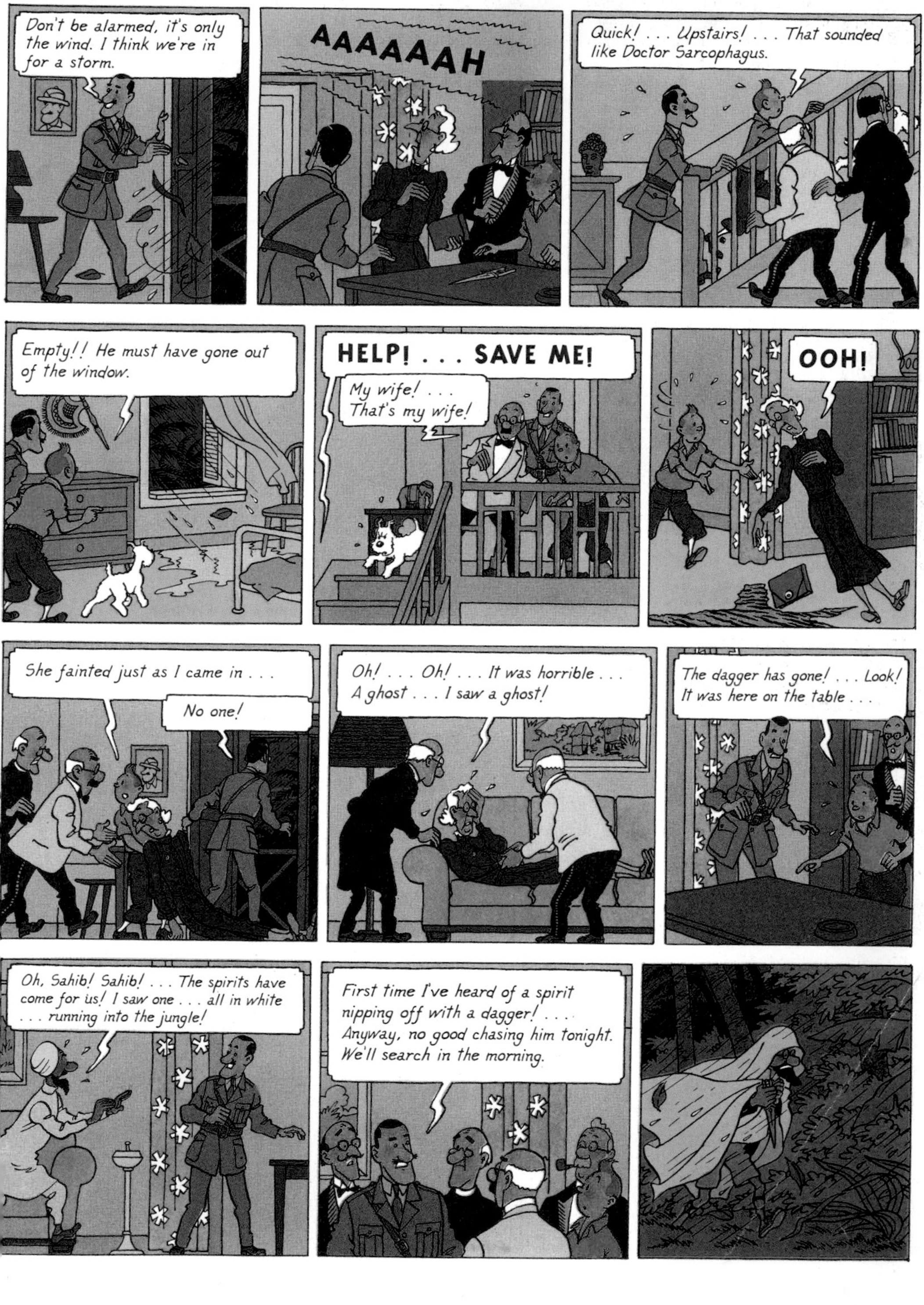
Don't be alarmed, it's only the wind. I think we're in for a storm.
AAAAAAH
Quick! . . . Upstairs! . . . That sounded like Doctor Sarcophagus.
Empty!! He must have gone out of the window.
HELP! . . . SAVE ME!
My wife! . . . That's my wife!
OOH!
She fainted just as I came in . . .
No one!
Oh! . . . Oh! . . . It was horrible . . . A ghost . . . I saw a ghost!
The dagger has gone! . . . Look! It was here on the table . . .
Oh, Sahib! Sahib! . . . The spirits have come for us! I saw one . . . all in white . . . running into the jungle!
First time I've heard of a spirit nipping off with a dagger! . . . Anyway, no good chasing him tonight. We'll search in the morning.

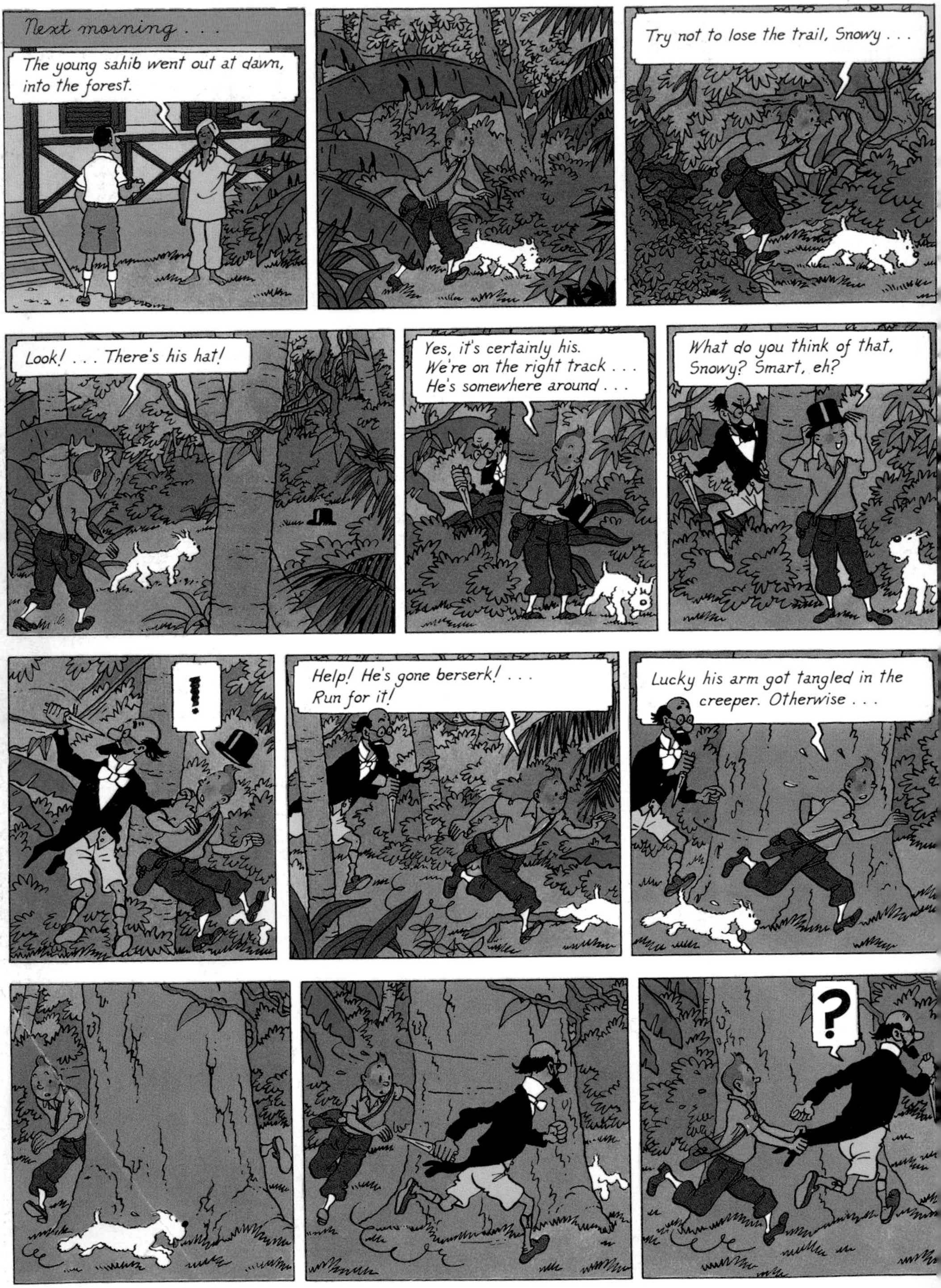
Next morning . . .
The young sahib went out at dawn, into the forest.
Try not to lose the trail, Snowy . . .
Look! . . . There's his hat!
Yes, it's certainly his. We're on the right track . . . He's somewhere around . . .
What do you think of that, Snowy? Smart, eh?
Help! He's gone berserk! . . . Run for it!
Lucky his arm got tangled in the creeper. Otherwise . . .
?

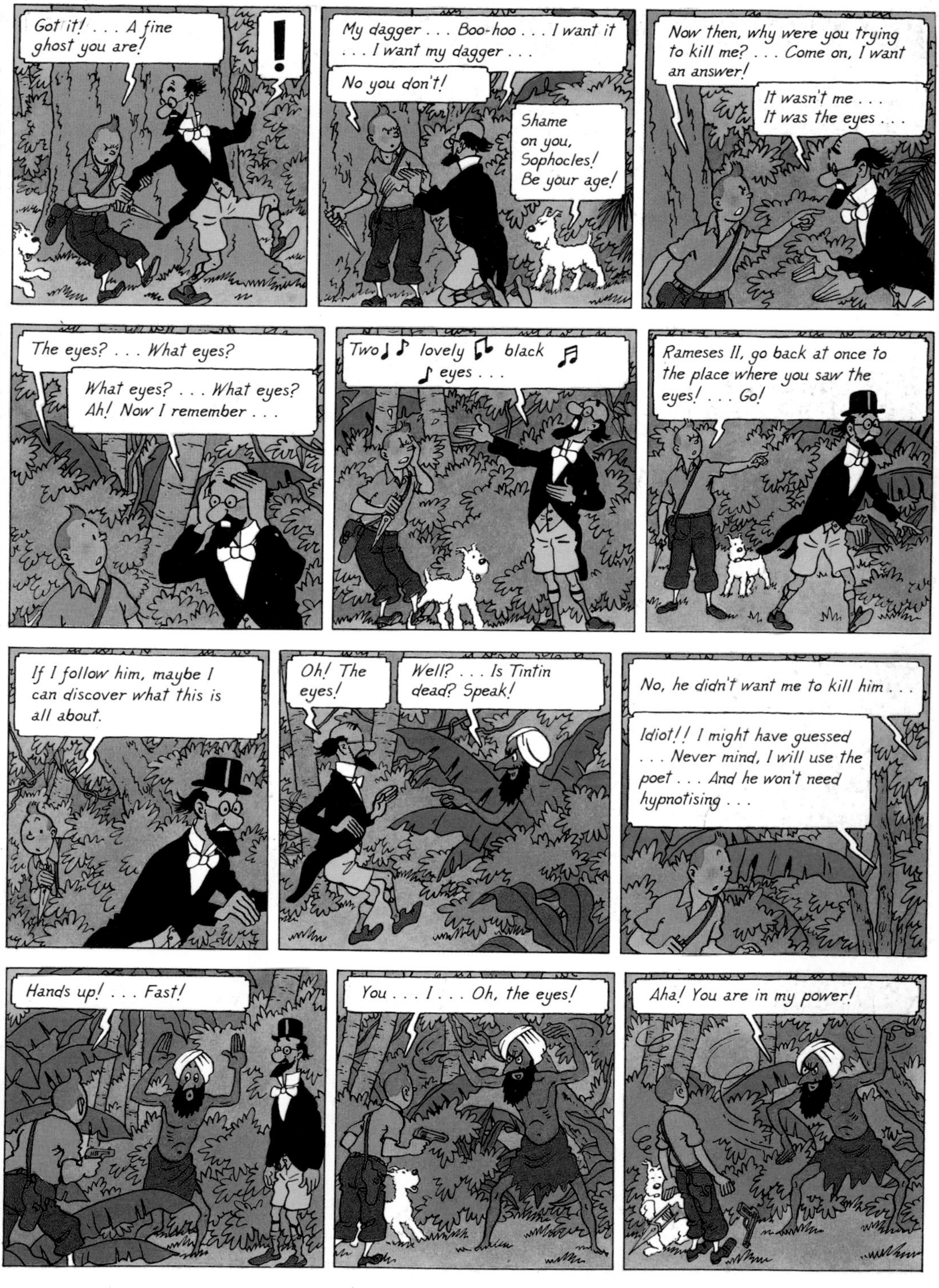
Got it! . . . A fine ghost you are!
!
My dagger . . . Boo-hoo . . . I want it . . . I want my dagger . . .
No you don't!
Shame on you, Sophocles! Be your age!
Now then, why were you trying to kill me? . . . Come on, I want an answer!
It wasn't me . . . It was the eyes . . .
The eyes? . . . What eyes?
What eyes? . . . What eyes? Ah! Now I remember . . .
Two lovely black eyes . . .
Rameses II, go back at once to the place where you saw the eyes! . . . Go!
If I follow him, maybe I can discover what this is all about.
Oh! The eyes!
Well? . . . Is Tintin dead? Speak!
No, he didn't want me to kill him . . .
Idiot!! I might have guessed . . . Never mind, I will use the poet . . . And he won't need hypnotising . . .
Hands up! . . . Fast!
You . . . I . . . Oh, the eyes!
Aha! You are in my power!

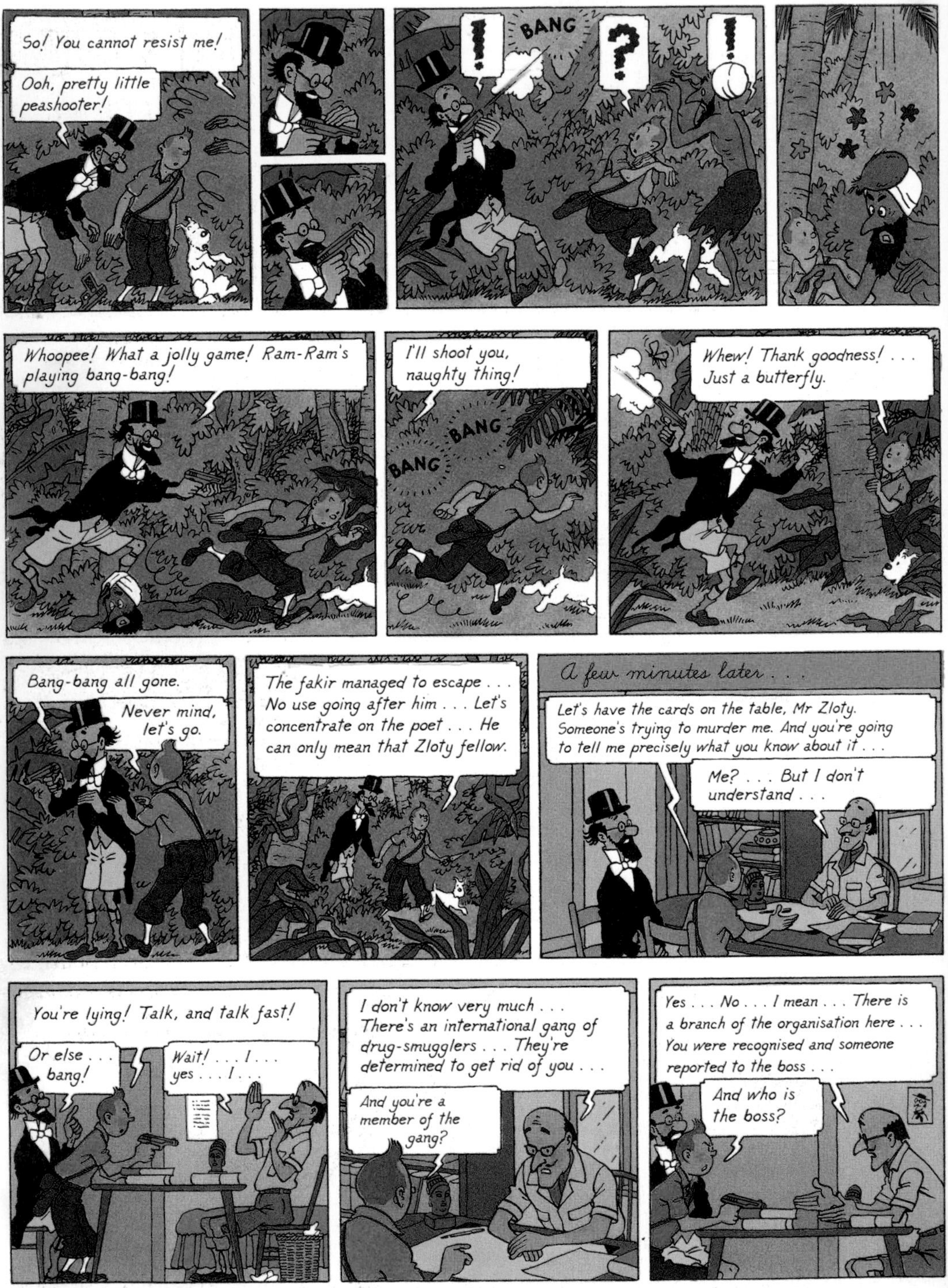
So! You cannot resist me!
Ooh, pretty little peashooter!
BANG
!
?
!
Whoopee! What a jolly game! Ram-Ram's playing bang-bang!
I'll shoot you, naughty thing!
BANG
BANG
Whew! Thank goodness! . . . Just a butterfly.
Bang-bang all gone.
Never mind, let's go.
The fakir managed to escape . . . No use going after him . . . Let's concentrate on the poet . . . He can only mean that Zloty fellow.
A few minutes later . . .
Let's have the cards on the table, Mr Zloty. Someone's trying to murder me. And you're going to tell me precisely what you know about it . . .
Me? . . . But I don't understand . . .
You're lying! Talk, and talk fast!
Or else . . . bang!
Wait! . . . I . . . yes . . . I . . .
I don't know very much . . . There's an international gang of drug-smugglers . . . They're determined to get rid of you . . .
And you're a member of the gang?
Yes . . . No . . . I mean . . . There is a branch of the organisation here . . . You were recognised and someone reported to the boss . . .
And who is the boss?

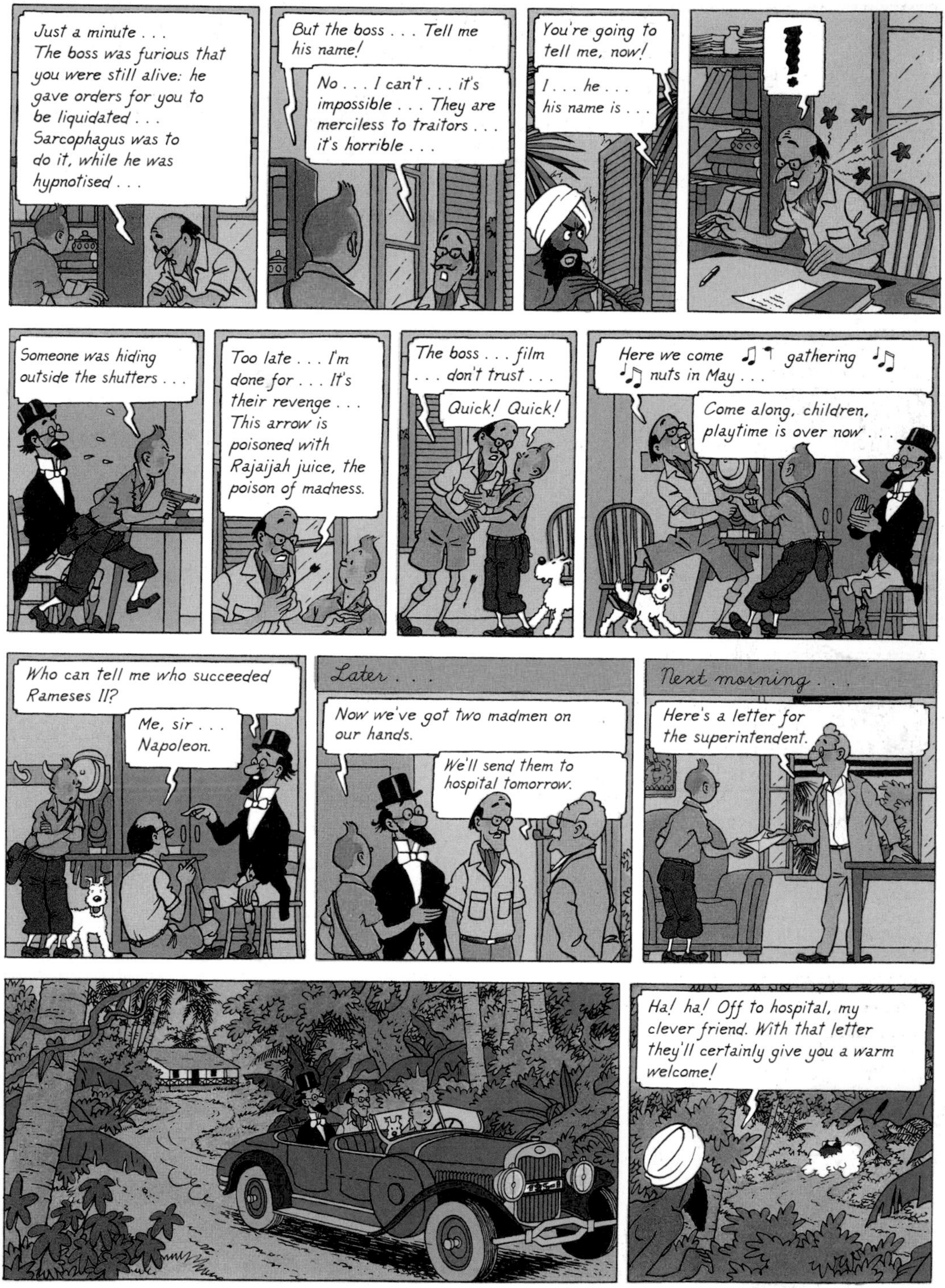
Just a minute . . . The boss was furious that you were still alive: he gave orders for you to be liquidated . . . Sarcophagus was to do it, while he was hypnotised . . .
But the boss . . . Tell me his name!
No . . . I can't . . . it's impossible . . . They are merciless to traitors . . . it's horrible . . .
You're going to tell me, now!
I . . . he . . . his name is . . .
!
Someone was hiding outside the shutters . . .
Too late . . . I'm done for . . . It's their revenge . . . This arrow is poisoned with Rajaijah juice, the poison of madness.
The boss . . . film . . . don't trust . . .
Quick! Quick!
Here we come ♫ gathering ♫ nuts in May . . .
Come along, children, playtime is over now . . .
Who can tell me who succeeded Rameses II?
Me, sir . . . Napoleon.
Later . . .
Now we've got two madmen on our hands.
We'll send them to hospital tomorrow.
Next morning . . .
Here's a letter for the superintendent.
Ha! ha! Off to hospital, my clever friend. With that letter they'll certainly give you a warm welcome!

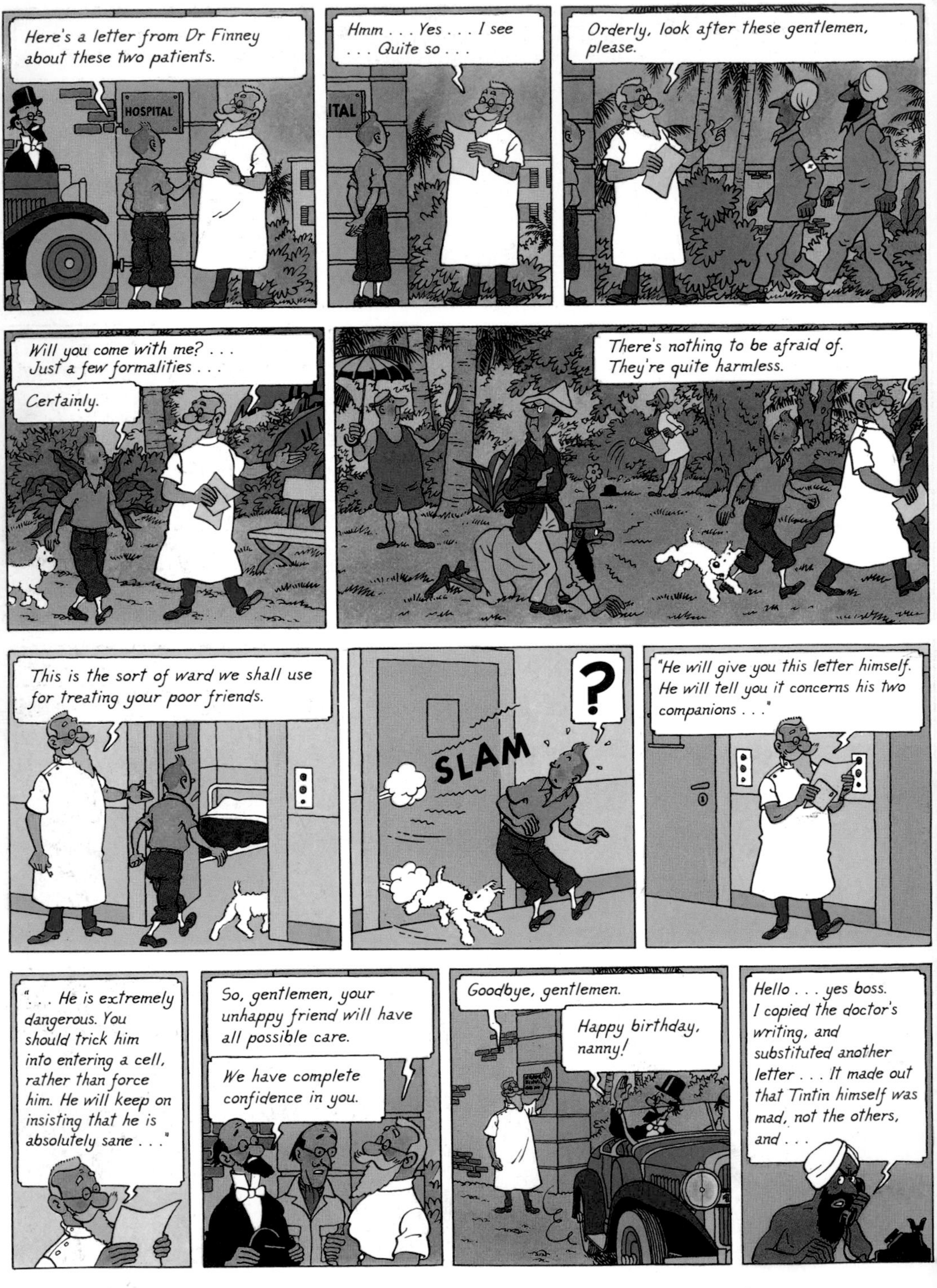
Here's a letter from Dr Finney about these two patients.
HOSPITAL
Hmm . . . Yes . . . I see . . . Quite so . . .
ITAL
Orderly, look after these gentlemen, please.
Will you come with me? . . . Just a few formalities . . .
Certainly.
There's nothing to be afraid of. They're quite harmless.
This is the sort of ward we shall use for treating your poor friends.
SLAM
?
"He will give you this letter himself. He will tell you it concerns his two companions . . ."
". . . He is extremely dangerous. You should trick him into entering a cell, rather than force him. He will keep on insisting that he is absolutely sane . . ."
So, gentlemen, your unhappy friend will have all possible care.
We have complete confidence in you.
Goodbye, gentlemen.
Happy birthday, nanny!
Hello . . . yes boss. I copied the doctor's writing, and substituted another letter . . . It made out that Tintin himself was mad, not the others, and . . .

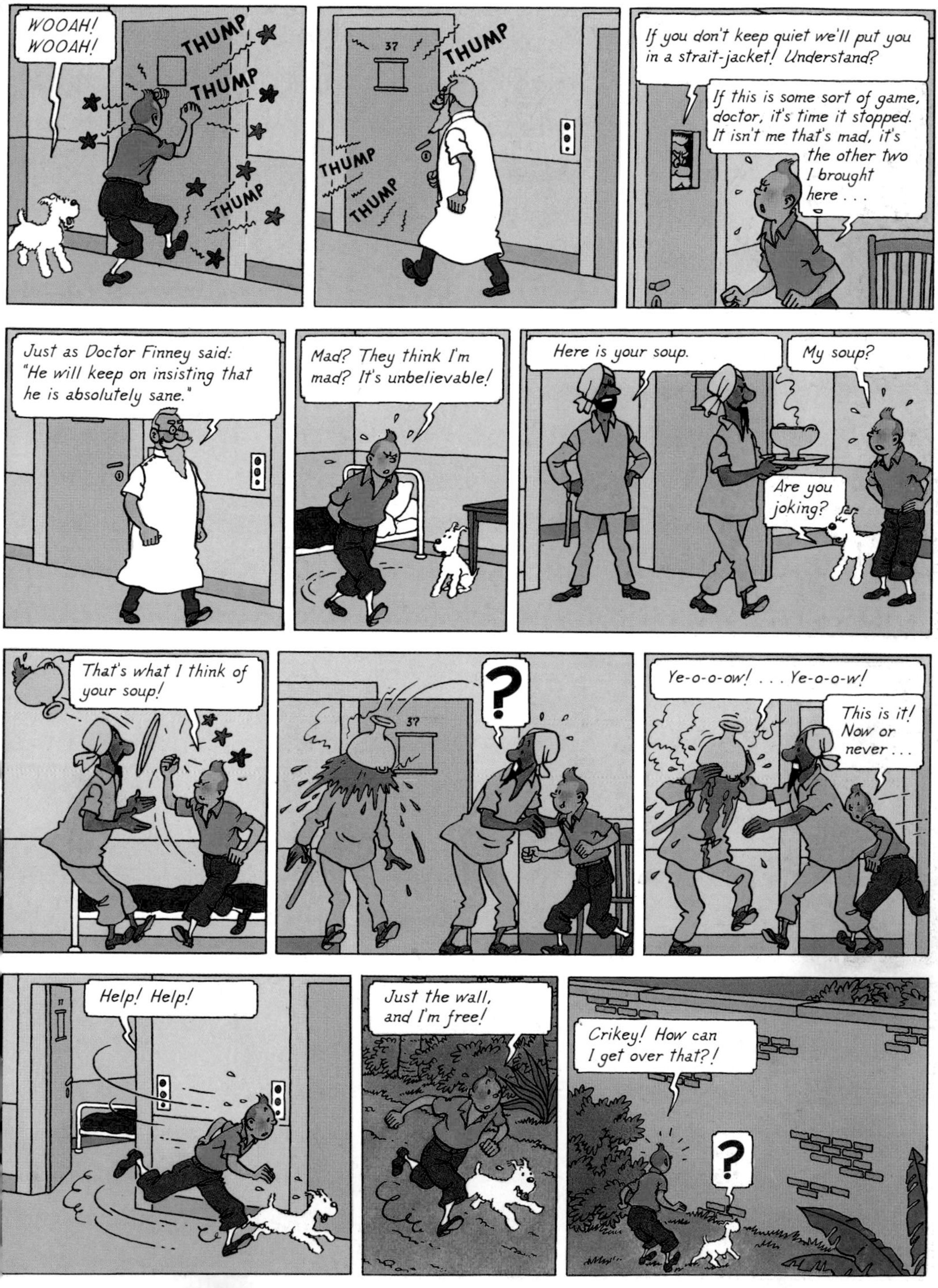
WOOAH! WOOAH!
THUMP
THUMP
THUMP
THUMP
THUMP
THUMP
If you don't keep quiet we'll put you in a strait-jacket! Understand?
If this is some sort of game, doctor, it's time it stopped. It isn't me that's mad, it's the other two I brought here . . .
Just as Doctor Finney said: "He will keep on insisting that he is absolutely sane."
Mad? They think I'm mad? It's unbelievable!
Here is your soup.
My soup?
Are you joking?
That's what I think of your soup!
?
Ye-o-o-ow! . . . Ye-o-o-w!
This is it! Now or never . . .
Help! Help!
Just the wall, and I'm free!
Crikey! How can I get over that?!
?

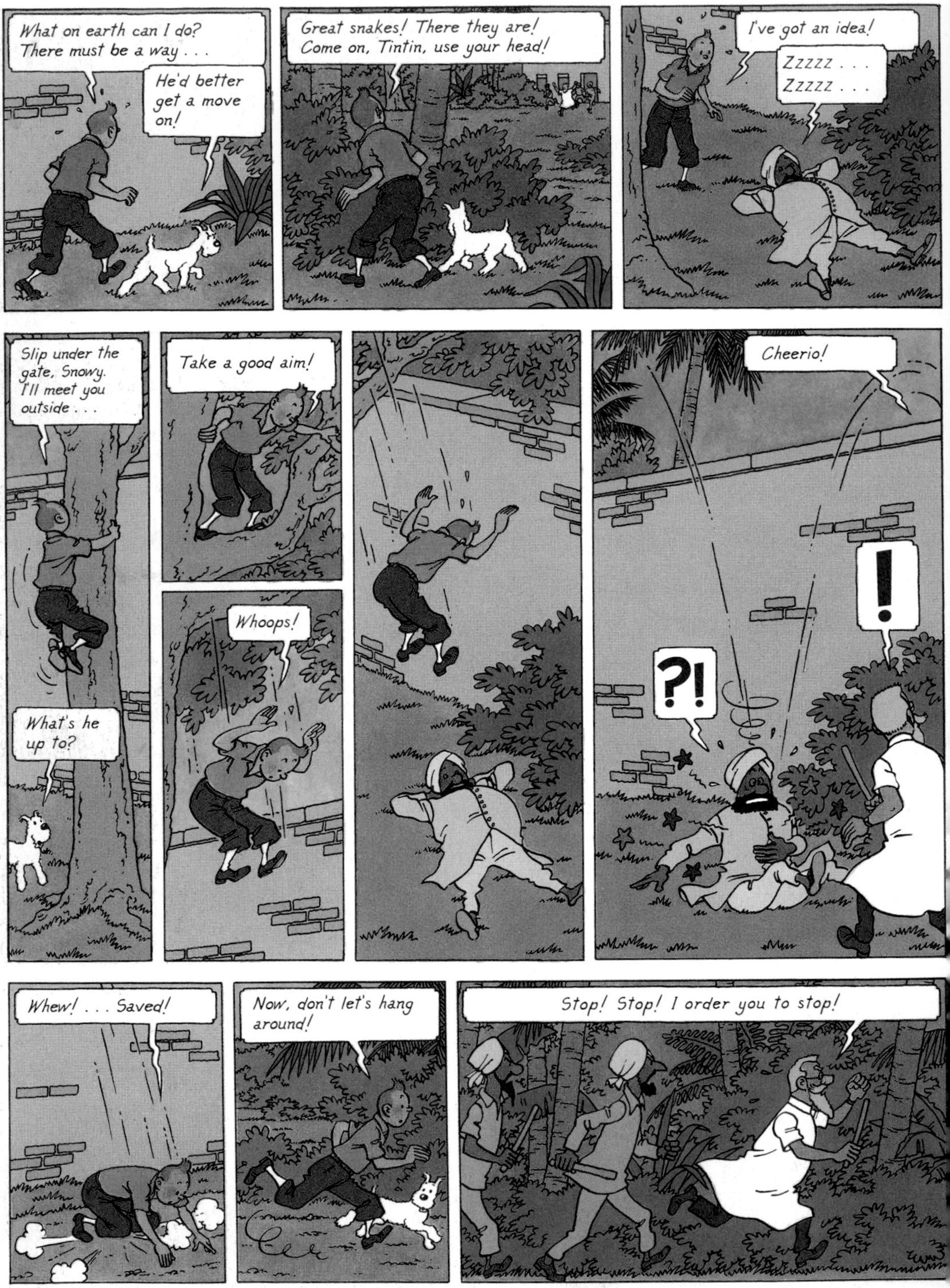
What on earth can I do? There must be a way . . .
He'd better get a move on!
Great snakes! There they are! Come on, Tintin, use your head!
I've got an idea!
Zzzzz . . . Zzzzz . . .
Slip under the gate, Snowy. I'll meet you outside . . .
What's he up to?
Take a good aim!
Whoops!
Cheerio!
?!
!
Whew! . . . Saved!
Now, don't let's hang around!
Stop! Stop! I order you to stop!

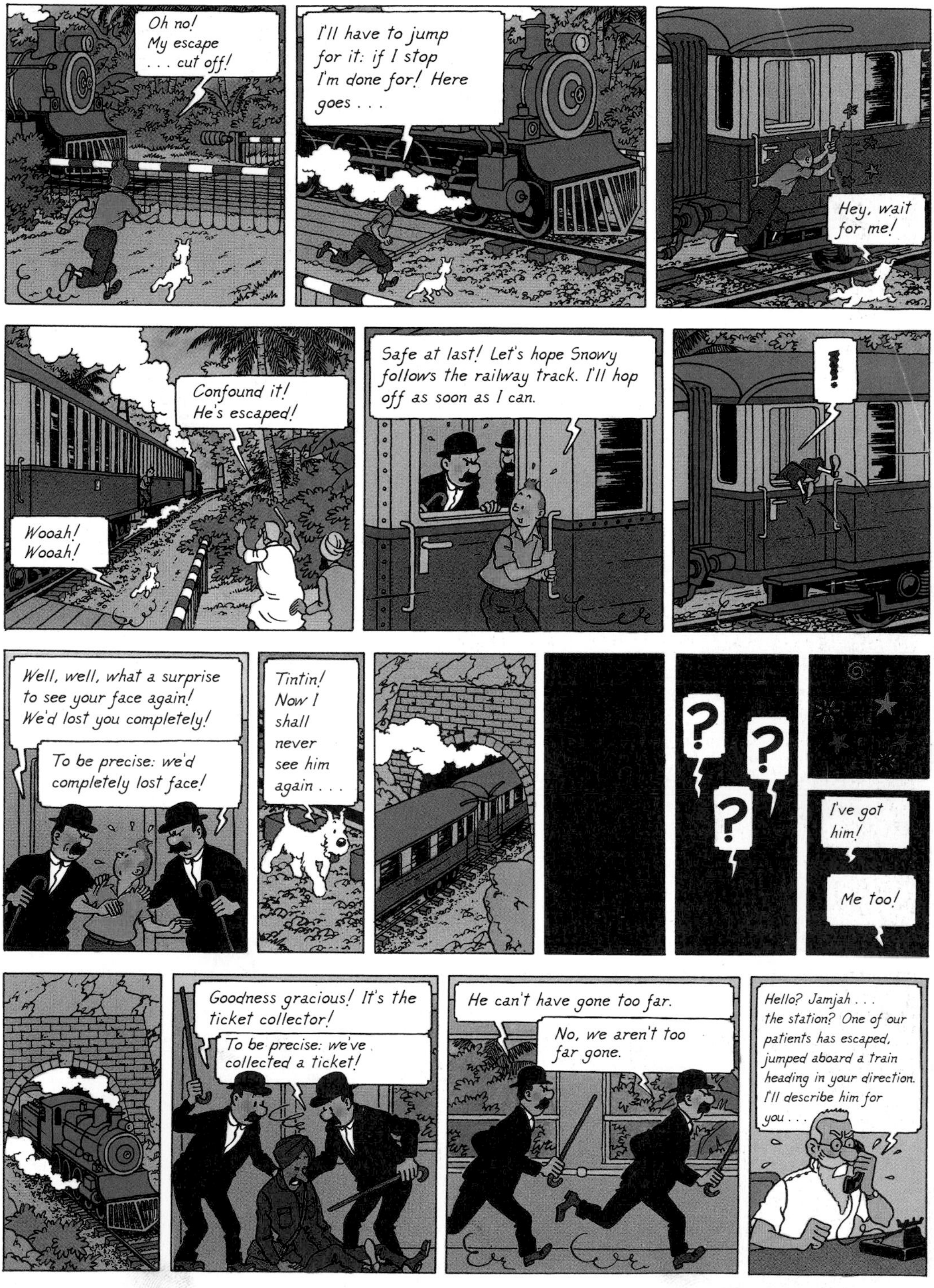
Oh no! My escape . . . cut off!
I'll have to jump for it: if I stop I'm done for! Here goes . . .
Hey, wait for me!
Confound it! He's escaped!
Wooah! Wooah!
Safe at last! Let's hope Snowy follows the railway track. I'll hop off as soon as I can.
!!!
Well, well, what a surprise to see your face again! We'd lost you completely!
To be precise: we'd completely lost face!
Tintin! Now I shall never see him again . . .
? ? ?
I've got him!
Me too!
Goodness gracious! It's the ticket collector!
To be precise: we've collected a ticket!
He can't have gone too far.
No, we aren't too far gone.
Hello? Jamjah . . . the station? One of our patients has escaped, jumped aboard a train heading in your direction. I'll describe him for you . . .

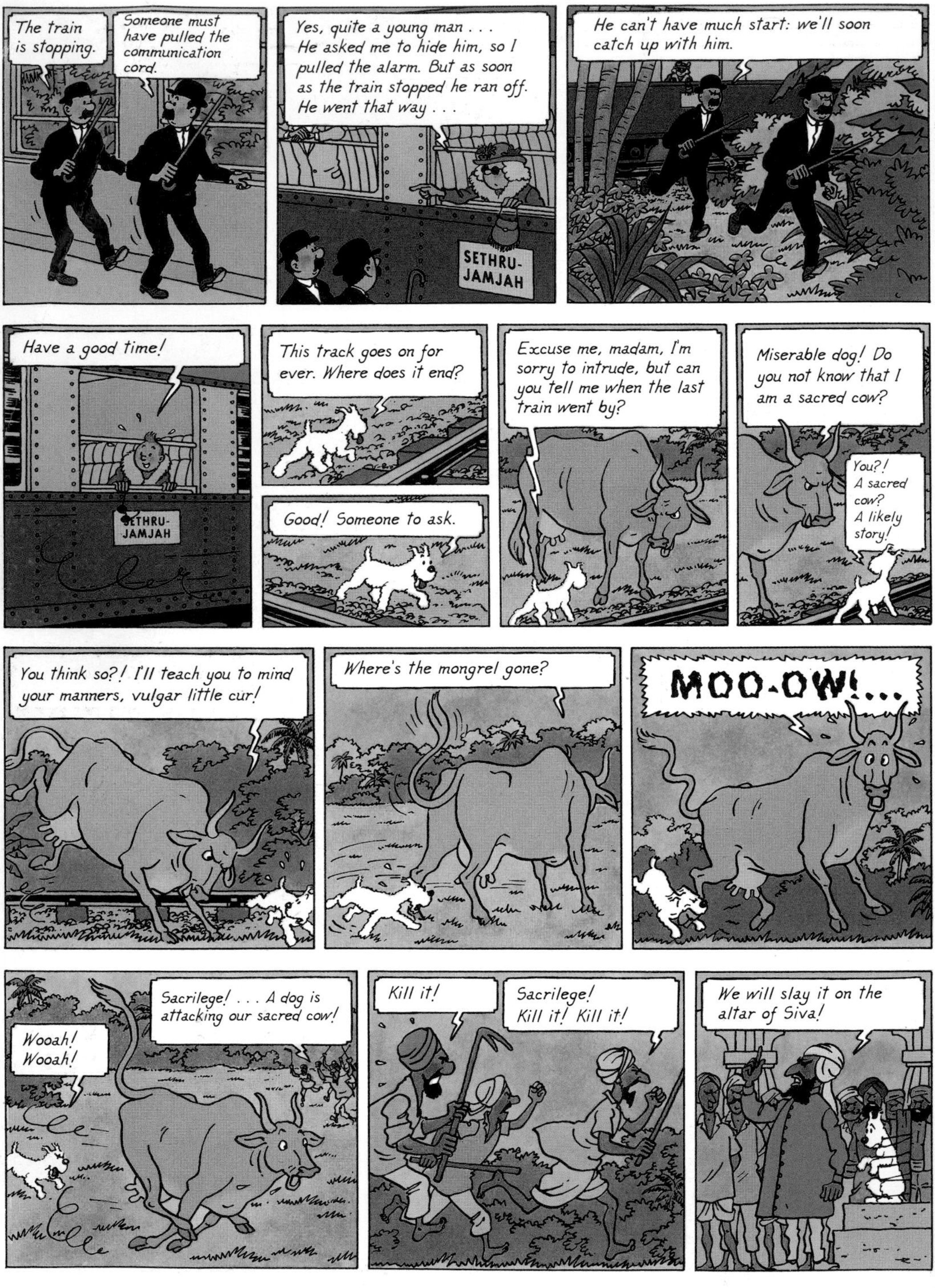
The train is stopping.
Someone must have pulled the communication cord.
Yes, quite a young man . . . He asked me to hide him, so I pulled the alarm. But as soon as the train stopped he ran off. He went that way . . .
SETHRU-JAMJAH
He can't have much start: we'll soon catch up with him.
Have a good time!
SETHRU-JAMJAH
This track goes on for ever. Where does it end?
Good! Someone to ask.
Excuse me, madam, I'm sorry to intrude, but can you tell me when the last train went by?
Miserable dog! Do you not know that I am a sacred cow?
You?! A sacred cow? A likely story!
You think so?! I'll teach you to mind your manners, vulgar little cur!
Where's the mongrel gone?
MOO-OW!...
Sacrilege! . . . A dog is attacking our sacred cow!
Wooah! Wooah!
Kill it!
Sacrilege! Kill it! Kill it!
We will slay it on the altar of Siva!

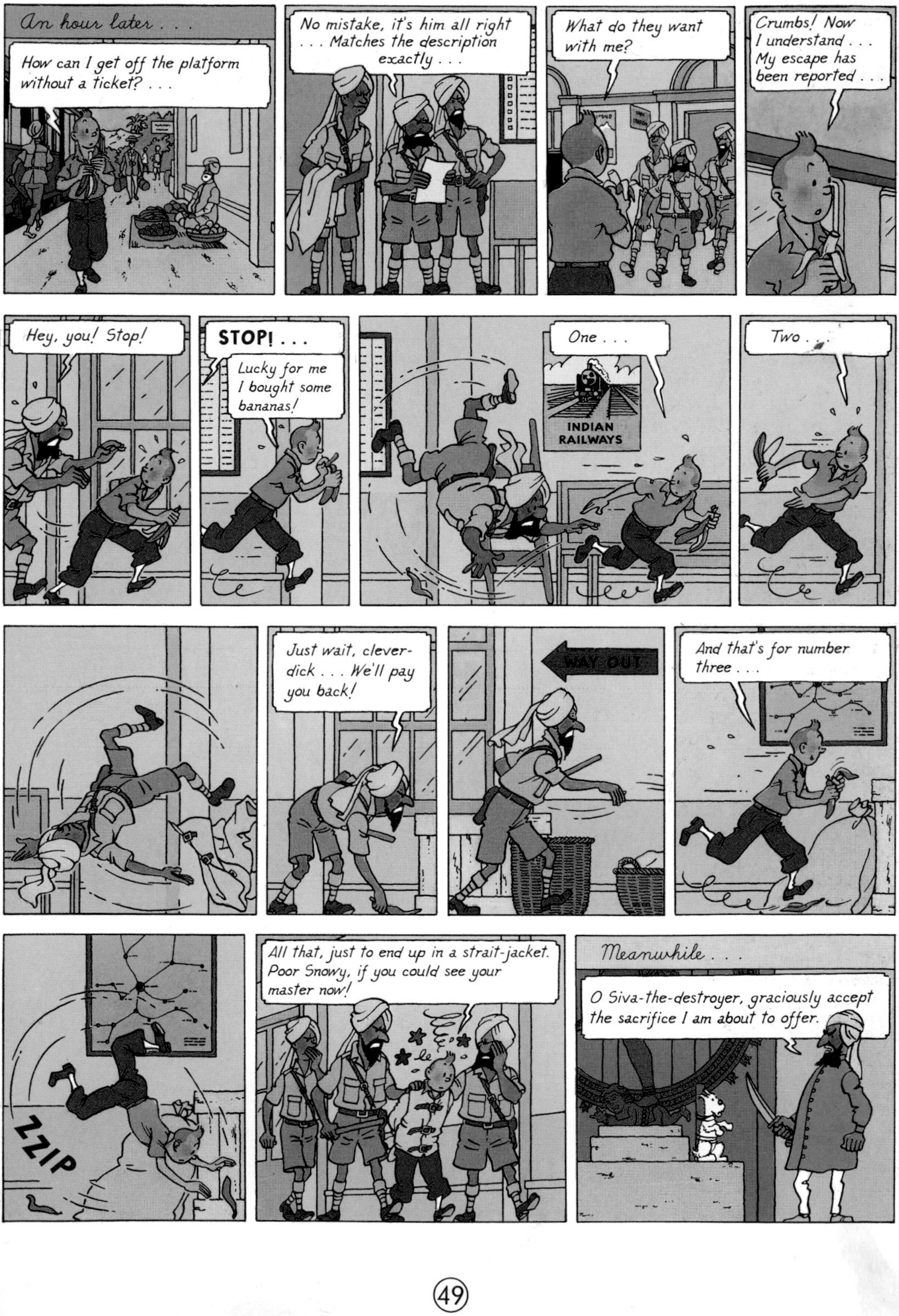
An hour later . . .
How can I get off the platform without a ticket? . . .
No mistake, it's him all right . . . Matches the description exactly . . .
What do they want with me?
Crumbs! Now I understand . . . My escape has been reported . . .
Hey, you! Stop!
STOP! . . .
Lucky for me I bought some bananas!
One . . .
INDIAN RAILWAYS
Two . . .
Just wait, clever-dick . . . We'll pay you back!
WAY OUT
And that's for number three . . .
ZZIP
All that, just to end up in a strait-jacket. Poor Snowy, if you could see your master now!
Meanwhile . . .
O Siva-the-destroyer, graciously accept the sacrifice I am about to offer.

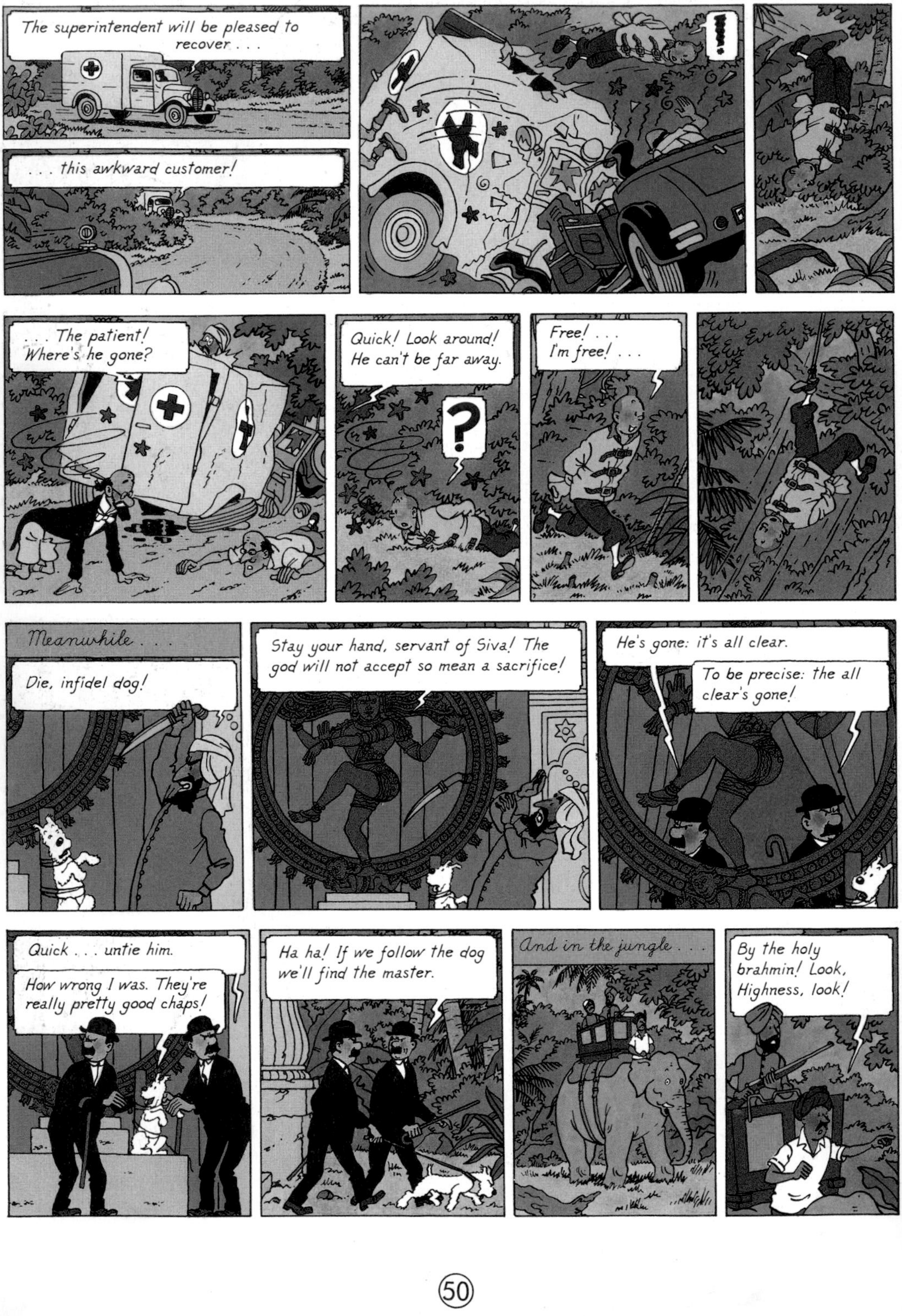
The superintendent will be pleased to recover . . .
. . . this awkward customer!
!!!!
. . . The patient! Where's he gone?
Quick! Look around! He can't be far away.
?
Free! . . . I'm free! . . .
Meanwhile . . .
Die, infidel dog!
Stay your hand, servant of Siva! The god will not accept so mean a sacrifice!
He's gone: it's all clear.
To be precise: the all clear's gone!
Quick . . . untie him.
How wrong I was. They're really pretty good chaps!
Ha ha! If we follow the dog we'll find the master.
And in the jungle . . .
By the holy brahmin! Look, Highness, look!

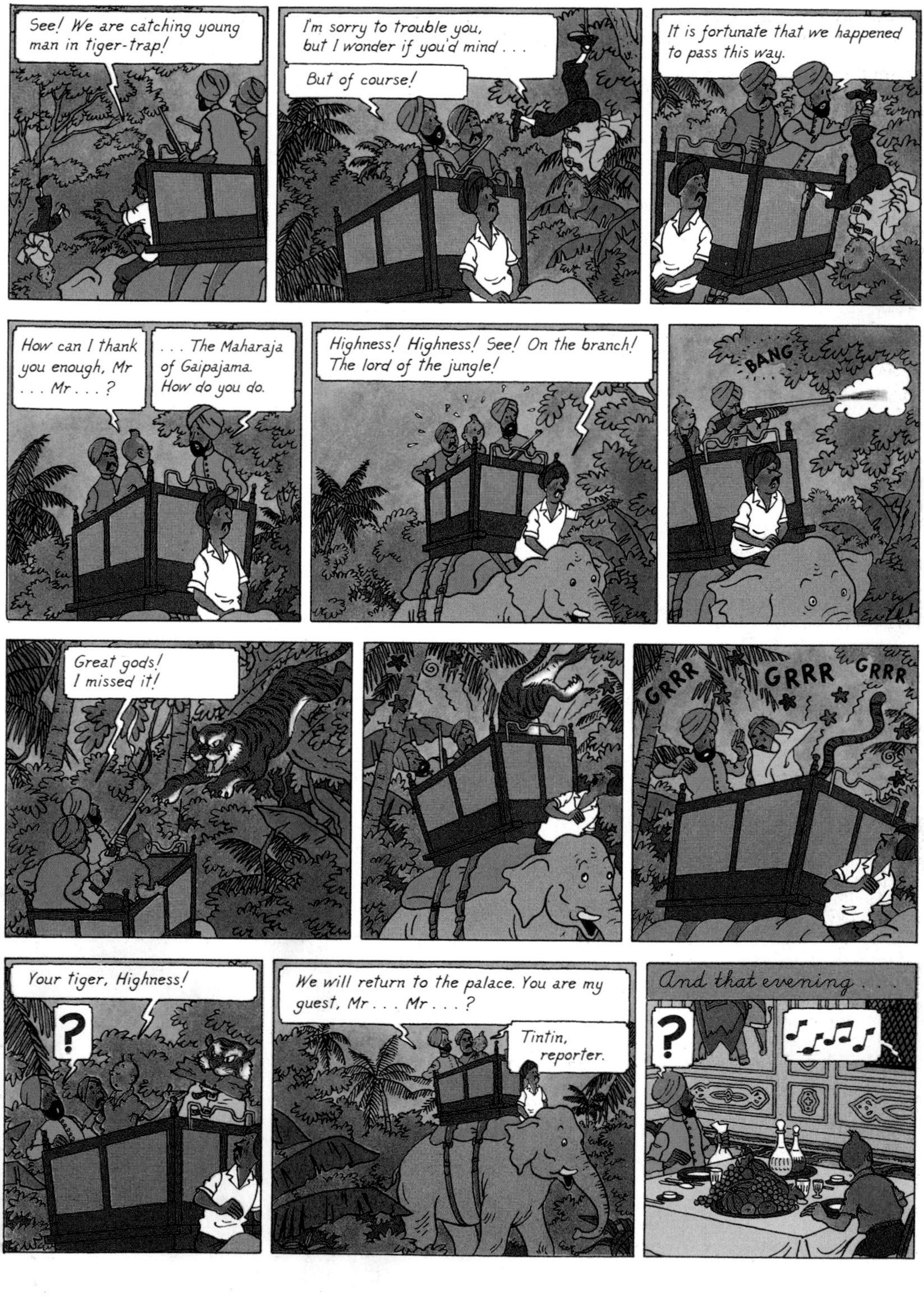

See! We are catching young man in tiger-trap!
I'm sorry to trouble you, but I wonder if you'd mind . . .
But of course!
It is fortunate that we happened to pass this way.
How can I thank you enough, Mr . . . Mr . . . ?
. . . The Maharaja of Gaipajama. How do you do.
Highness! Highness! See! On the branch! The lord of the jungle!
BANG
Great gods! I missed it!
GRRR
GRRR
GRRR
Your tiger, Highness!
?
We will return to the palace. You are my guest, Mr . . . Mr . . . ?
Tintin, reporter.
And that evening . . .
?

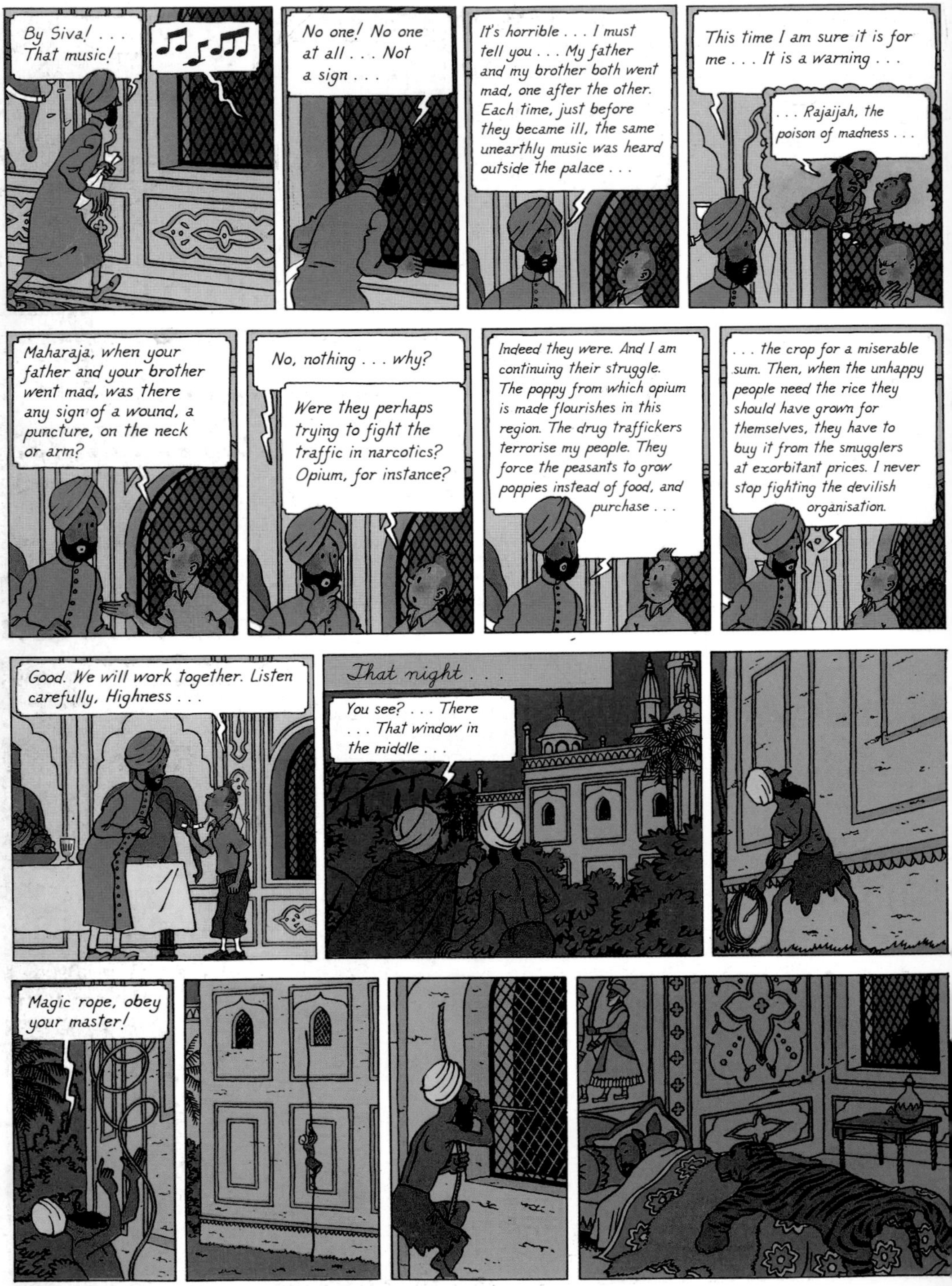

By Siva! . . . That music!
It's horrible . . . I must tell you . . . My father and my brother both went mad, one after the other. Each time, just before they became ill, the same unearthly music was heard outside the palace . . .
No one! No one at all . . . Not a sign . . .
This time I am sure it is for me . . . It is a warning . . .
. . . Rajaijah, the poison of madness . . .
Maharaja, when your father and your brother went mad, was there any sign of a wound, a puncture, on the neck or arm?
No, nothing . . . why?
Were they perhaps trying to fight the traffic in narcotics? Opium, for instance?
Indeed they were. And I am continuing their struggle. The poppy from which opium is made flourishes in this region. The drug traffickers terrorise my people. They force the peasants to grow poppies instead of food, and purchase . . .
. . . the crop for a miserable sum. Then, when the unhappy people need the rice they should have grown for themselves, they have to buy it from the smugglers at exorbitant prices. I never stop fighting the devilish organisation.
Good. We will work together. Listen carefully, Highness . . .
That night . . .
You see? . . . There . . . That window in the middle . . .
Magic rope, obey your master!

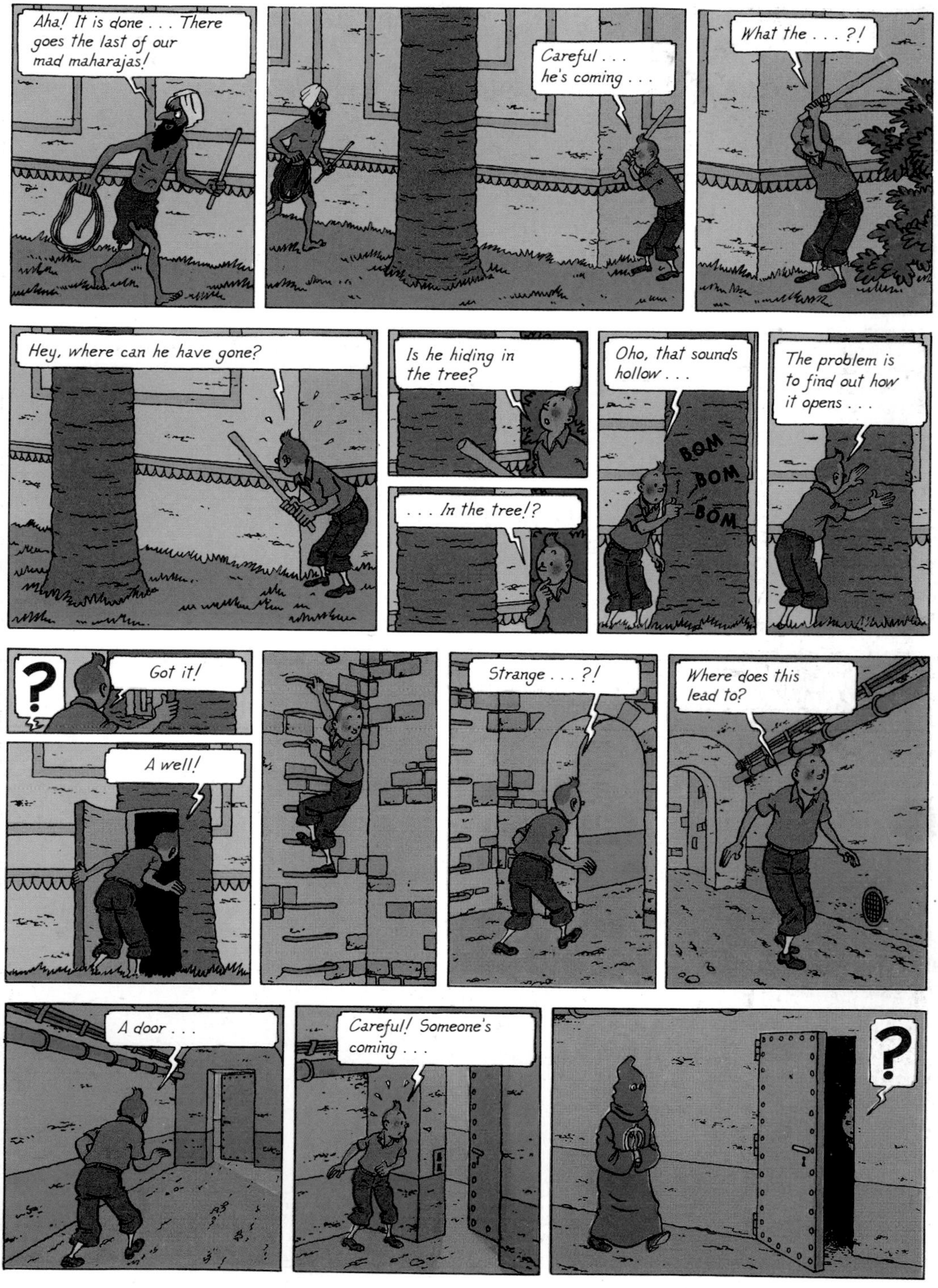
Aha! It is done . . . There goes the last of our mad maharajas!
Careful . . . he's coming . . .
What the . . . ?!
Hey, where can he have gone?
Is he hiding in the tree?
. . . In the tree!?
Oho, that sounds hollow . . .
BOM
BOM
BOM
The problem is to find out how it opens . . .
?
Got it!
A well!
Strange . . . ?!
Where does this lead to?
A door . . .
Careful! Someone's coming . . .
?

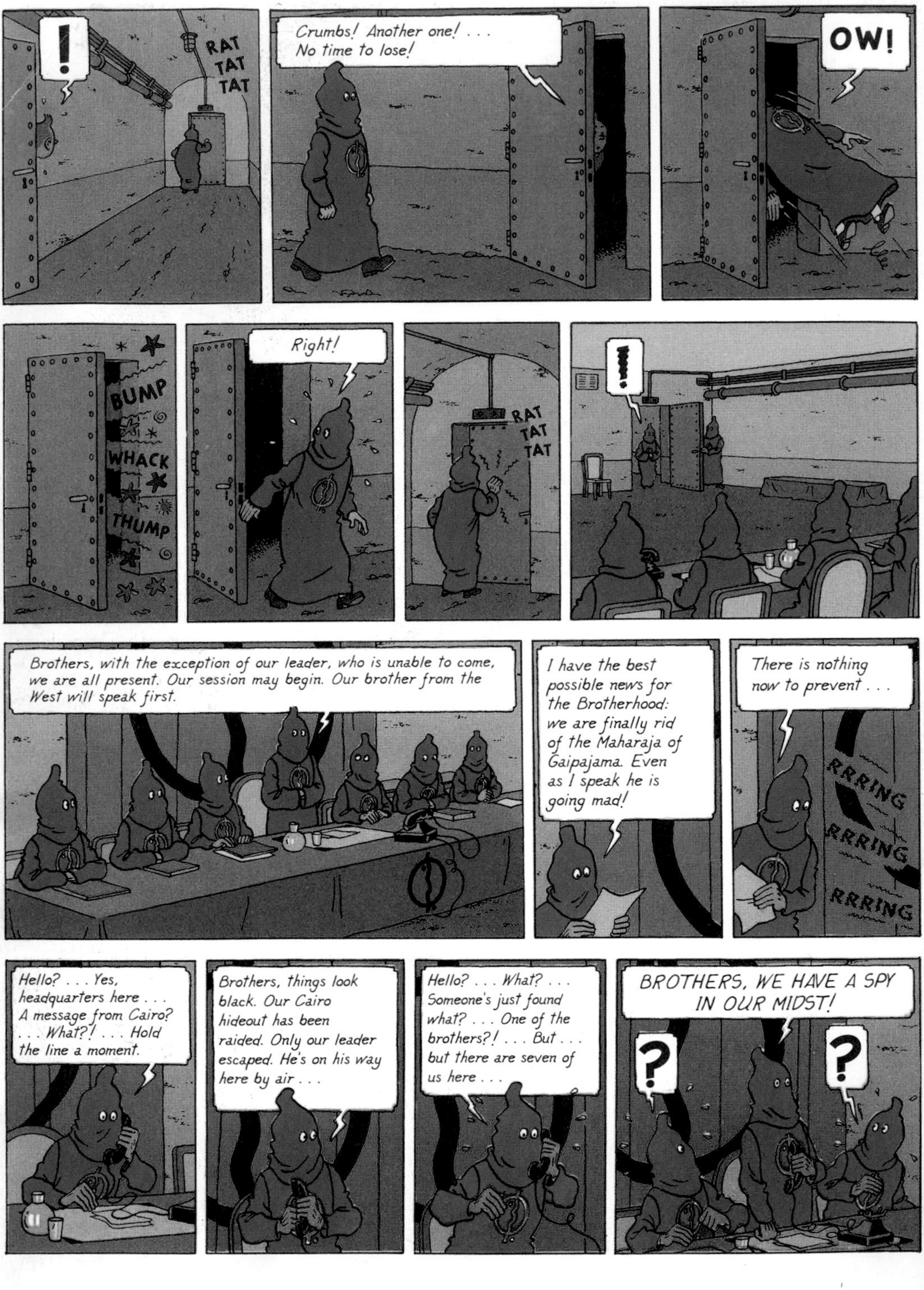
!
RAT TAT TAT
Crumbs! Another one! . . . No time to lose!
OW!
BUMP
WHACK
THUMP
Right!
RAT TAT TAT
!
Brothers, with the exception of our leader, who is unable to come, we are all present. Our session may begin. Our brother from the West will speak first.
I have the best possible news for the Brotherhood: we are finally rid of the Maharaja of Gaipajama. Even as I speak he is going mad!
There is nothing now to prevent . . .
RRRING
RRRING
RRRING
Hello? . . . Yes, headquarters here . . . A message from Cairo? . . . What?! . . . Hold the line a moment.
Brothers, things look black. Our Cairo hideout has been raided. Only our leader escaped. He's on his way here by air . . .
Hello? . . . What? . . . Someone's just found what? . . . One of the brothers?! . . . But . . . but there are seven of us here . . .
BROTHERS, WE HAVE A SPY IN OUR MIDST!
?
?

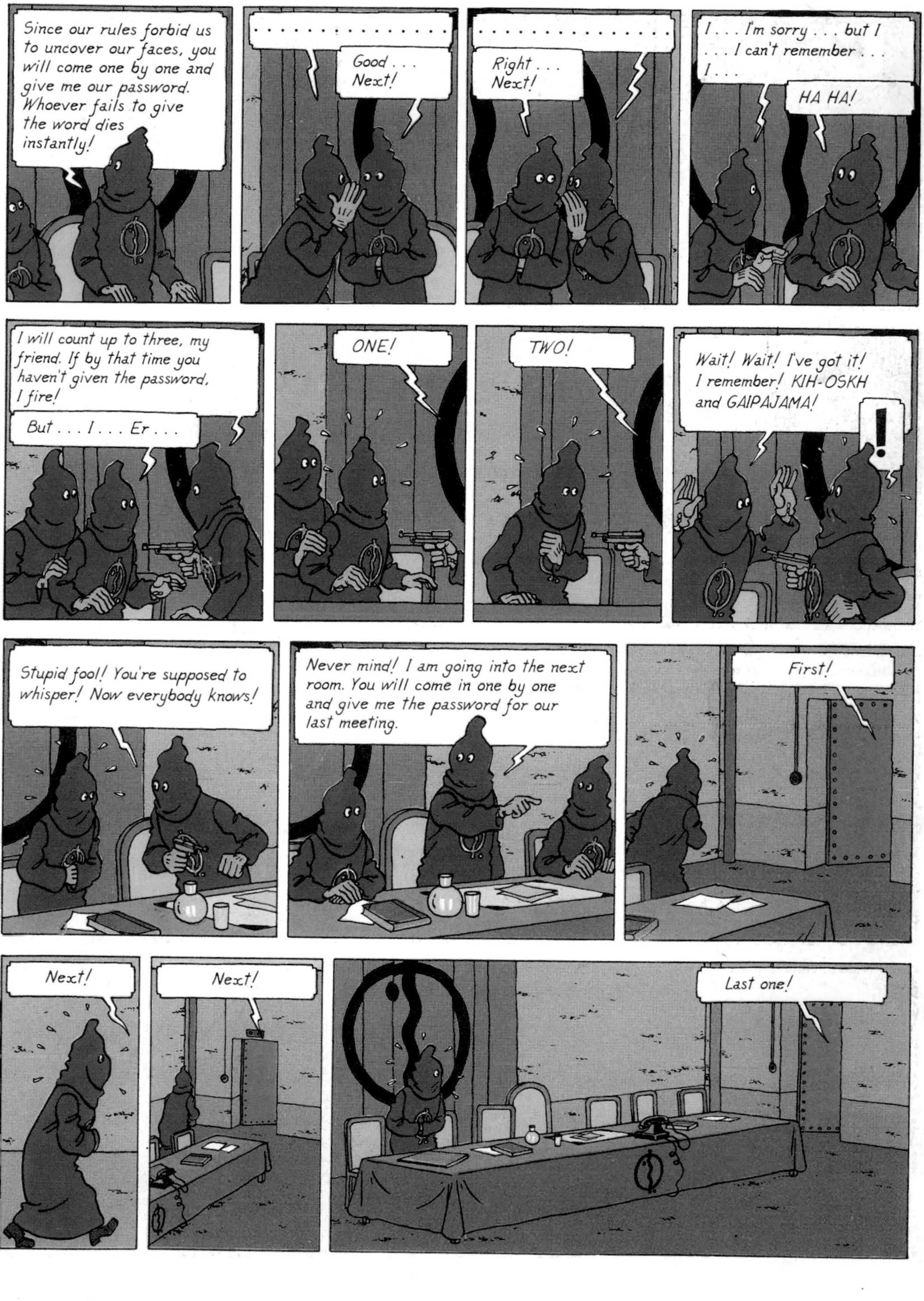
Since our rules forbid us to uncover our faces, you will come one by one and give me our password. Whoever fails to give the word dies instantly!
. . . .
Good . . . Next!
. . . .
Right . . . Next!
I . . . I'm sorry . . . but I . . . I can't remember . . . I . . .
HA HA!
I will count up to three, my friend. If by that time you haven't given the password, I fire!
But . . . I . . . Er . . .
ONE!
TWO!
Wait! Wait! I've got it! I remember! KIH-OSKH and GAIPAJAMA!
!
Stupid fool! You're supposed to whisper! Now everybody knows!
Never mind! I am going into the next room. You will come in one by one and give me the password for our last meeting.
First!
Next!
Next!
Last one!

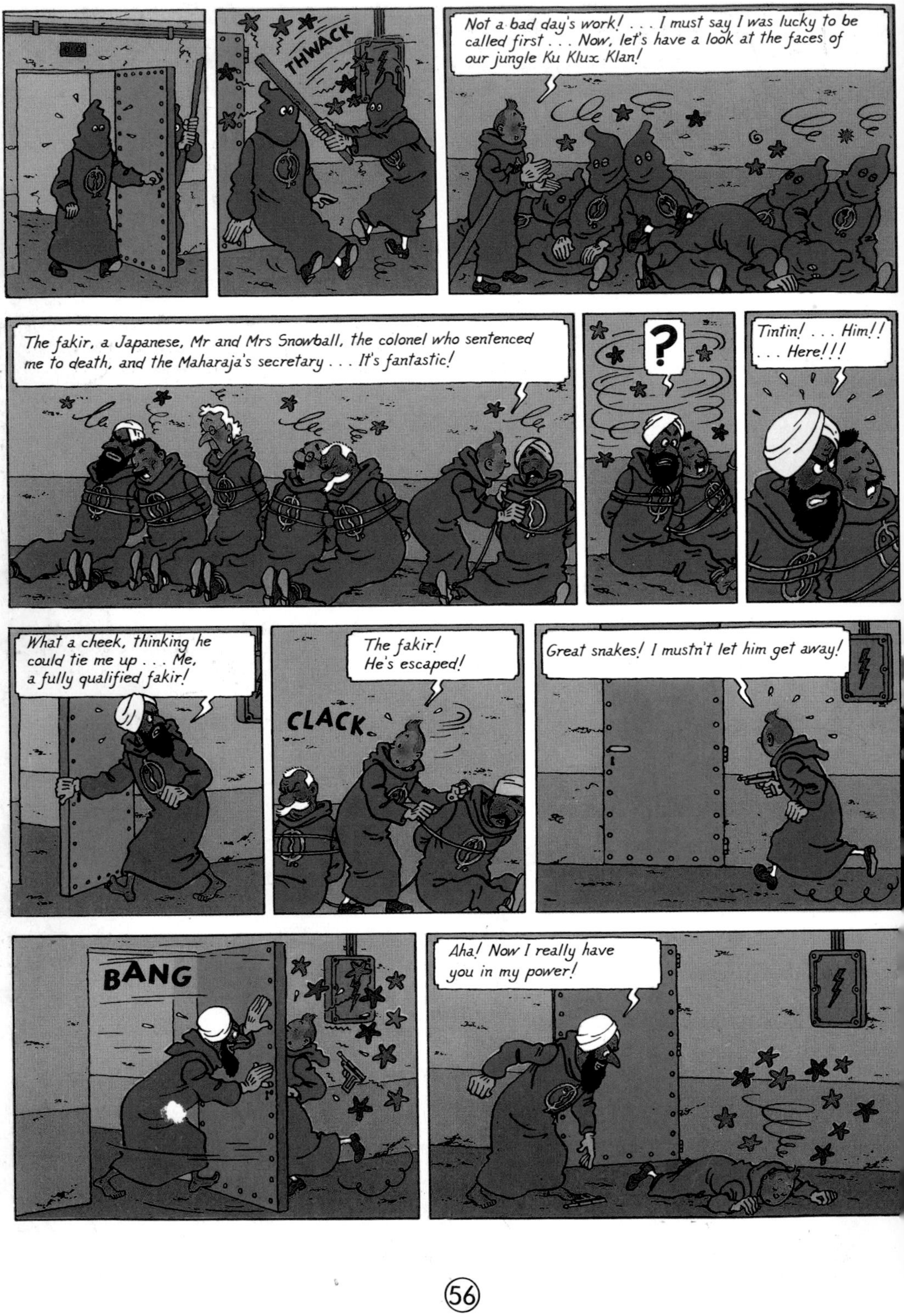
THWACK
Not a bad day's work! . . . I must say I was lucky to be called first . . . Now, let's have a look at the faces of our jungle Ku Klux Klan!
The fakir, a Japanese, Mr and Mrs Snowball, the colonel who sentenced me to death, and the Maharaja's secretary . . . It's fantastic!
?
Tintin! . . . Him!! . . . Here!!!
What a cheek, thinking he could tie me up . . . Me, a fully qualified fakir!
CLACK
The fakir! He's escaped!
Great snakes! I mustn't let him get away!
BANG
Aha! Now I really have you in my power!

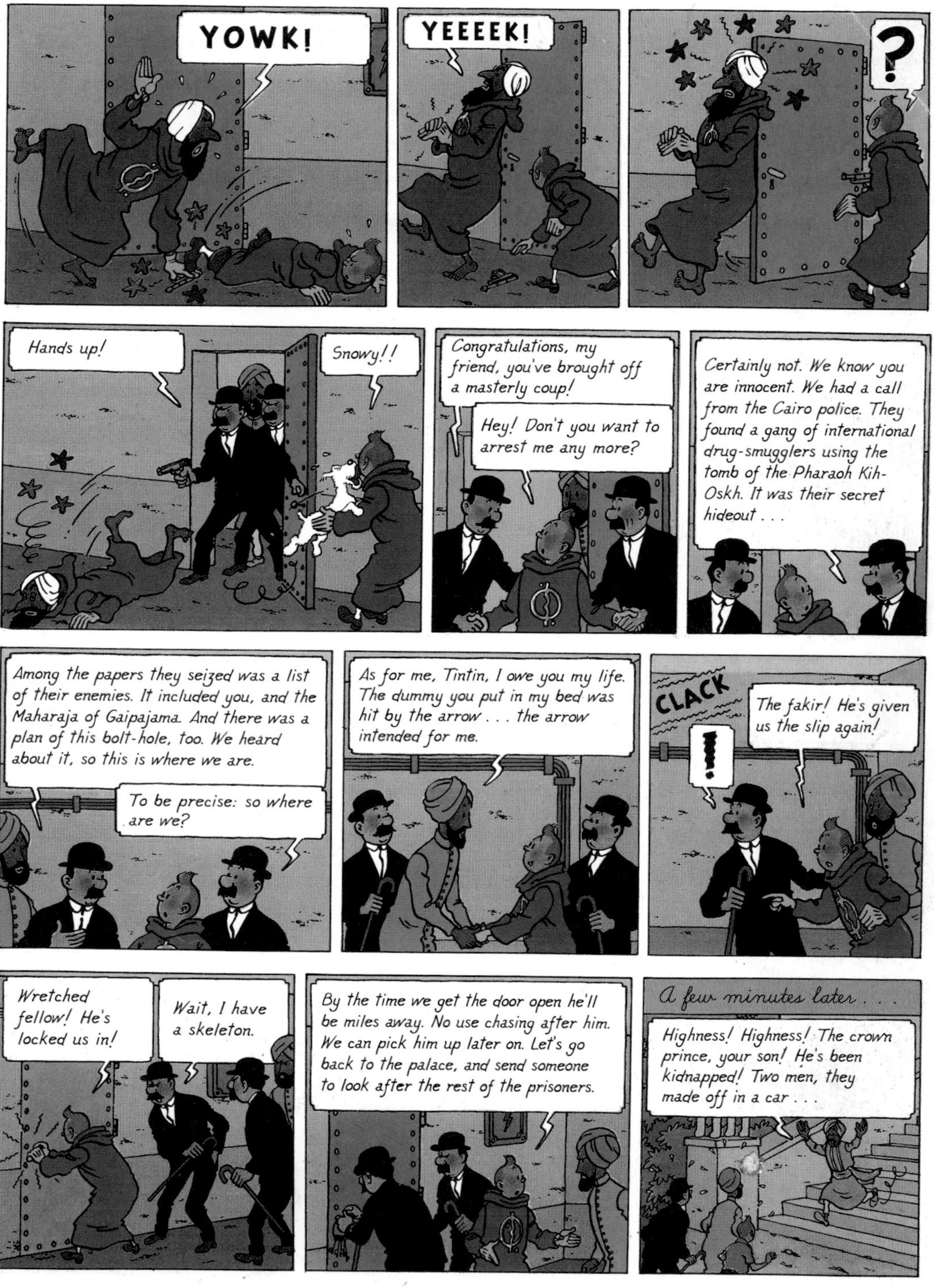
YOWK!
YEEEEK!
?
Hands up!
Snowy!!
Congratulations, my friend, you've brought off a masterly coup!
Hey! Don't you want to arrest me any more?
Certainly not. We know you are innocent. We had a call from the Cairo police. They found a gang of international drug-smugglers using the tomb of the Pharaoh Kih-Oskh. It was their secret hideout . . .
Among the papers they seized was a list of their enemies. It included you, and the Maharaja of Gaipajama. And there was a plan of this bolt-hole, too. We heard about it, so this is where we are.
To be precise: so where are we?
As for me, Tintin, I owe you my life. The dummy you put in my bed was hit by the arrow . . . the arrow intended for me.
CLACK
!
The fakir! He's given us the slip again!
Wretched fellow! He's locked us in!
Wait, I have a skeleton.
By the time we get the door open he'll be miles away. No use chasing after him. We can pick him up later on. Let's go back to the palace, and send someone to look after the rest of the prisoners.
A few minutes later . . .
Highness! Highness! The crown prince, your son! He's been kidnapped! Two men, they made off in a car . . .

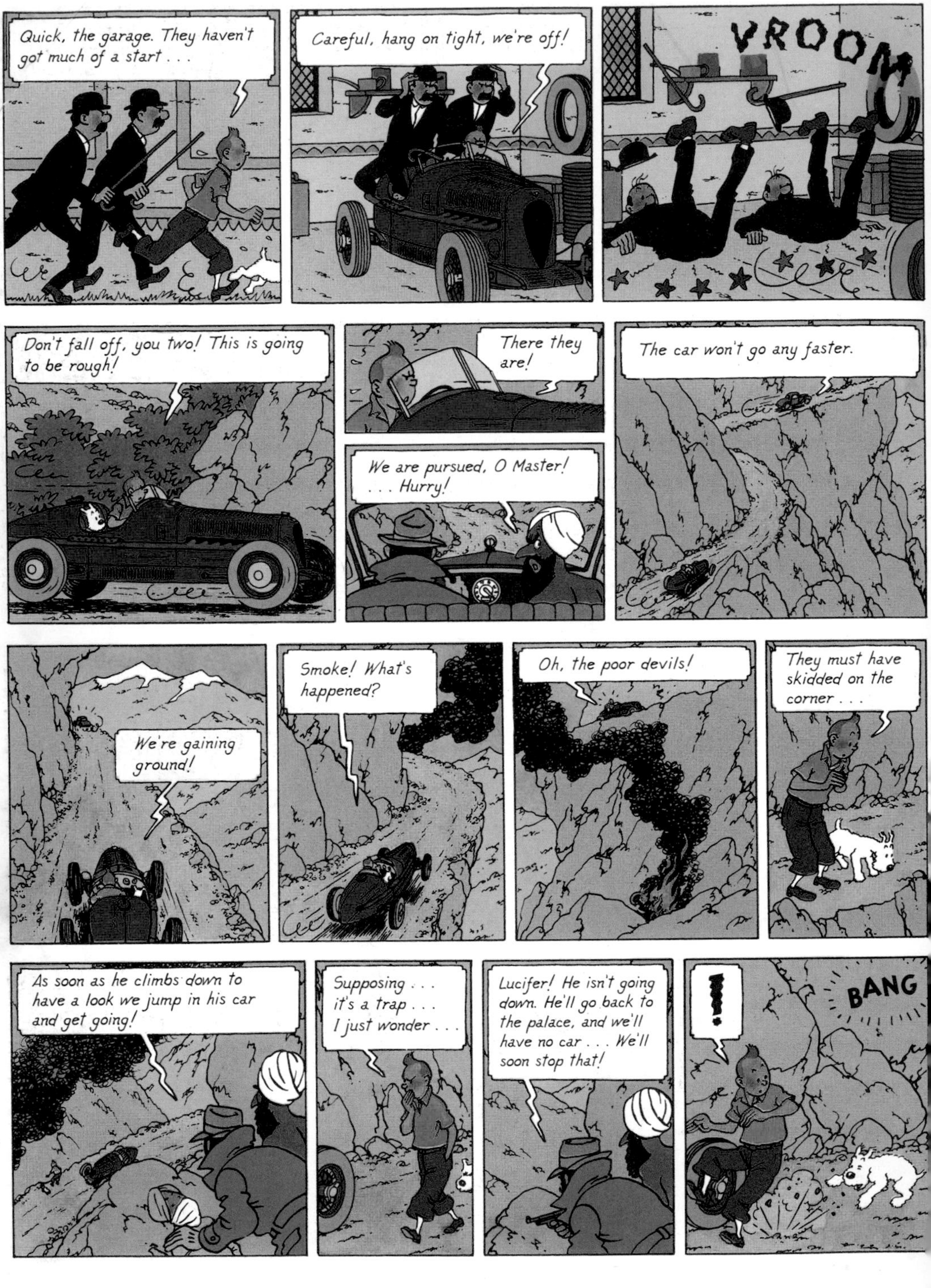

Quick, the garage. They haven't got much of a start . . .
Careful, hang on tight, we're off!
VROOM
Don't fall off, you two! This is going to be rough!
There they are!
We are pursued, O Master! . . . Hurry!
The car won't go any faster.
We're gaining ground!
Smoke! What's happened?
Oh, the poor devils!
They must have skidded on the corner . . .
As soon as he climbs down to have a look we jump in his car and get going!
Supposing . . . it's a trap . . . I just wonder . . .
Lucifer! He isn't going down. He'll go back to the palace, and we'll have no car . . . We'll soon stop that!
!
BANG

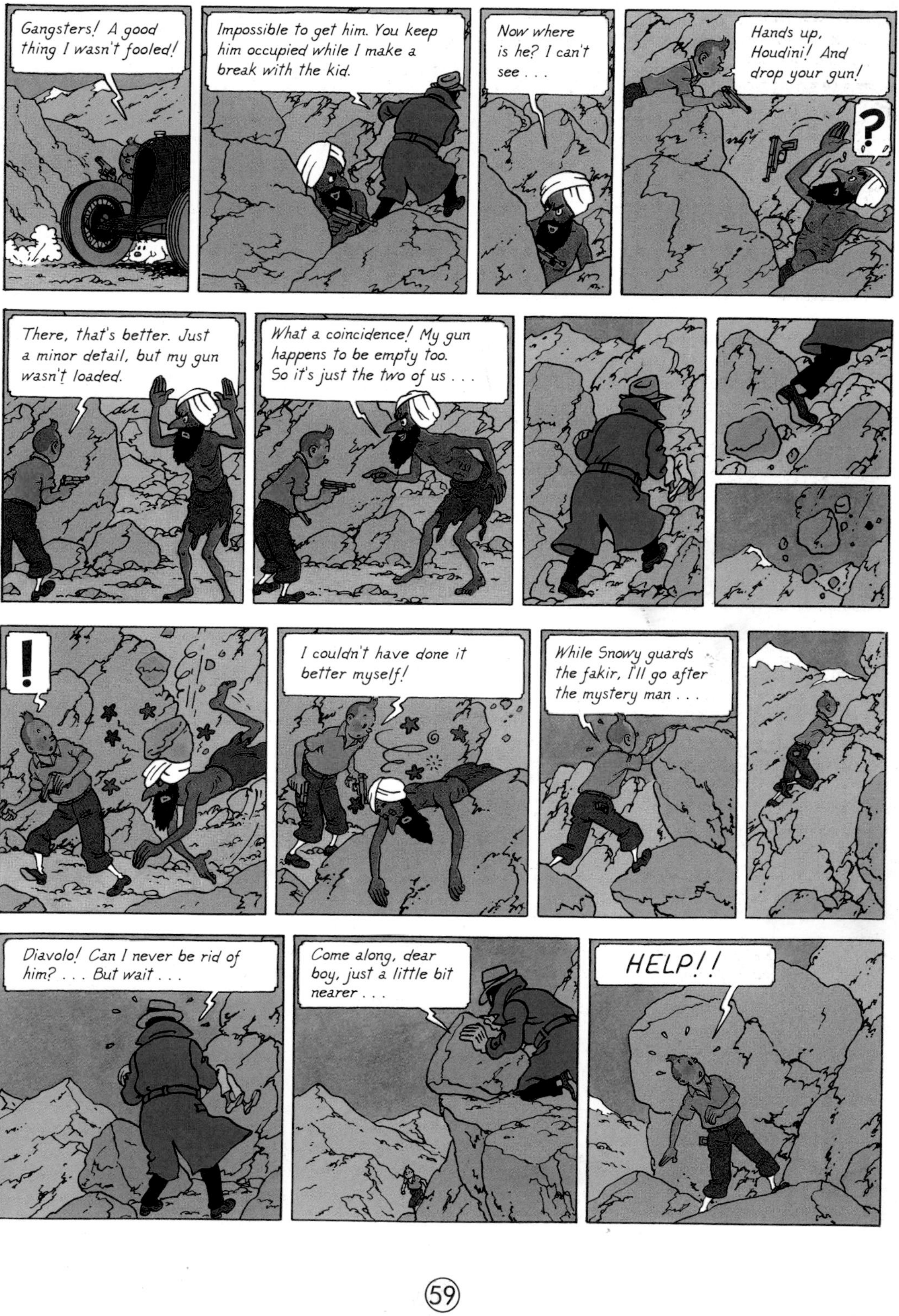
Gangsters! A good thing I wasn't fooled!
Impossible to get him. You keep him occupied while I make a break with the kid.
Now where is he? I can't see . . .
Hands up, Houdini! And drop your gun!
?
There, that's better. Just a minor detail, but my gun wasn't loaded.
What a coincidence! My gun happens to be empty too. So it's just the two of us . . .
!
I couldn't have done it better myself!
While Snowy guards the fakir, I'll go after the mystery man . . .
Diavolo! Can I never be rid of him? . . . But wait . . .
Come along, dear boy, just a little bit nearer . . .
HELP!!

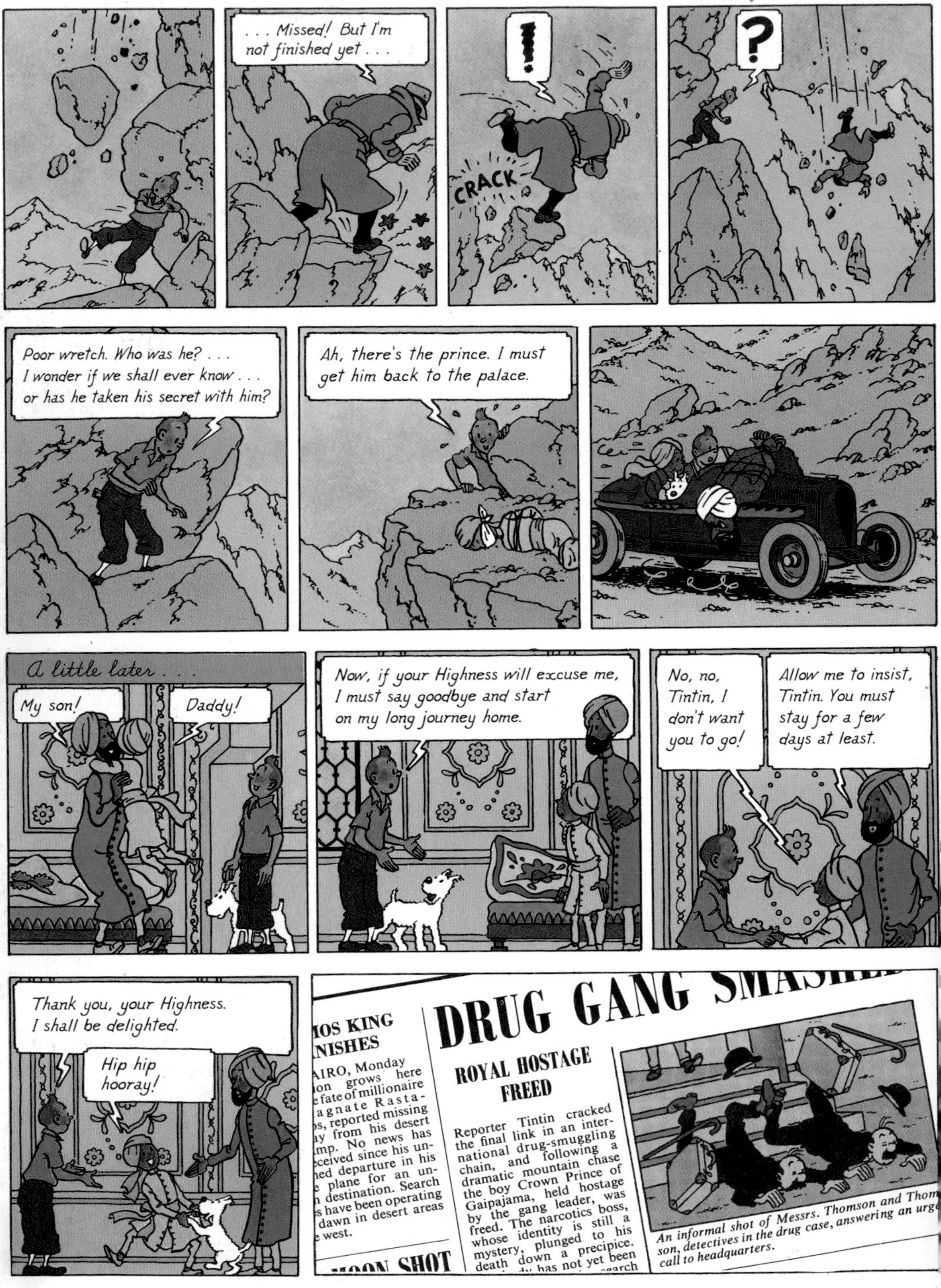

. . . Missed! But I'm not finished yet . . .
!
CRACK
?
Poor wretch. Who was he? . . . I wonder if we shall ever know . . . or has he taken his secret with him?
Ah, there's the prince. I must get him back to the palace.
A little later . . .
My son!
Daddy!
Now, if your Highness will excuse me, I must say goodbye and start on my long journey home.
No, no, Tintin, I don't want you to go!
Allow me to insist, Tintin. You must stay for a few days at least.
Thank you, your Highness. I shall be delighted.
Hip hip hooray!
DRUG GANG SMASHE
IOS KING
NISHES
AIRO, Monday
ion grows here
e fate of millionaire
agnate Rasta-
ps, reported missing
ay from his desert
mp. No news has
ceived since his un-
hed departure in his
e plane for an un-
h destination. Search
s have been operating
dawn in desert areas
e west.
ROYAL HOSTAGE FREED
Reporter Tintin cracked the final link in an international drug-smuggling chain, and following a dramatic mountain chase the boy Crown Prince of Gaipajama, held hostage by the gang leader, was freed. The narcotics boss, whose identity is still a mystery, plunged to his death down a precipice.
An informal shot of Messrs. Thomson and Thom son, detectives in the drug case, answering an urge call to headquarters.
MOON SHOT

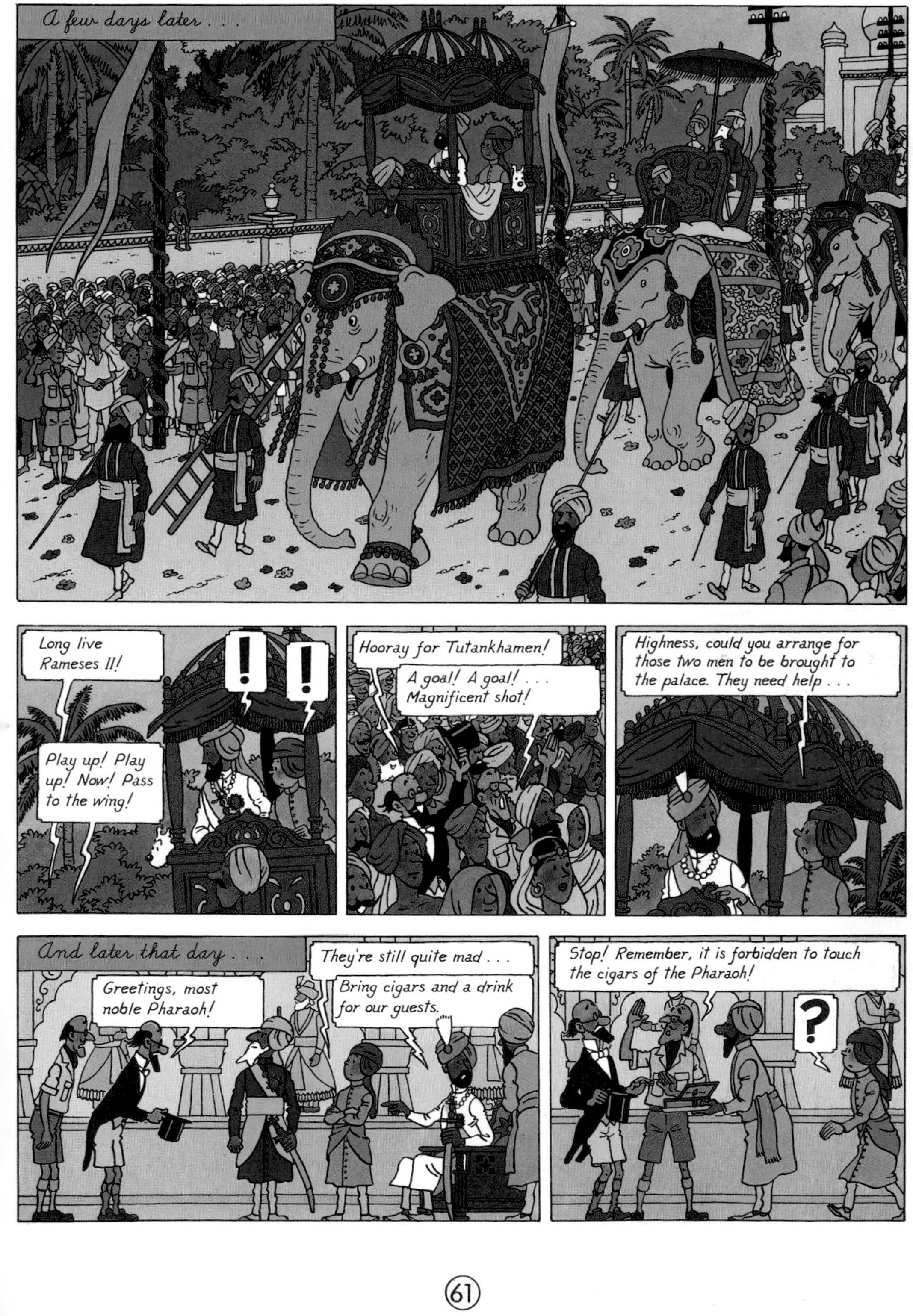
A few days later . . .
Long live Rameses II!
!
!
Play up! Play up! Now! Pass to the wing!
Hooray for Tutankhamen!
A goal! A goal! . . . Magnificent shot!
Highness, could you arrange for those two men to be brought to the palace. They need help . . .
And later that day . . .
Greetings, most noble Pharaoh!
They're still quite mad . . .
Bring cigars and a drink for our guests.
Stop! Remember, it is forbidden to touch the cigars of the Pharaoh!
?

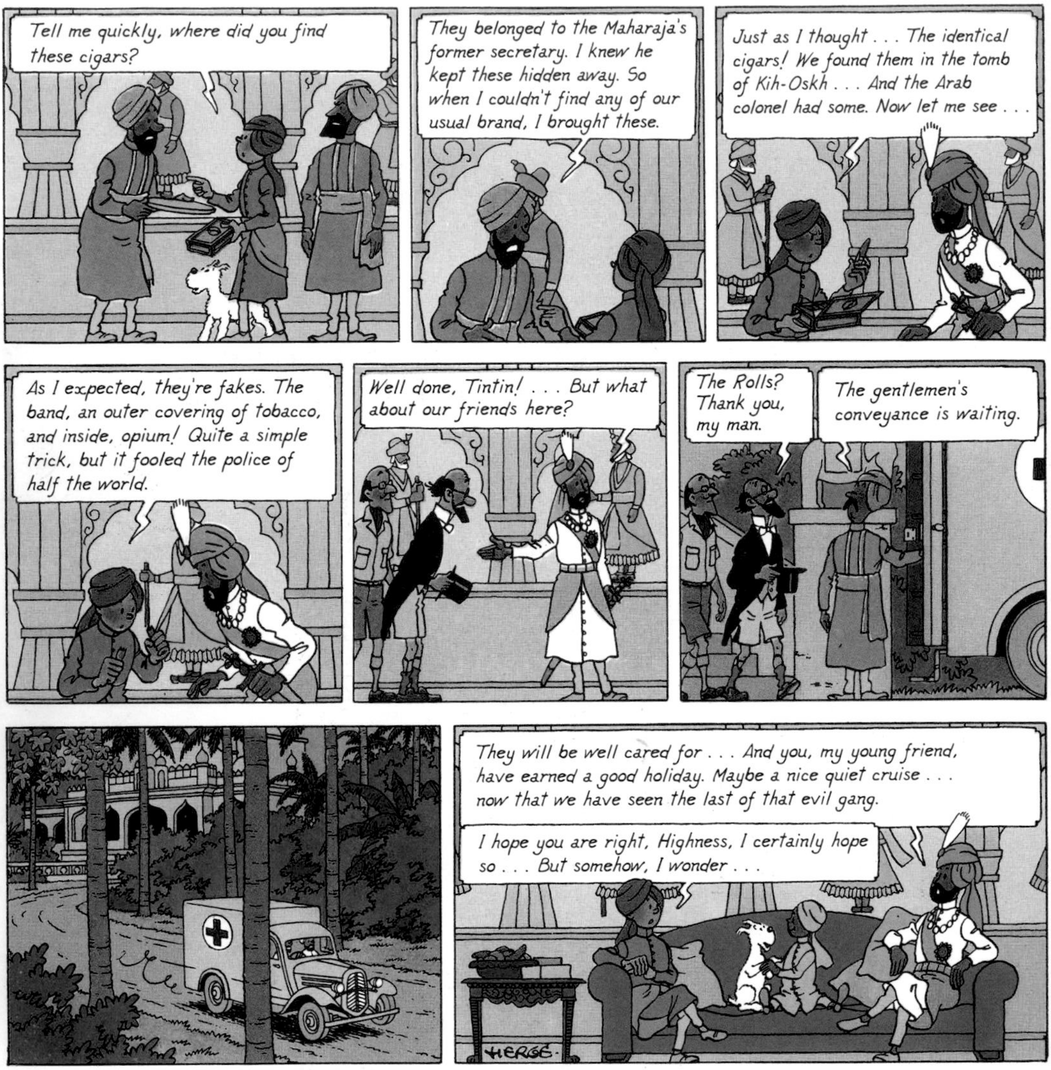
Tell me quickly, where did you find these cigars?
They belonged to the Maharaja's former secretary. I knew he kept these hidden away. So when I couldn't find any of our usual brand, I brought these.
Just as I thought . . . The identical cigars! We found them in the tomb of Kih-Oskh . . . And the Arab colonel had some. Now let me see . . .
As I expected, they're fakes. The band, an outer covering of tobacco, and inside, opium! Quite a simple trick, but it fooled the police of half the world.
Well done, Tintin! . . . But what about our friends here?
The Rolls? Thank you, my man.
The gentlemen's conveyance is waiting.
They will be well cared for . . . And you, my young friend, have earned a good holiday. Maybe a nice quiet cruise . . . now that we have seen the last of that evil gang.
I hope you are right, Highness, I certainly hope so . . . But somehow, I wonder . . .
HERGÉ

THE END

THE REAL-LIFE INSPIRATION
BEHIND
TINTIN'S ADVENTURES

Written by Stuart Tett
with the collaboration of Studio Moulinsart.

1907	1924	1925	1928	1929
GEORGES REMI BORN IN BELGIUM	CHOOSES PEN-NAME "HERGÉ" – HIS INITIALS "G.R." REVERSED	HERGÉ LEAVES SCHOOL	HERGÉ HELPS TO CREATE CHILDREN'S MAGAZINE *LE PETIT VINGTIÈME*	TINTIN'S FIRST ADVENTURE, *TINTIN IN THE LAND OF THE SOVIETS*, APPEARS IN *LE PETIT VINGTIÈME*

HERGÉ

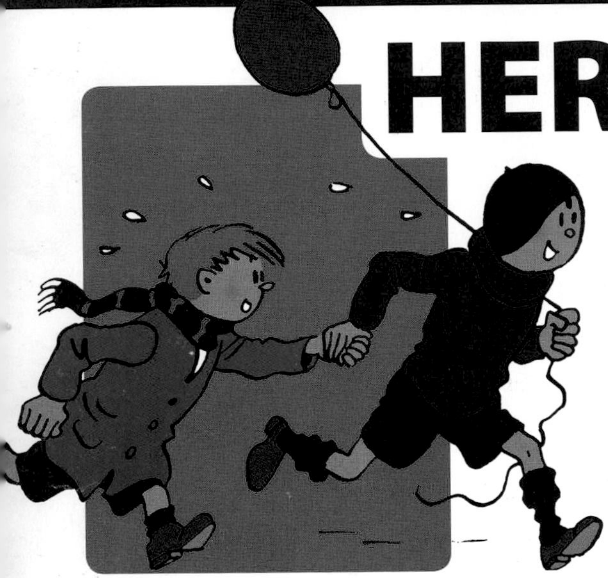

Other series

Hergé had already created several other comic strips by the time he began writing Tintin's fourth adventure, *Cigars of the Pharaoh*, in 1932. The most successful of these was *Quick and Flupke*, a series of short stories about two Belgian scalawags from the streets of Brussels.

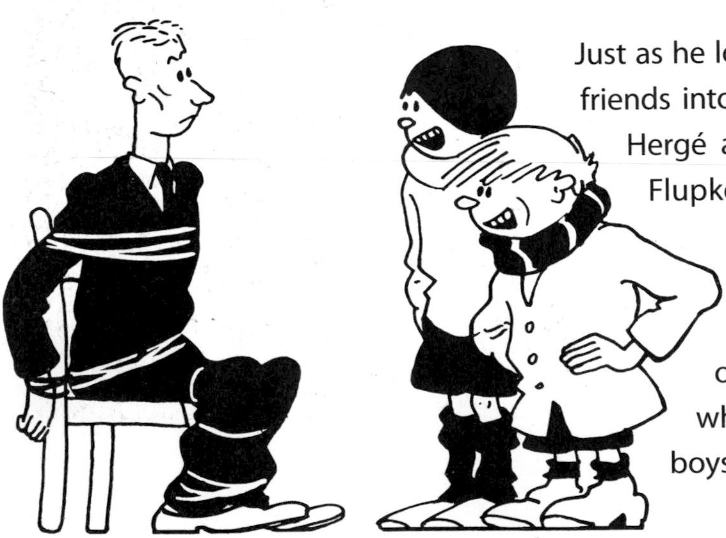

Just as he loved to draw his real friends into Tintin's adventures, Hergé also gave Quick and Flupke small roles in one or two Tintin stories. The author even drew one episode of *Quick and Flupke* in which the two naughty boys kidnap him!

1934	1946	1971	1976	1983
PUBLICATION OF *CIGARS OF THE PHARAOH*	LAUNCH OF *TINTIN* MAGAZINE	HERGÉ VISITS AMERICA	PUBLICATION OF TINTIN'S LAST ADVENTURE, *TINTIN AND THE PICAROS*	HERGÉ DIES AGED 75

about Tintin and his creator Hergé!

TINTIN

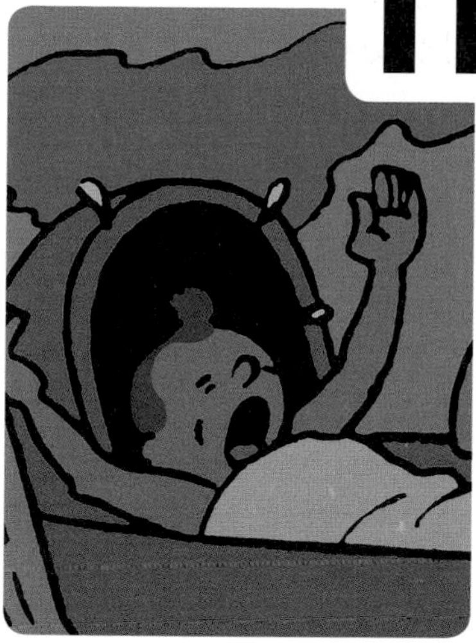

Dreams

Cigars of the Pharaoh is the first adventure in which we see Tintin dreaming, and what a nightmare! From now on dreams become regular events in the reporter's adventures.

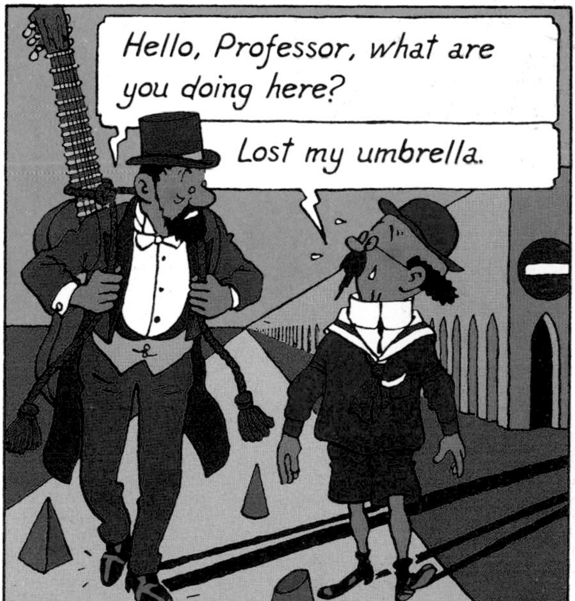
Hello, Professor, what are you doing here?
Lost my umbrella.

The story of *Tintin in Tibet* begins when Tintin has a dream. Later on, Captain Haddock (who makes his first appearance in *The Crab with the Golden Claws*) also has a dream, when he falls asleep while hiking in the Himalayas!

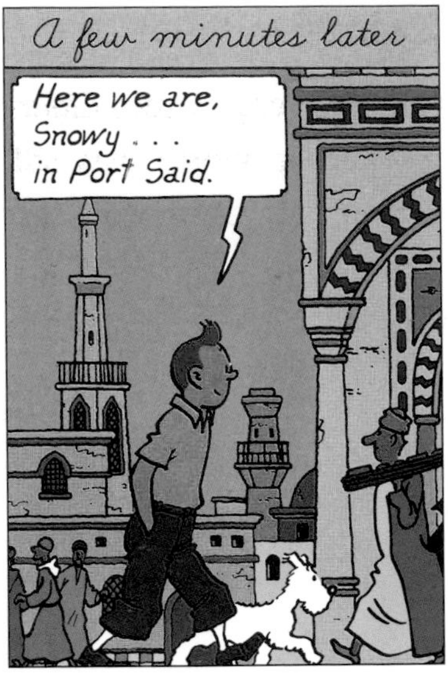
A few minutes later
Here we are, Snowy . . . in Port Said.

THE TRUE STORY
... behind *Cigars of the Pharaoh*

Tintin has barely begun his holiday cruise when he meets an eccentric professor named Sophocles Sarcophagus, who invites him to join a search for the lost tomb of an Ancient Egyptian pharaoh. But before Tintin sets off on the hunt for the tomb of the fictional Pharaoh Kih-Oskh, he disembarks at Port Said, an Egyptian city that was built in 1859 during the construction of the Suez Canal.

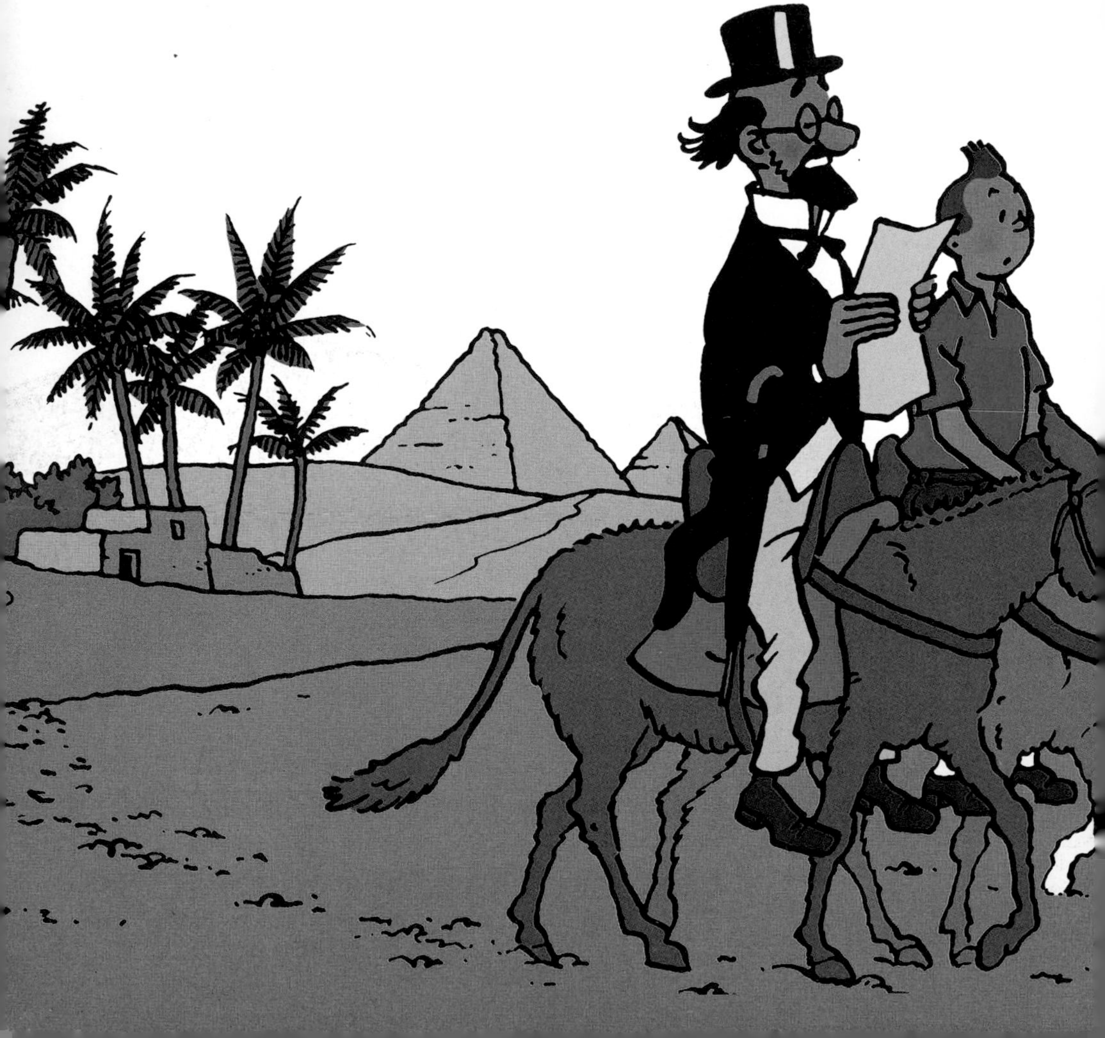

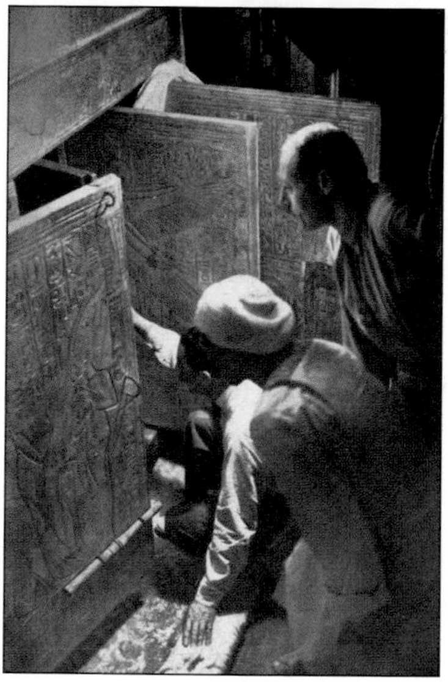

Once upon a time...

In the early 1930s, when Hergé wrote *Cigars of the Pharaoh*, the whole world was still excited about the discovery of the tomb of Pharaoh Tutankhamun. The photo on the left shows the moment in 1922 when the tomb was opened by British Egyptologist Howard Carter (1874–1939).

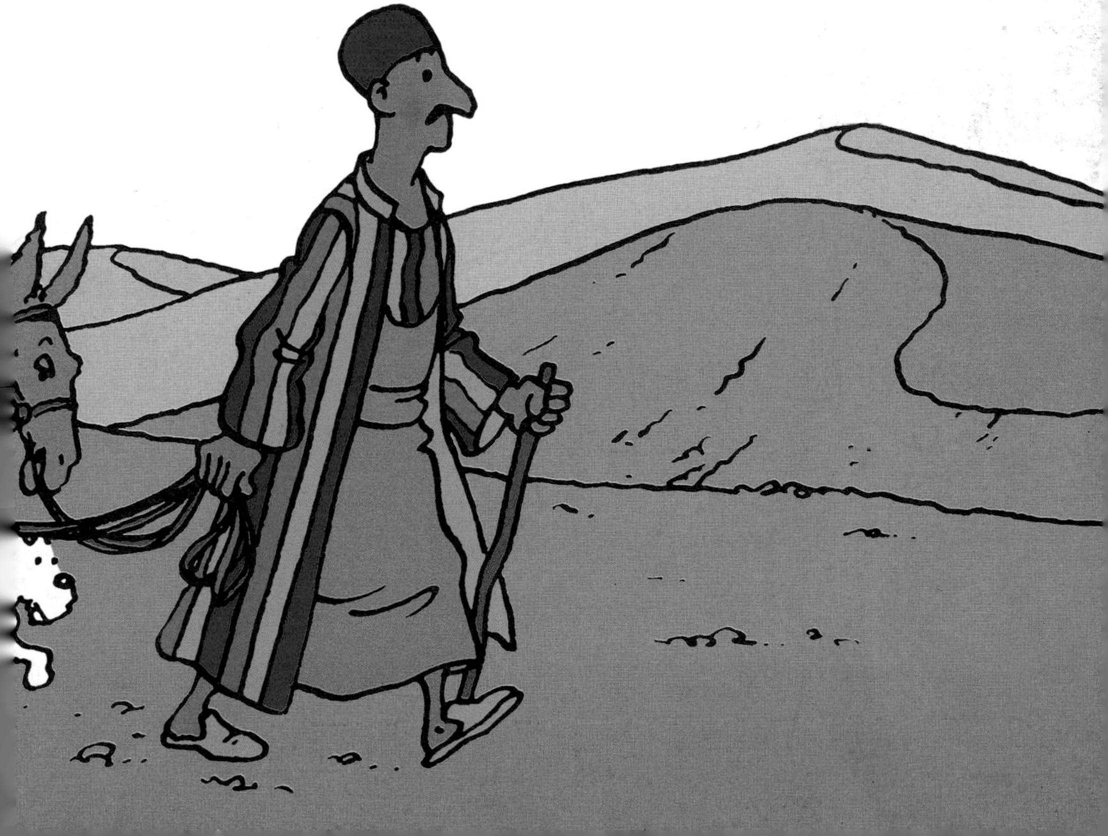

THE ARABIAN PENINSULA

As soon as Tintin finds his way into the tomb of Kih-Oskh, things begin to go wrong. His nightmare of being mummified seems to have come true when he wakes up in a coffin, but why is he floating on the Red Sea? It looks like all hope is lost until a dhow (a traditional Arab boat) picks him up. The dhow drops anchor off the coast of the Arabian Peninsula, and Tintin sets off to explore.

TURKEY
TURKMENISTAN
IRAQ
IRAN
AFGHANISTAN
PAKISTAN
NEPAL
EGYPT
TINTIN LANDS HERE
SAUDI
ARABIA
INDIA
SUDAN
ETHIOPIA

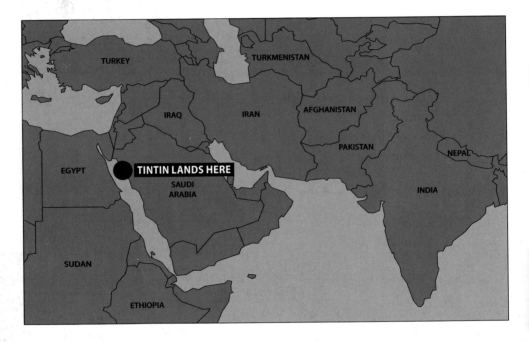

Once upon a time…

Although it doesn't say so in the story, in reality Tintin would now be in the country of Saudi Arabia. From the beginning of the twentieth century, Abdul-Aziz bin Saud—the leader of the House of Saud (a lineage of monarchs)—began armed campaigns against various tribes in the region. By 1932 he had consolidated his power over much of the Arabian Peninsula and renamed it Saudi Arabia.

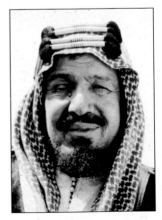

THE DESERT TOWN

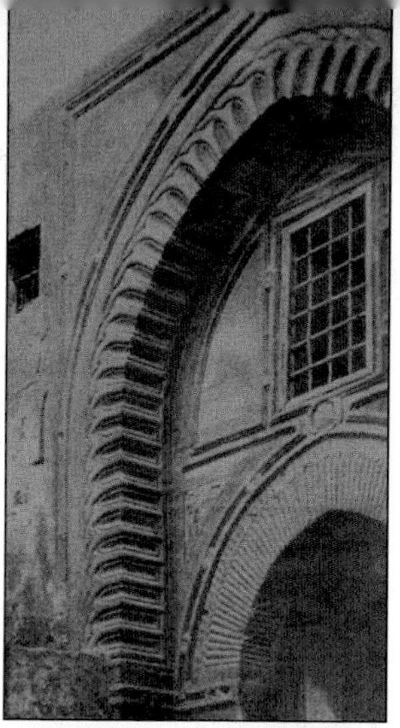

The courageous reporter makes his way to the fictional town of Abudin. Sometimes Hergé based his drawings on several sources: in this case he copied some details from an arch in Cairo for the Abudin city gate. While Tintin was in Arabia, part of Hergé was still in Egypt! ▶

Once upon a time…

In Abudin Tintin gets drawn into a desert conflict, just like real-life British army officer T. E. Lawrence (1888–1935), who was also known as Lawrence of Arabia. But while T. E. Lawrence willingly fought alongside—and led—the Arabs against the Ottoman Empire in the Arab Revolt (1916–1918), Tintin is less enthusiastic about his new position as Army Private Ali-Bhai.

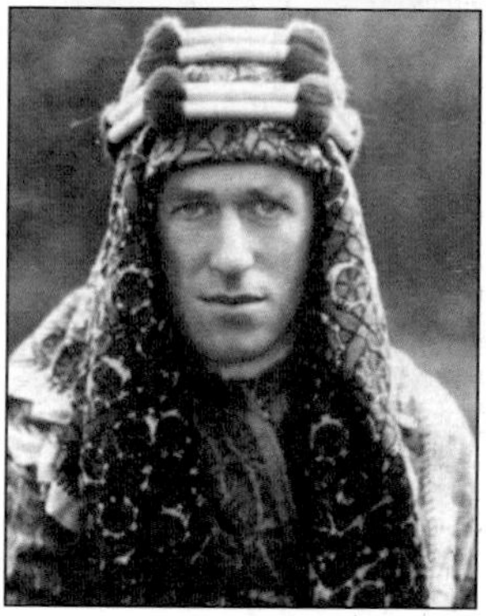

Lawrence of Arabia

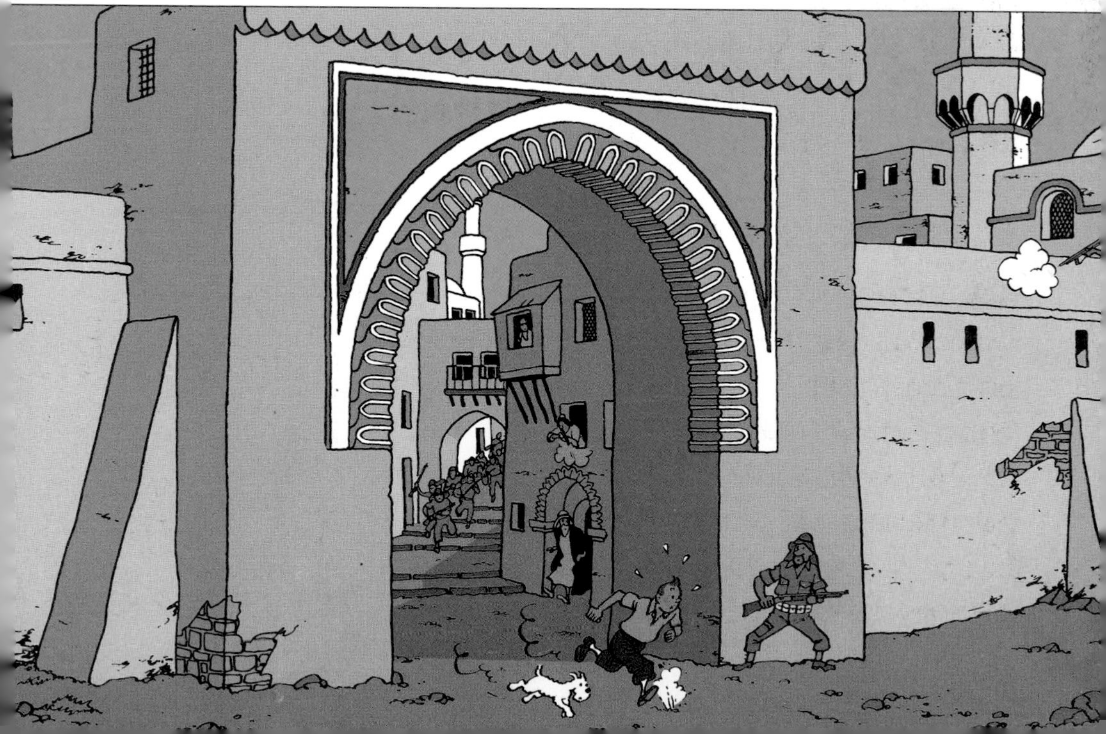

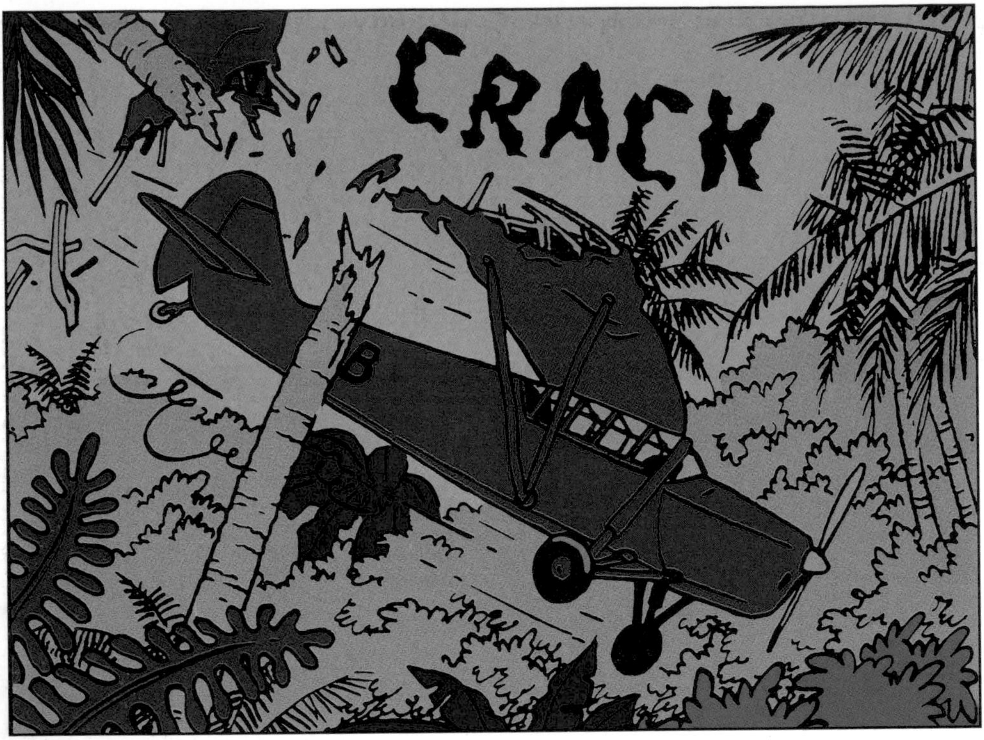
CRACK

"Hold tight, Snowy! Here we go!"

Tintin thinks that he has managed to escape, but it is not long before enemy fighter planes are spraying bullets at him. Spinning his airplane so that it looks like he has been hit, Tintin manages to escape once again. But then he runs out of fuel while flying over India. It's time for a crash landing!

Once upon a time…

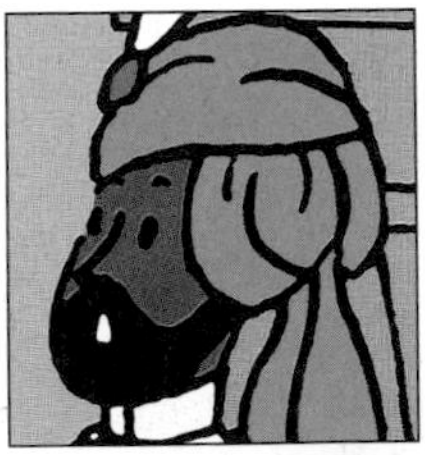

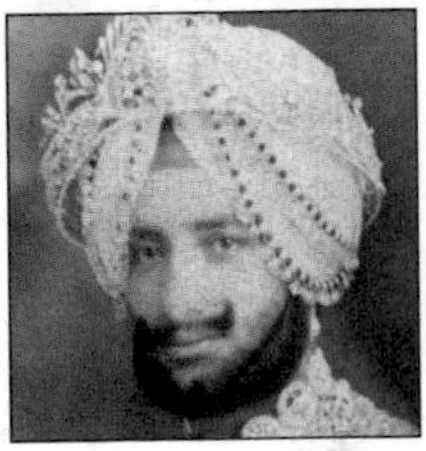

Cigars of the Pharaoh is set in a time when India was governed by the British Empire. The period (1858–1947) of British colonial rule in India is known as the Raj. Britain directly controlled two-thirds of the country while exercising influence over the remaining third, which was made up of hundreds of small states. These states were ruled by Indian kings known as maharajas. Look at this photo of the Maharaja of Patiala in 1938. ▶

Overpowering a tiger!

While in India Tintin tries to escape from doctors and policemen who are convinced that he is mad. Tintin even gets put in a straitjacket, which actually comes in very handy during a life-or-death struggle with a ferocious tiger!

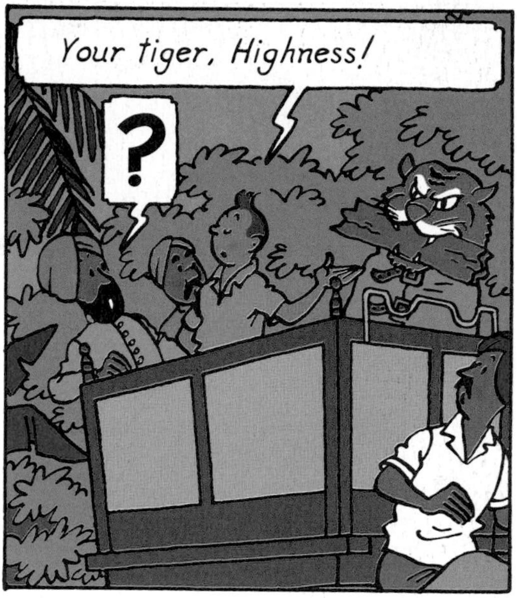
Your tiger, Highness!
?

Once upon a time...

There used to be high numbers of the Bengal tiger living in India: an estimated 40,000 at the turn of the century. Hunting tigers became very popular during the twentieth century, however, and numbers decreased to merely 1,900 in the late 1960s. Since 1970, tiger hunting has been banned throughout India.

It's amazing how much traveling Tintin does in this adventure.
Now it's time for us to **Explore and Discover!**

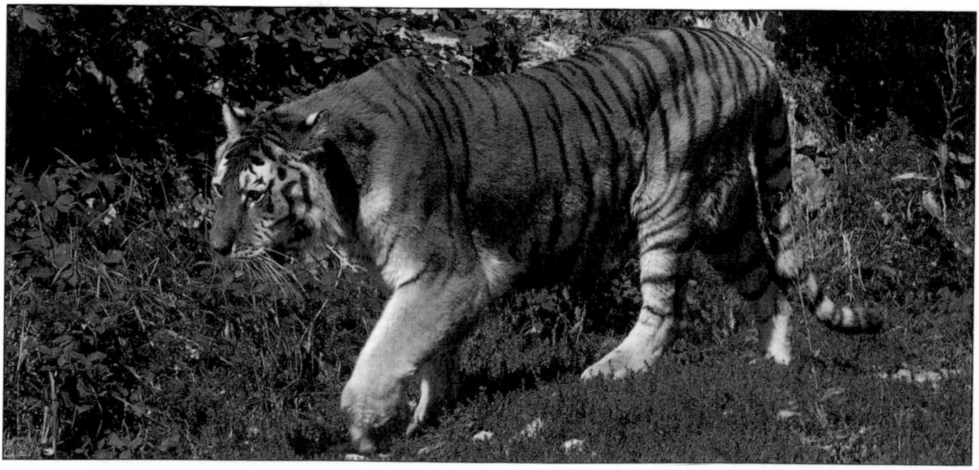

EXPLORE AND DISCOVER

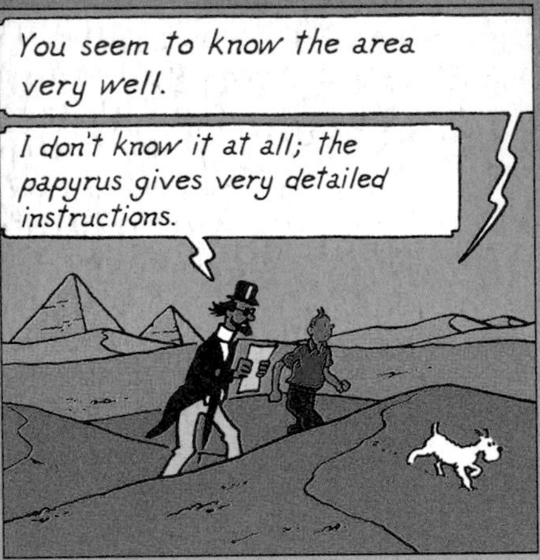
You seem to know the area very well.
I don't know it at all; the papyrus gives very detailed instructions.

It all begins with a piece of papyrus, on which are written detailed instructions leading to the tomb of Pharaoh Kih-Oskh. Papyrus is thick paper made from strips of the papyrus plant, stuck together in rows. Symbols were inscribed onto scrolls of papyrus from as far back as 4,000 B.C. The material was also used in the manufacture of mattresses, boats and sandals.

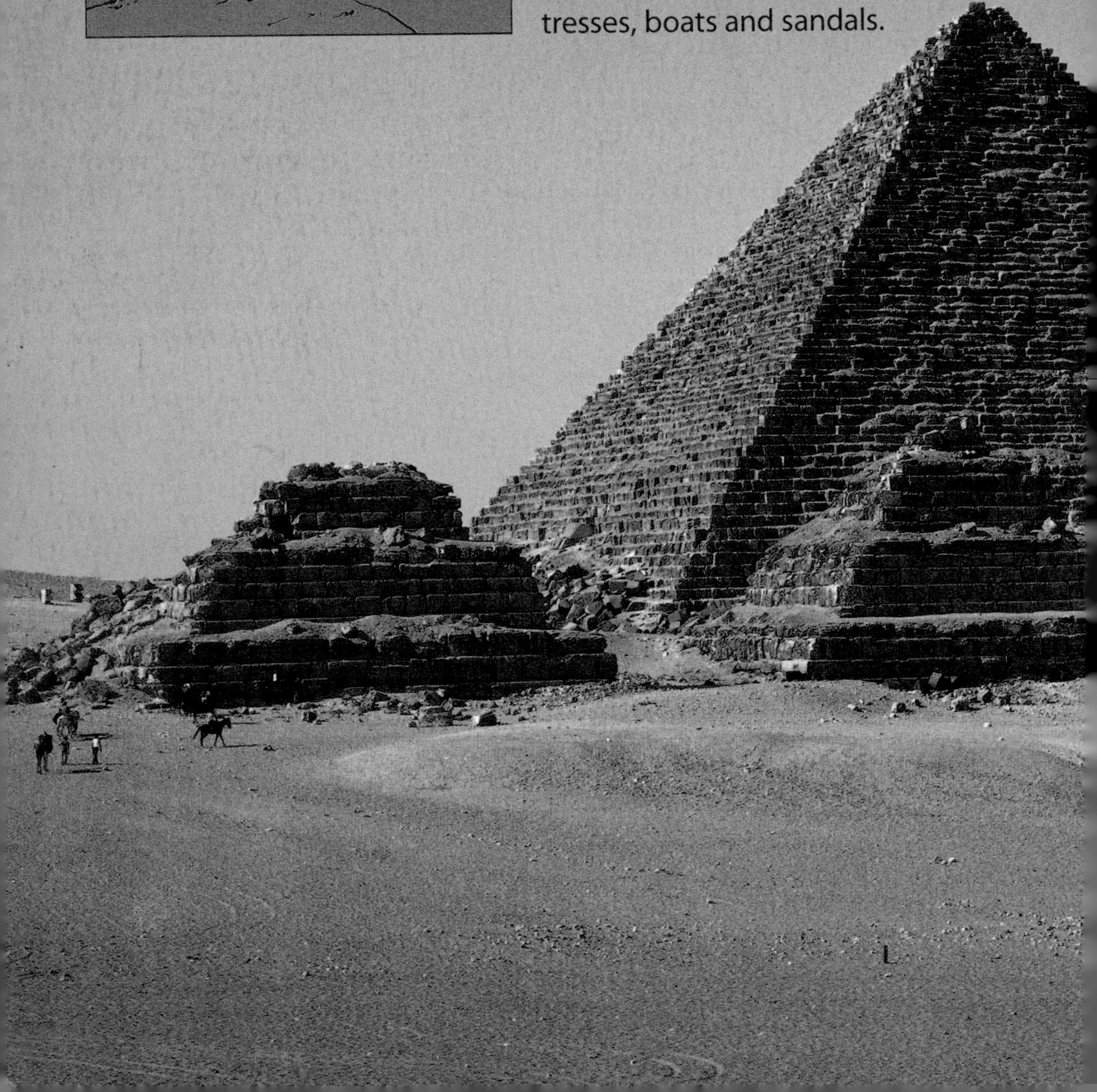

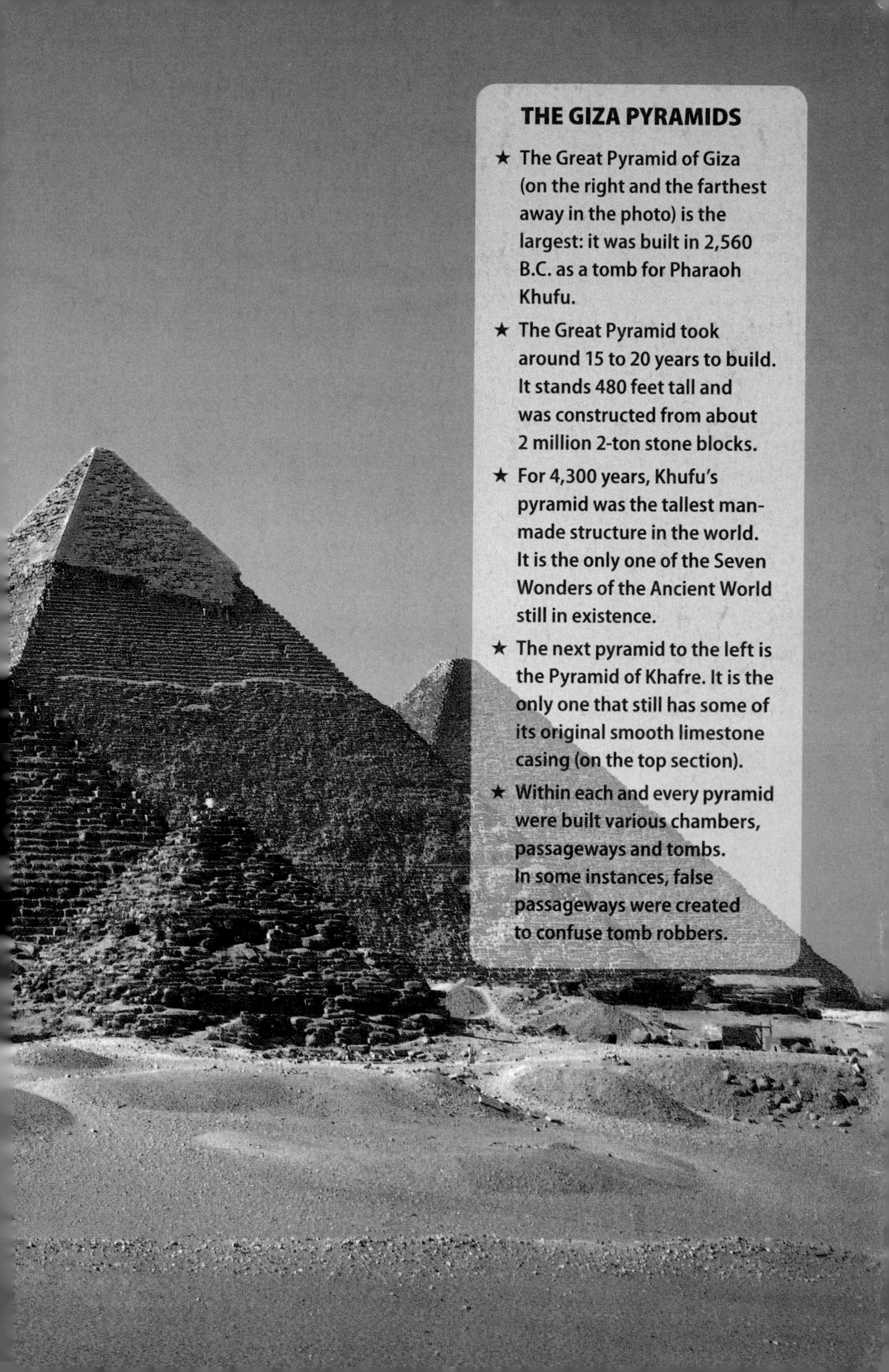

THE GIZA PYRAMIDS

- ★ The Great Pyramid of Giza (on the right and the farthest away in the photo) is the largest: it was built in 2,560 B.C. as a tomb for Pharaoh Khufu.
- ★ The Great Pyramid took around 15 to 20 years to build. It stands 480 feet tall and was constructed from about 2 million 2-ton stone blocks.
- ★ For 4,300 years, Khufu's pyramid was the tallest man-made structure in the world. It is the only one of the Seven Wonders of the Ancient World still in existence.
- ★ The next pyramid to the left is the Pyramid of Khafre. It is the only one that still has some of its original smooth limestone casing (on the top section).
- ★ Within each and every pyramid were built various chambers, passageways and tombs. In some instances, false passageways were created to confuse tomb robbers.

THE DISCOVERY OF TUTANKHAMUN

Tutankhamun was a pharaoh who lived from 1,341 to 1,323 B.C. He became king when he was nine years old and ruled for nearly ten years before falling ill and dying at a young age. Although he was a relatively minor pharaoh, in 1922 Tutankhamun became famous all over the world when his tomb was unearthed by Howard Carter. Today his death mask (shown opposite) is the most recognizable symbol of Ancient Egypt.

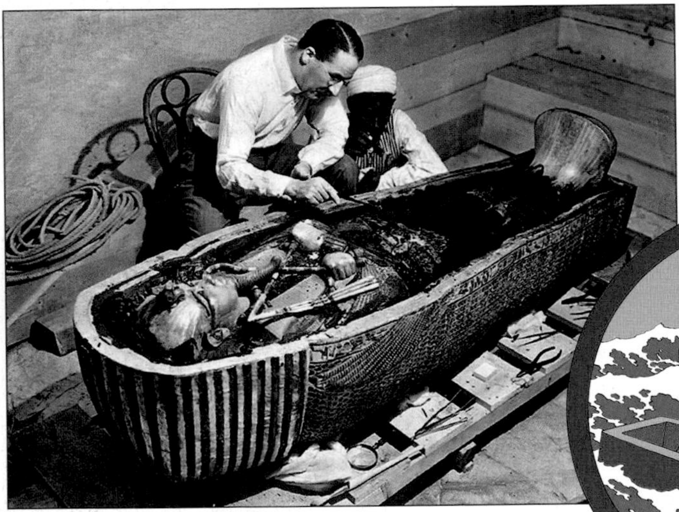

Howard Carter looks inside Tutankhamum's coffin

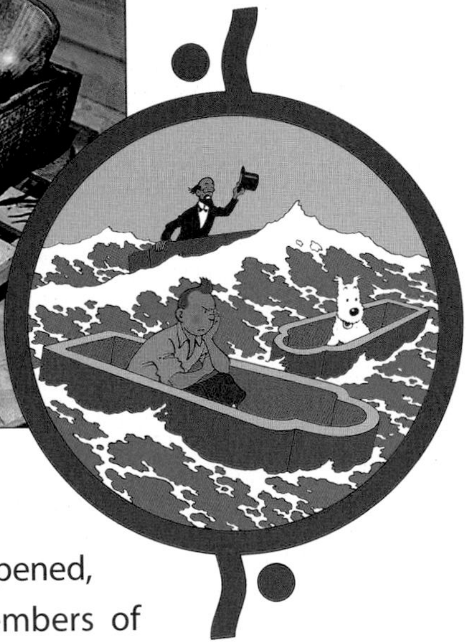

The Curse of the Pharaoh

Not long after Tutankhamun's tomb was opened, a rumor began circulating that the members of Howard Carter's team had been cursed. The main sponsor of the expedition, Lord Carnarvon, fell sick and died six weeks after entering the tomb. Two years later anthropologist Henry Field's house burned down. One of Carter's friends had recently given Field a mummified hand with a bracelet inscribed, "Cursed be the one who moves my body!" Hergé was enthralled by these spooky stories. On the other hand, Tintin looks pretty annoyed: perhaps he doesn't have time for curses!

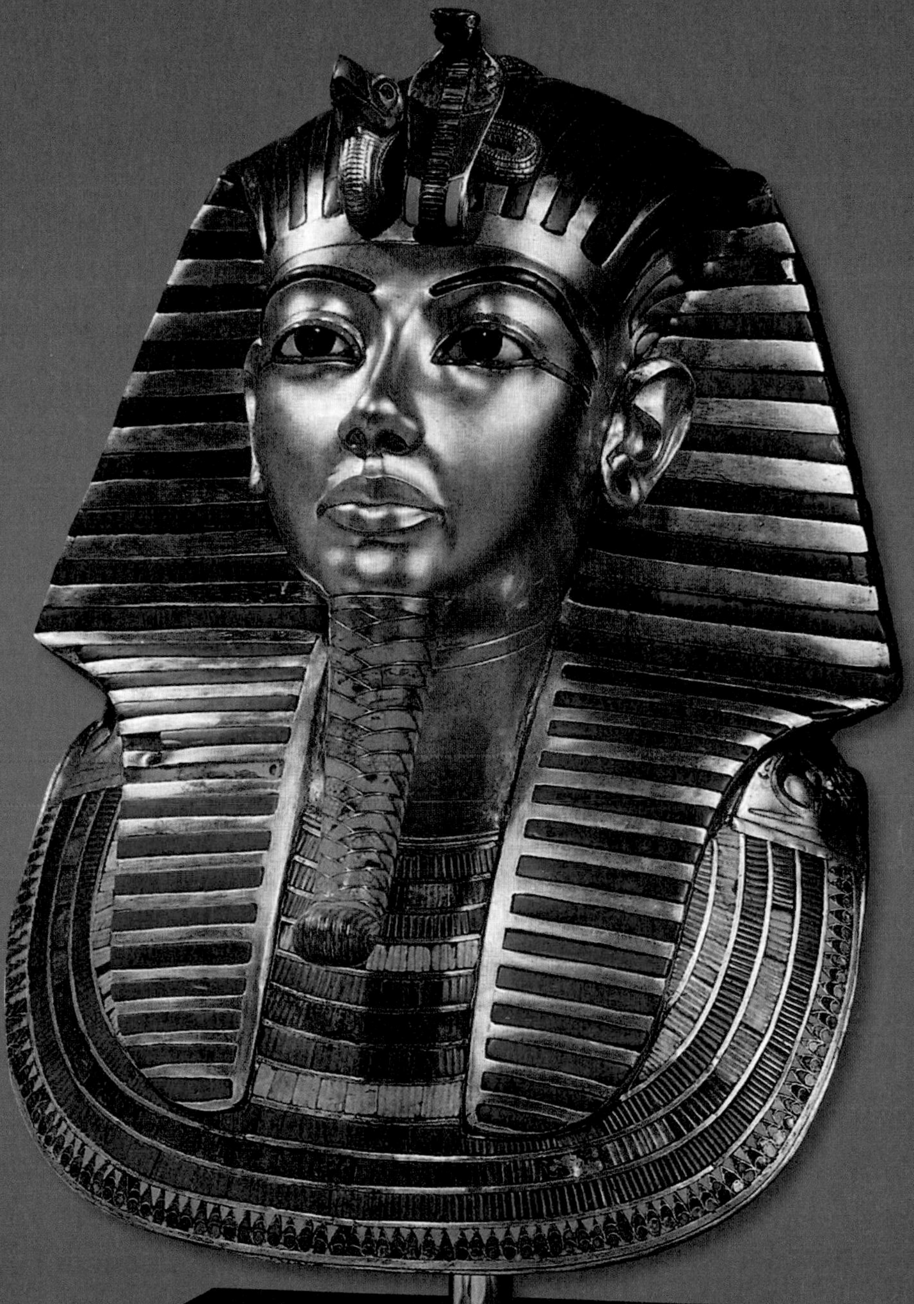

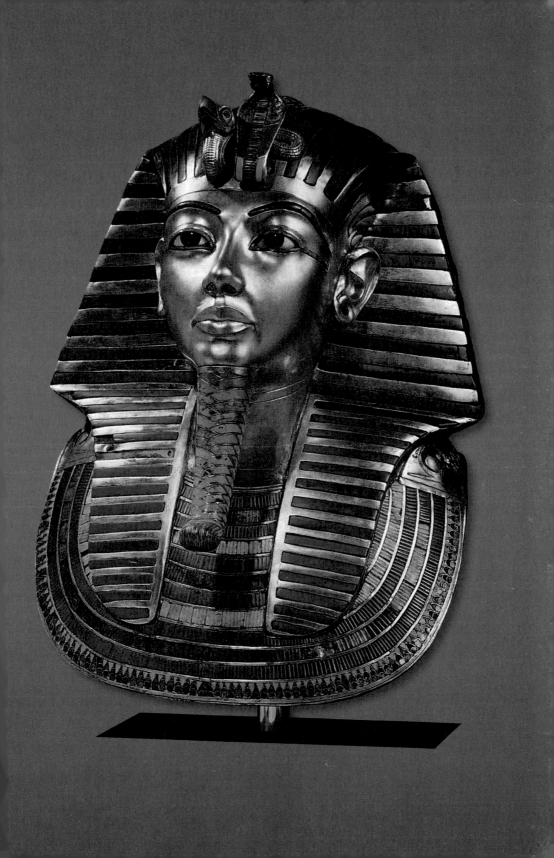

THE PHARAOH'S REVENGE!

Just before he wakes up floating on the Red Sea, Tintin comes across the scary sight of an empty coffin with his name on it!

19
20
21
20 A
SANDYS
PTOLOGIST
S. SARCOPHAGUS
GYPTOLOGIST
SNOWY
DOG
TINTIN
JOURNALIST

14
E. P. JACOBINI
EGYPTOLOGIST

© Studio Artos

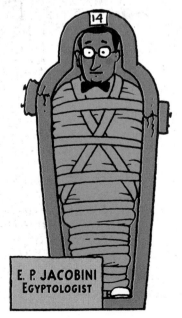

E.P. JACOBINI

You know that Hergé sometimes drew himself into his cartoons, but on this occasion the creator of Tintin sketched a friend into the story. Edgar-Pierre Jacobs was a comic strip artist who helped Hergé to reformat the early Tintin books in the 1940s. To return the favor, Hergé immortalized his friend as a mummy!

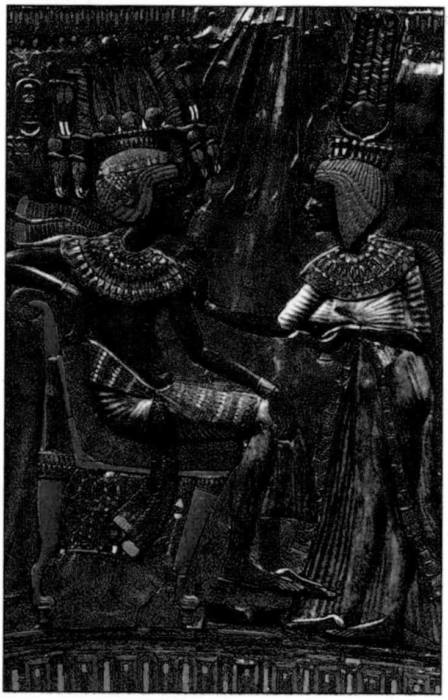

NIGHTMARE

Overcome by fumes, Tintin falls into a strange and disturbing sleep. He begins dreaming: first he sees Snowy and himself mummified in coffins, then Thomson and Thompson dressed up as Ancient Egyptians, one lighting the other's cigar. Cleverly, Hergé based the drawing of the Thom(p)sons on a real picture that was found on the back of one of the chairs in Tutankhamun's tomb. Check it out!

◀

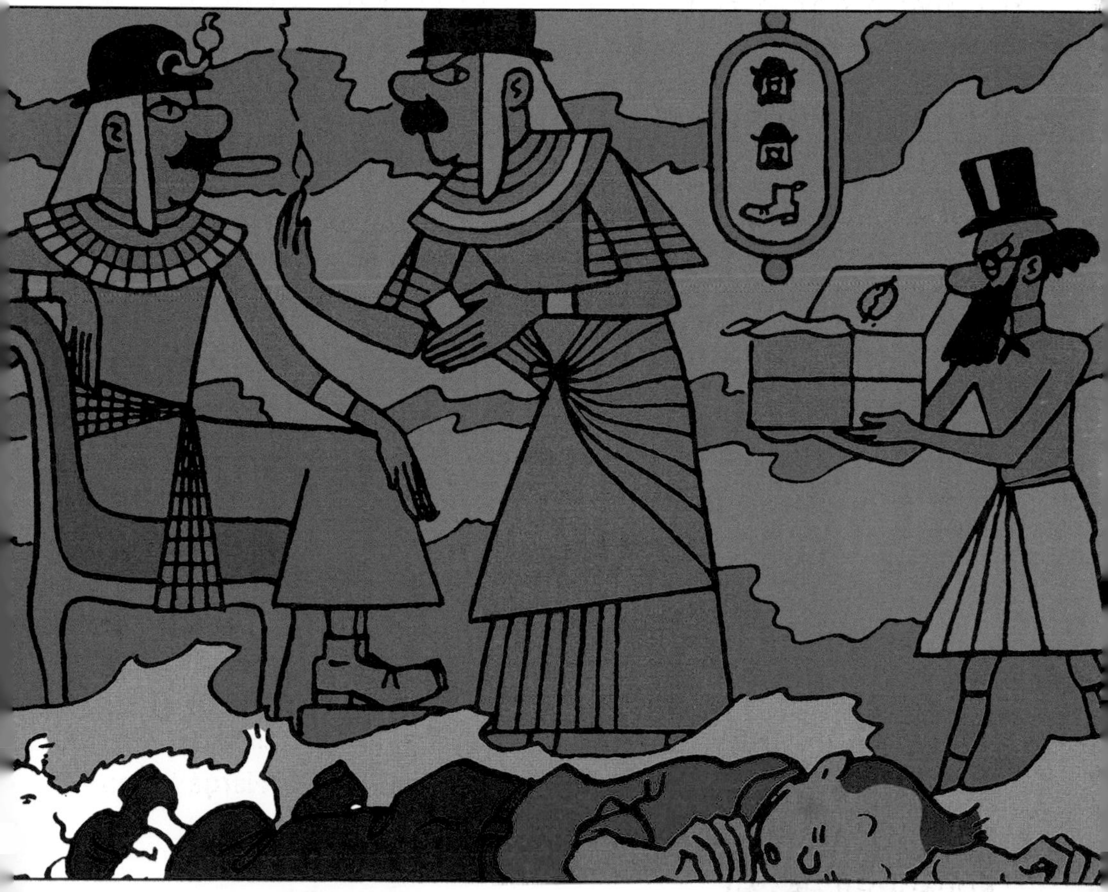

SAVED FROM THE RED SEA

Tintin is locked inside a coffin and tossed into the Red Sea by the crooked Captain Allan. Luckily he is picked up by a small dhow. Hergé based the captain of this boat on a notorious French adventurer and gun-runner named Henry de Monfreid (1879–1974).

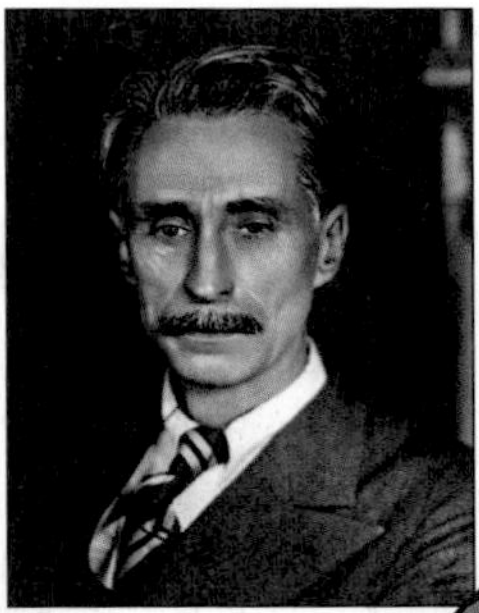

© Henri Manuel

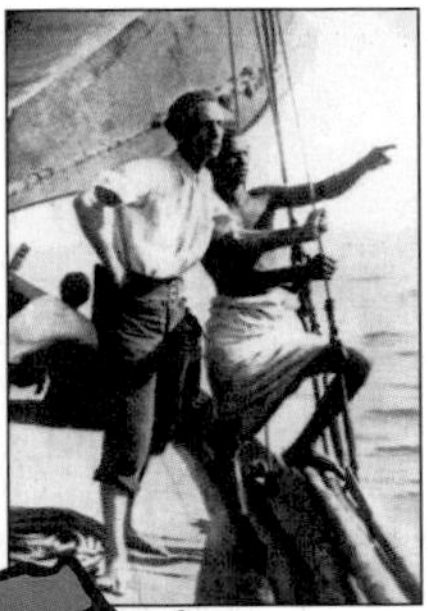

HENRY DE MONFREID

- ★ In 1911 Henry de Monfreid traveled to Djibouti, a small East African country located at the southern entrance to the Red Sea, where he planned to trade coffee.
- ★ Realizing that guns were more profitable than coffee in the unstable Middle East, it wasn't long before de Monfreid got in on the action.
- ★ Although he went to prison several times, on one occasion de Monfreid narrowly escaped justice when a coast guard decided not to search his boat for fear of offending a crowd of Muslim women on deck, who were on a pilgrimage.

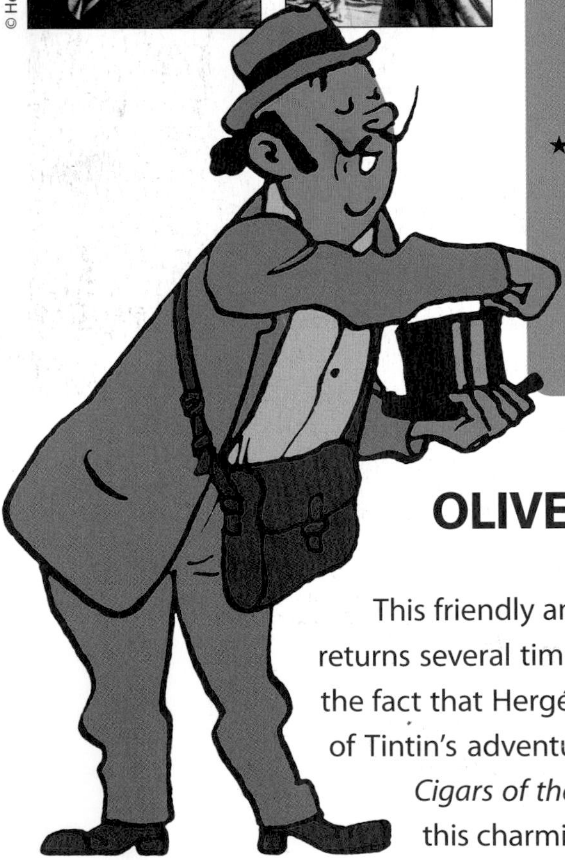

OLIVEIRA DA FIGUEIRA

This friendly and talkative Portuguese character returns several times in Tintin's adventures. Perhaps the fact that Hergé was negotiating the publication of Tintin's adventures in Portuguese (while writing *Cigars of the Pharaoh*) inspired him to create this charming salesman!

ESCAPE FROM ARABIA!

Tintin's luck runs out. First he interrupts the filming of a movie, and then the captain of the dhow he has traveled on turns out to be a ruthless arms trader. After narrowly escaping being blown sky-high, Tintin is drafted into an Arab army against his will. Even when he manages to flee in an airplane, his troubles are still not over. Two enemy aircraft are dispatched to shoot him down. Look at this picture of a Hawker Hart, the biplane that Hergé copied and sent after Tintin!

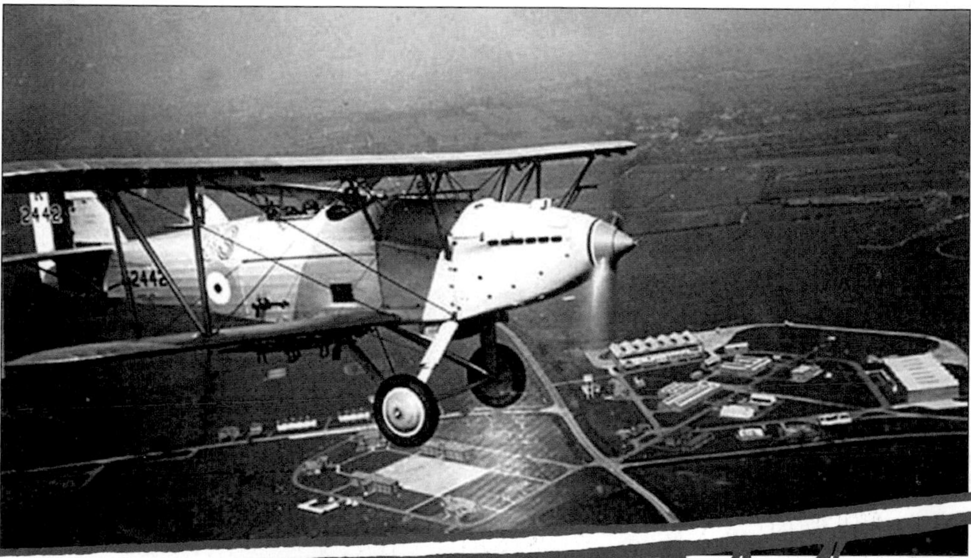

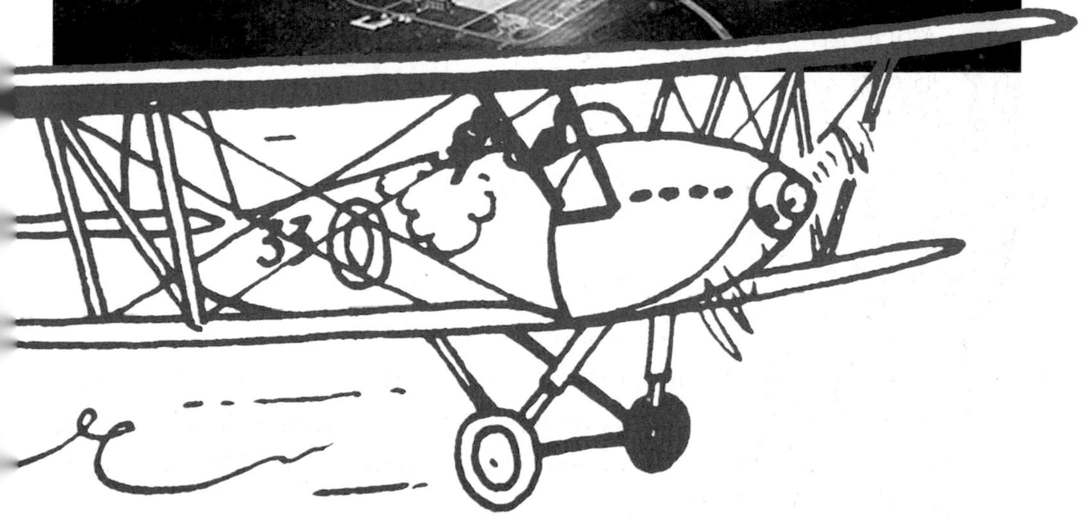

THE THOM(P)SONS

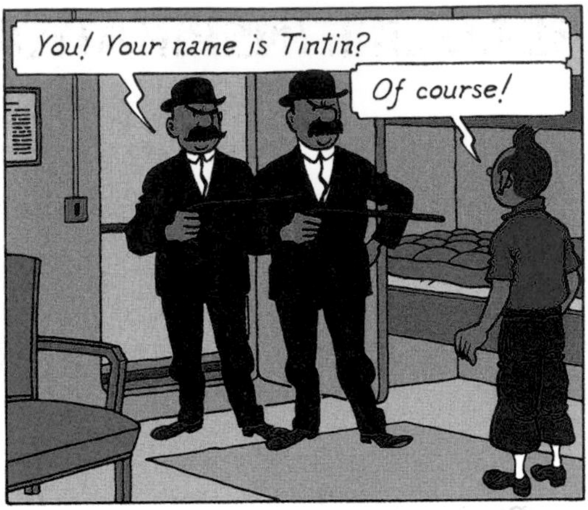
You! Your name is Tintin?
Of course!

Hergé introduces several important characters in *Cigars of the Pharaoh*, including the world's clumsiest policemen, Thomson and Thompson. Apart from Tintin and Snowy, the Thom(p)sons are the longest-running characters in the series, appearing in 20 of the 24 Tintin books.

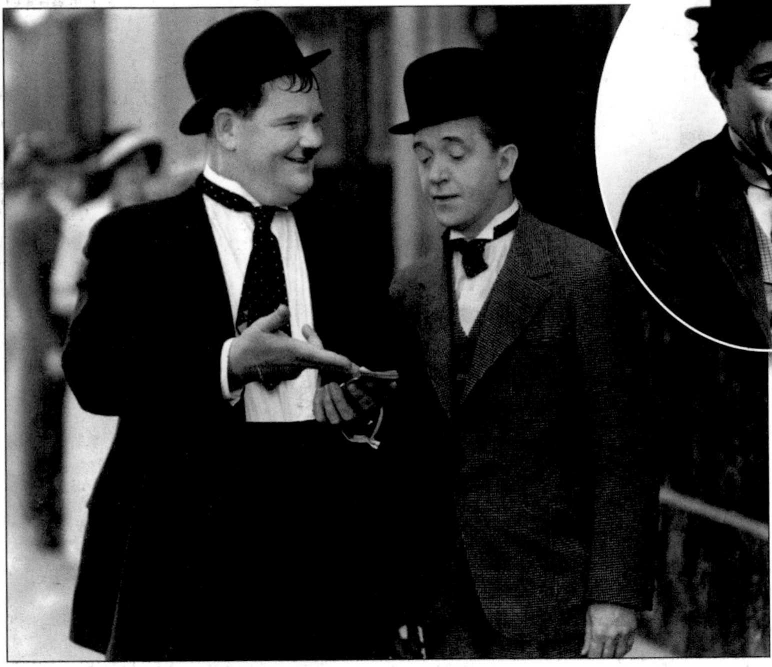

Laurel & Hardy, *Thicker than Water*, MGM 1935

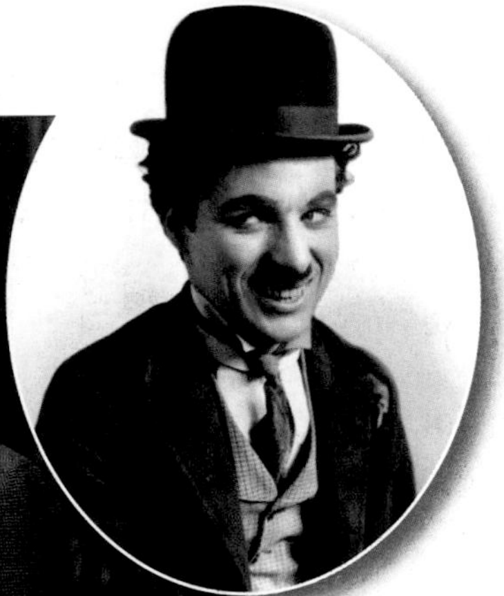

Charlie Chaplin, "The Tramp," 1915

The dim-witted detectives bring the slapstick comedy of actor Charlie Chaplin, whose films Hergé knew well, to the world of Tintin. As the reporter's adventures go on, the Thom(p)sons' whining and petty arguing bring to mind another pair of bowler-hatted nitwits, the popular film characters Laurel and Hardy!

REAL-LIFE INSPIRATION

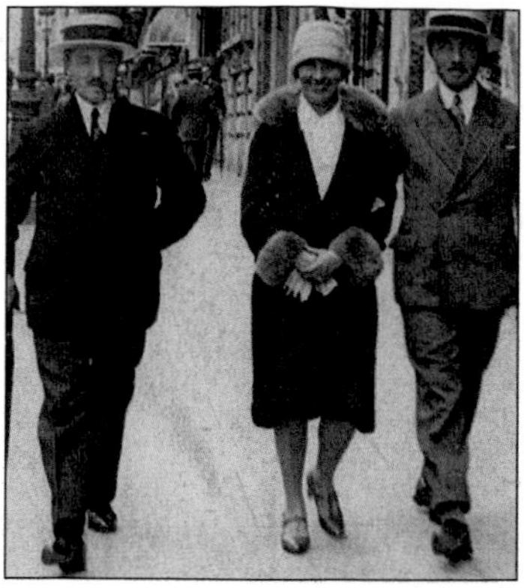

Hergé's father Alexis Remi (on the right) had a twin brother called Léon. They sometimes dressed in similar hats and suits when they went out together, walking sticks in hand. The two brothers even liked to repeat the French equivalent of the Thom(p)son's catchphrase: "To be precise!" The men's antics made an impression on the young Georges Remi!

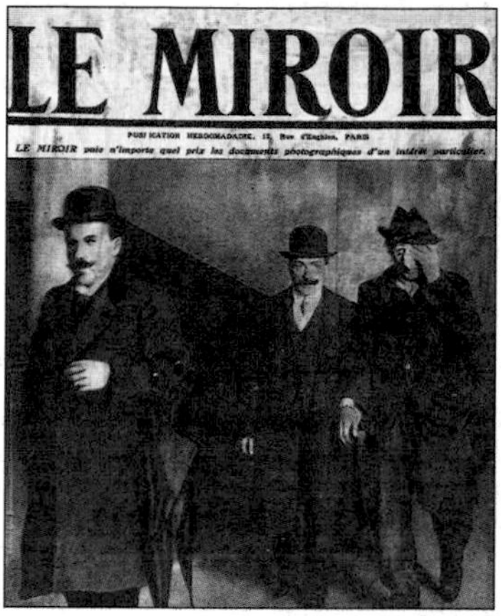
LE MIROIR
LE MIROIR paie n'importe quel prix les documents photographiques d'un intérêt particulier.

But perhaps there is even more behind the appearance of the silliest law enforcers in the world: check out the front cover of the March 1919 issue of French magazine *Le Miroir*, from Hergé's archives. ▶

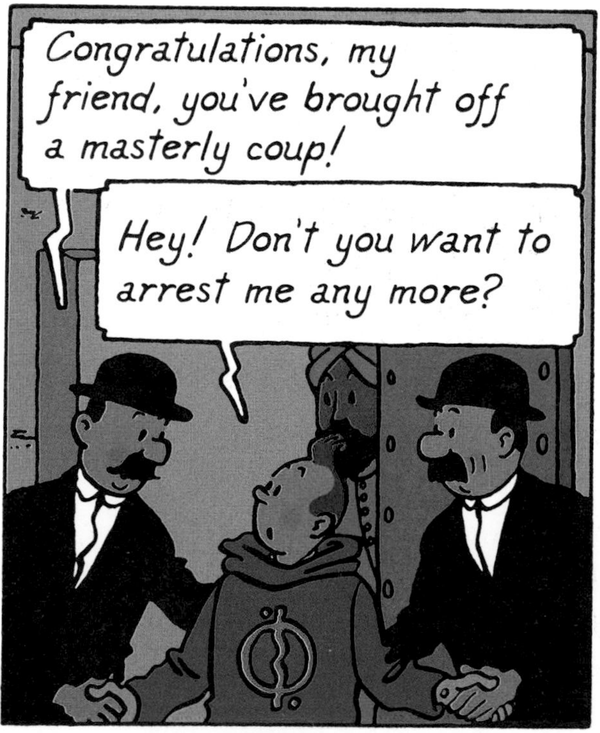
Congratulations, my friend, you've brought off a masterly coup!
Hey! Don't you want to arrest me any more?

Despite the fact that they spend most of their time failing to solve crimes, dressing up in hopeless disguises and falling flat on their faces, Thomson and Thompson always end up on Tintin's side, even if they do have to arrest him first!

TINTIN IN INDIA

When Tintin arrives in India he makes friends with a herd of elephants and finds Dr. Sarcophagus, who is even nuttier than usual.

Tintin takes Dr. Sarcophagus to the hospital, but the medical staff think that Tintin is the patient! Snowy gets lost as his master escapes, and soon gets captured by a group of men who want to sacrifice him to the Hindu god Siva. Check out a real statue below the drawing of Siva, who speaks thanks to the Thom(p)sons' skills in ventriloquism!

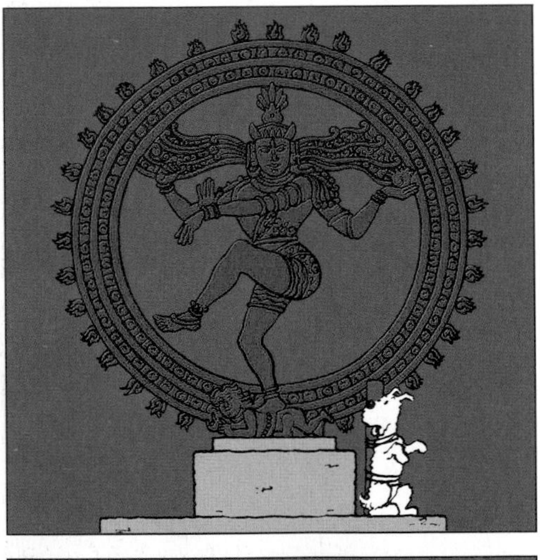

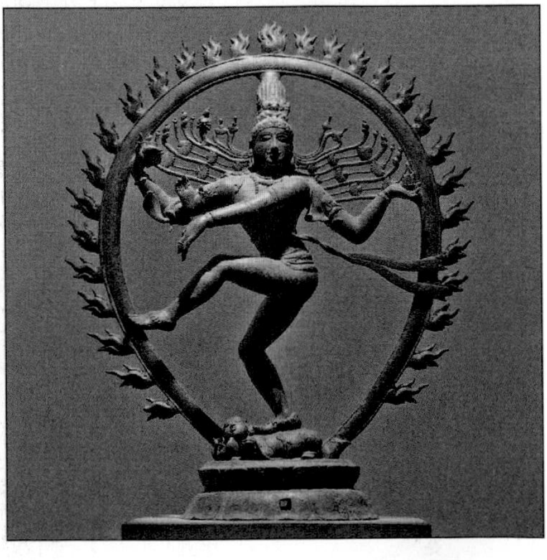

But there is someone in the story even more menacing than the Siva statue, a person who is also based on reality: the fakir!

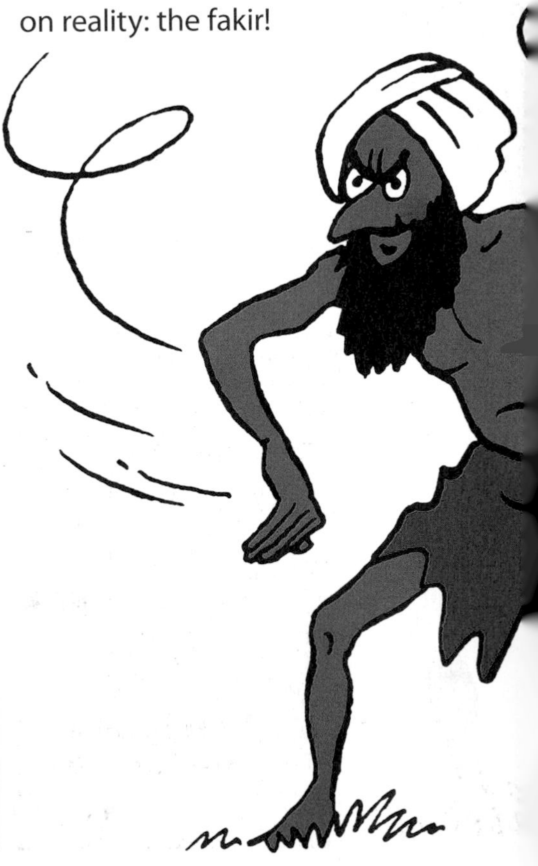

FAKIRS

★ The name fakir originally meant a Muslim Sufi ascetic: a wandering religious devotee who begged for food.

★ The term fakir has also come to refer to any Indian holy man who lives in poverty as a path to enlightenment.

★ Some fakirs are well-known for lying down on beds of nails, piercing their skin with knives and walking on hot coals—all things that you shouldn't try at home!

★ There are many stories of fakirs performing such magic as the Indian rope trick, which the fakir in Tintin's adventure uses to get near the maharaja.

★ In the photo on this page, the "fakir" is actually British magician "Karachi" (real name Arthur Claude Derby), performing the rope trick in 1935 with his son "Kyder"!

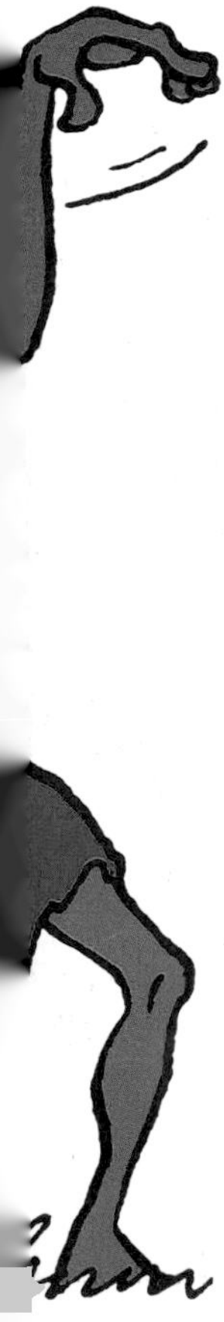

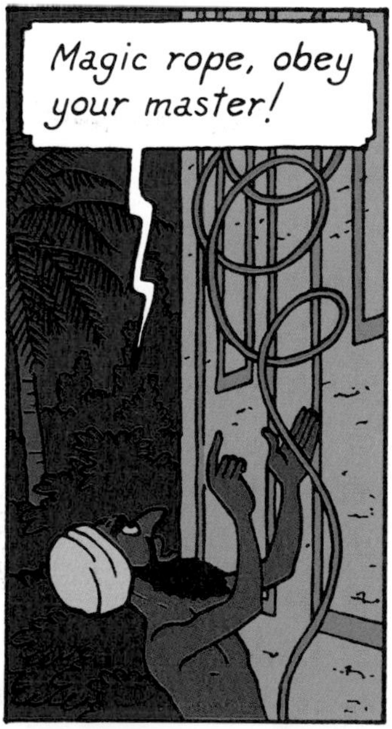
Magic rope, obey your master!

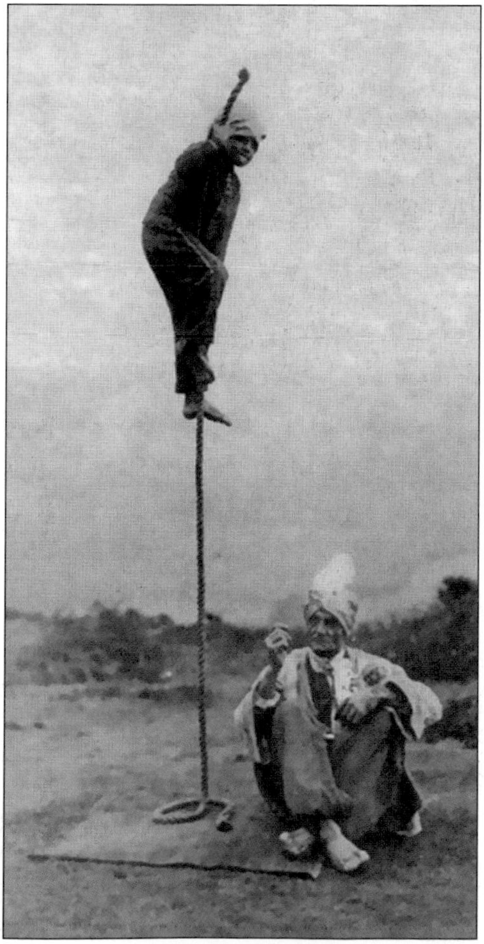

A TRIUMPHANT ELEPHANT PROCESSION!

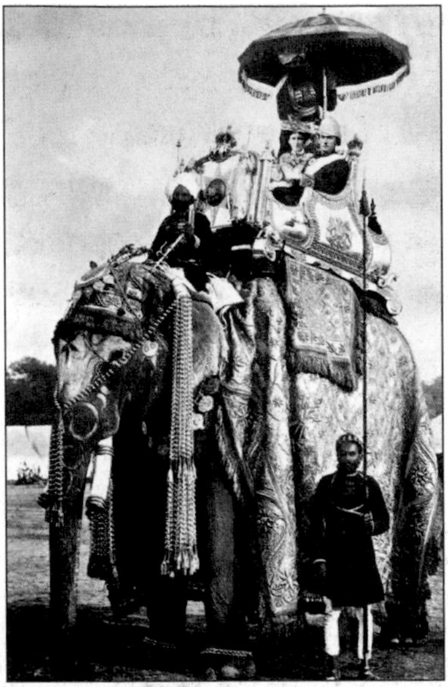

Tintin unmasks a gang of smugglers and rescues the Crown Prince of Gaipajama from the fakir and his master. It's time to celebrate, maharaja-style. Look at the real photo of a decorated elephant compared to Hergé's drawing below! ▼

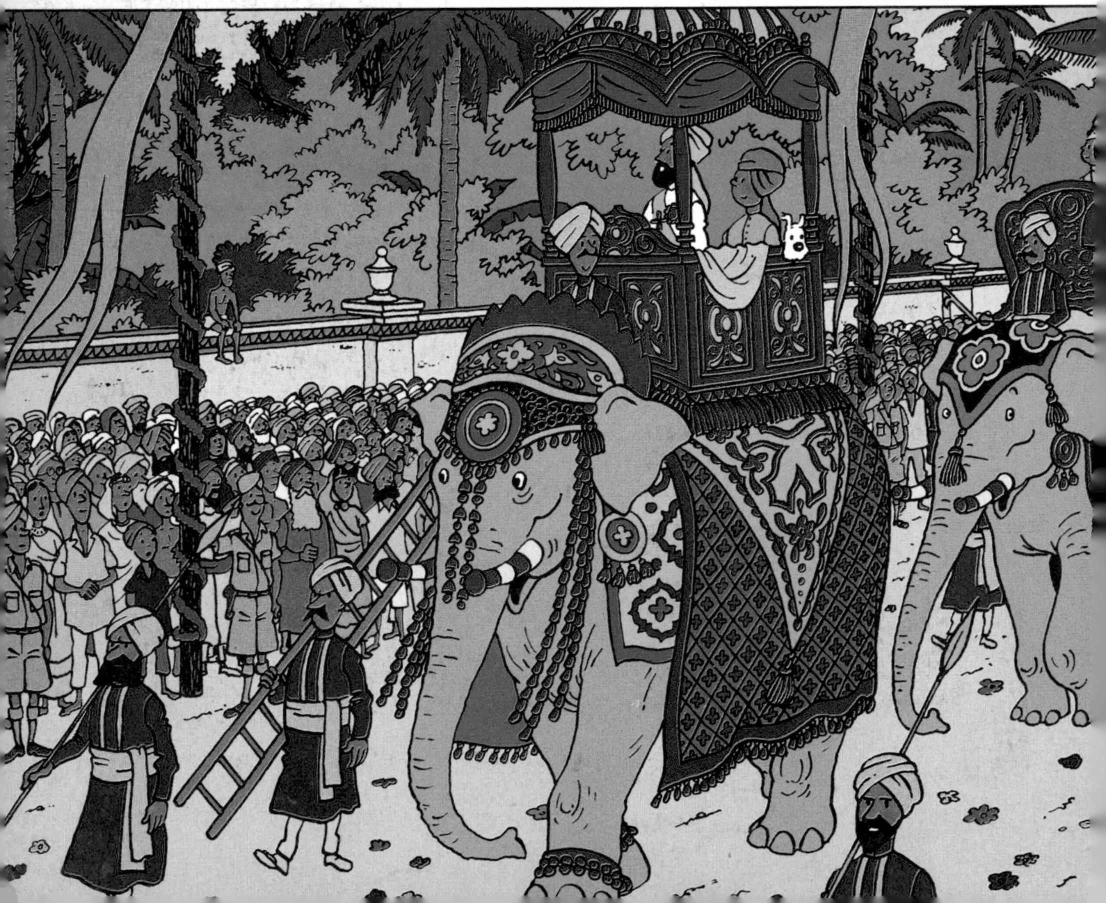

TINTIN'S GRAND ADVENTURE

Hergé was growing in confidence as he wrote Tintin's fourth adventure, *Cigars of the Pharaoh*. It was the first book to be published exclusively by Casterman, who would publish Tintin for the rest of the series. Hergé used the adventure to develop new characters who would become enduring members of the cast. He also left a cliffhanger at the end: what happened to the gang leader, who plunged off the cliff? Read *The Blue Lotus* to find out!

Trivia: *Cigars of the Pharaoh*

While conducting his research, Hergé was inspired by the work of Jean Capart (1877–1947), a Belgian Egyptologist who later inspired the character of Professor Tarragon in The Seven Crystal Balls.

The scene where Tintin floats on the sea in a coffin can be traced to the French novel Les Cinq Sous de Lavarède *(1894), by Paul d'Ivoi and H. Chabrillat.*

The captain's words on page 19, when he threatens to blow up his own boat, are directly inspired by a passage in Henry de Monfreid's book, Les Secrets de la Mer Rouge *(1931).*

In the first edition of the story, the tall mummified scholar with the top of his coffin cut away is labeled Lord Carnaval, in reference to Lord Carnarvon, who sponsored Howard Carter's search for Tutankhamun!

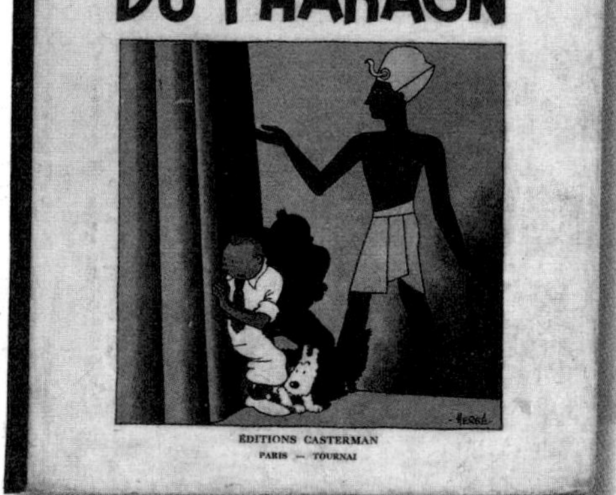
les aventures de
TINTIN
reporter
EN ORIENT
LES CIGARES DU PHARAON
EDITIONS CASTERMAN
PARIS — TOURNAI

The original cover for *Cigars of the Pharaoh* (1934)

GO ON MORE ADVENTURES WITH TINTIN!

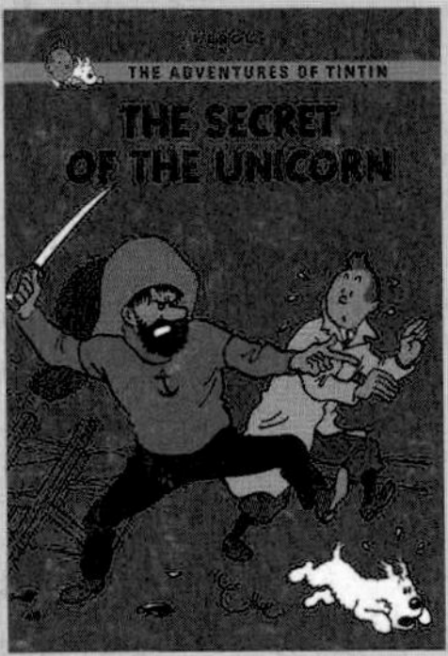
HERGÉ
THE ADVENTURES OF TINTIN
THE SECRET OF THE UNICORN

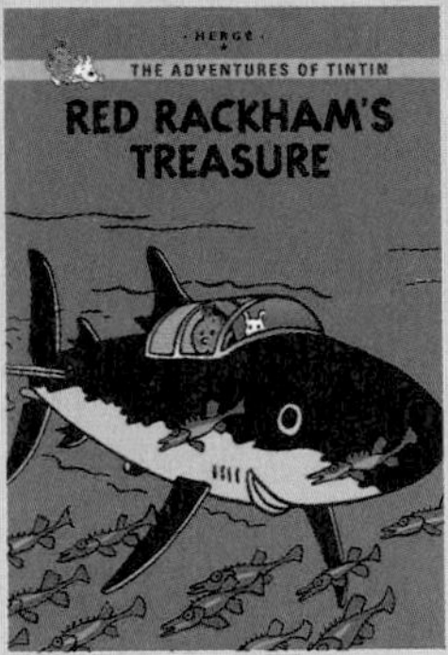
HERGÉ
THE ADVENTURES OF TINTIN
RED RACKHAM'S TREASURE

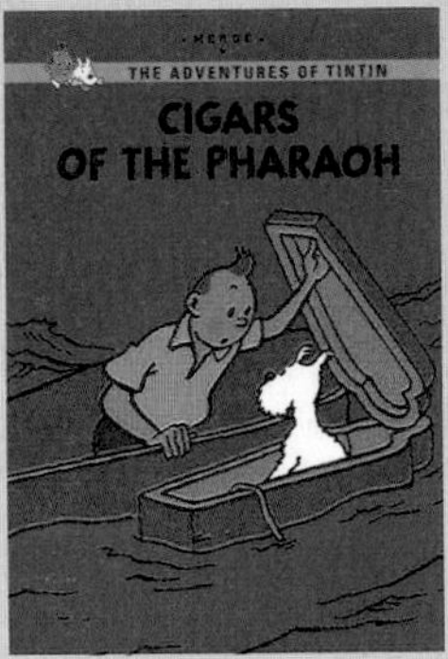
HERGÉ
THE ADVENTURES OF TINTIN
CIGARS OF THE PHARAOH

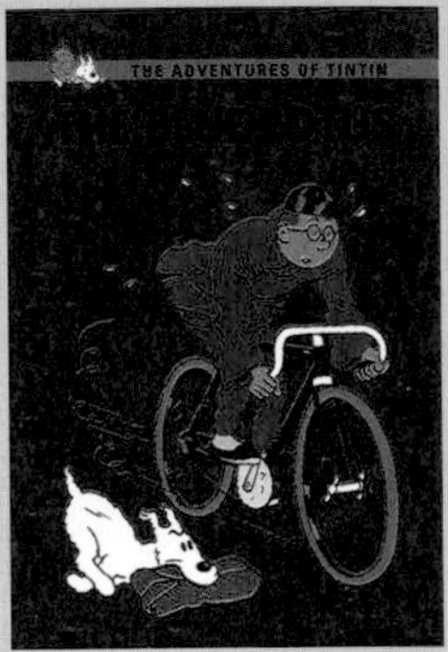
THE ADVENTURES OF TINTIN

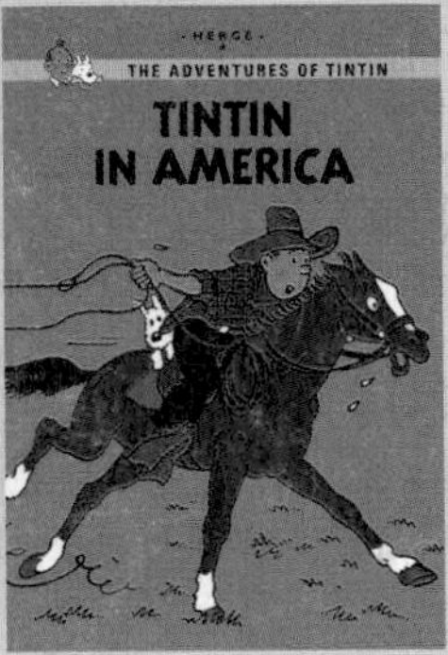
HERGÉ
THE ADVENTURES OF TINTIN
TINTIN IN AMERICA

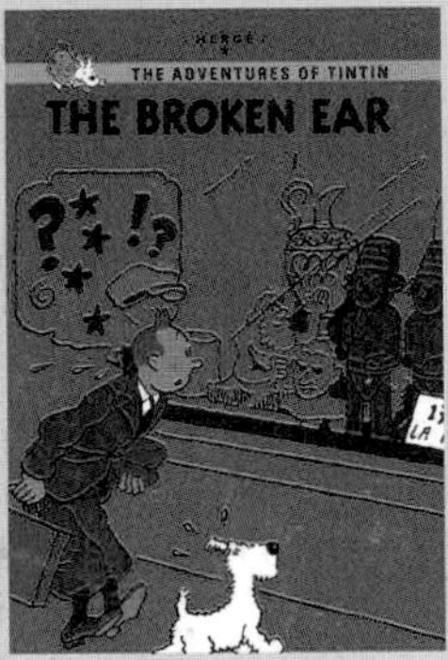
HERGÉ
THE ADVENTURES OF TINTIN
THE BROKEN EAR

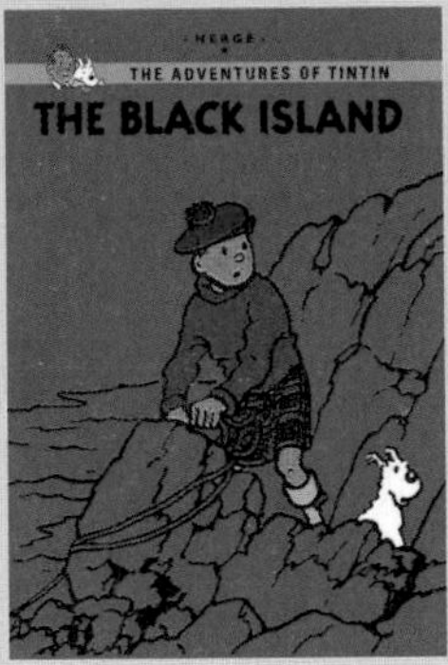
HERGÉ
THE ADVENTURES OF TINTIN
THE BLACK ISLAND

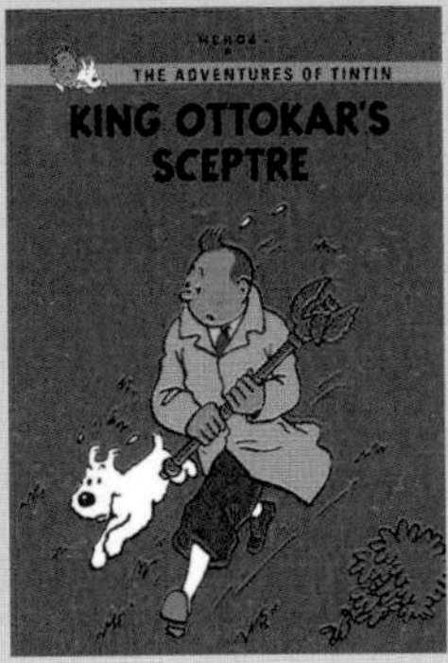
HERGÉ
THE ADVENTURES OF TINTIN
KING OTTOKAR'S SCEPTRE

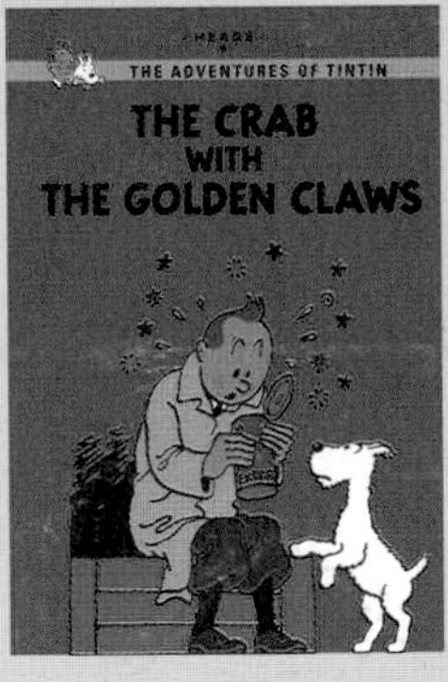
HERGÉ
THE ADVENTURES OF TINTIN
THE CRAB WITH THE GOLDEN CLAWS

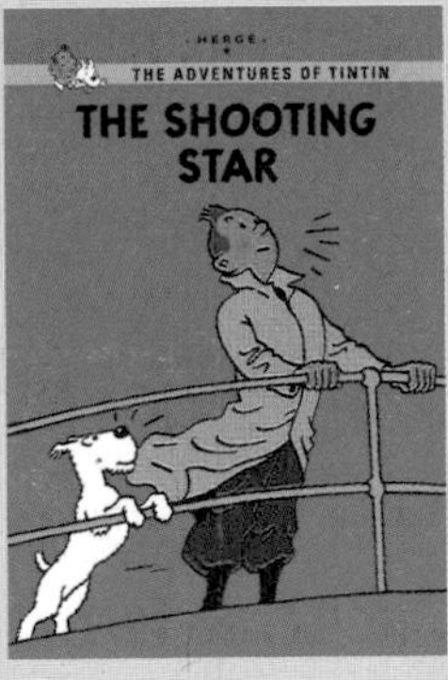
HERGÉ
THE ADVENTURES OF TINTIN
THE SHOOTING STAR

ALSO AVAILABLE

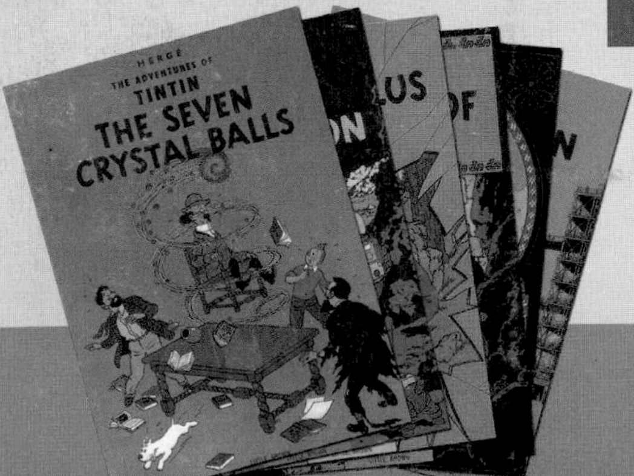
HERGÉ
THE ADVENTURES OF
TINTIN
THE SEVEN CRYSTAL BALLS

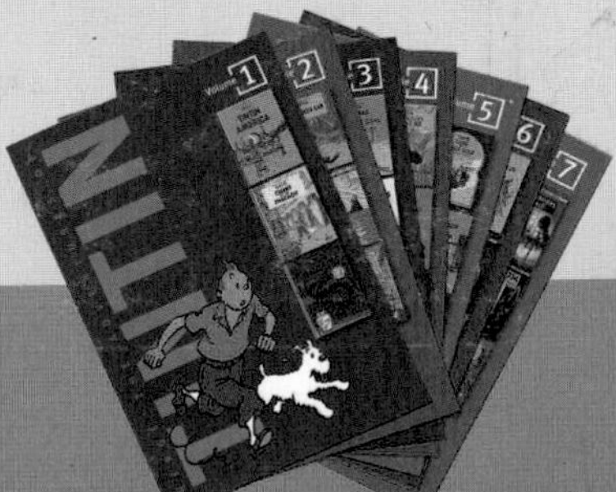
TINTIN